Beautiful.

The thought came to Sarah unheralded as she watched the man clear the embankment and stride out into the middle of the road. He made something in her thrill and quicken.

Every movement he made was graceful—graceful in the way of a wild animal...unconscious, unaffected, natural.

The one image that came instantly to her mind was that of a great jungle predator. He wasn't a big man, but there was an air of command in the way he held his head, something about the lines of his neck and shoulders, the set of his jaw. There was self-assurance in the way he stood, feet apart and hands on his hips, and arrogance in the way he waved her on, as if he owned the road and it was only by his grace that she was granted passage.

As she came closer to him, Sarah could see how his long dark hair clung to his sweat-glazed neck. His face was shaded by his hat, so she didn't see his eyes until she was directly opposite him. When she did, she felt a current pass through her, as if she'd just received a low-voltage electrical charge.

The man's eyes were blue.

And filled with naked desire. Primitive—and unmistakable.

Dear Reader,

When two people fall in love, the world is suddenly new and exciting, and it's that same excitement we bring to you in Silhouette Intimate Moments. These are stories with scope and grandeur. The characters lead lives we all dream of, and everything they do reflects the wonder of being in love.

Longer and more sensuous than most romances, Silhouette Intimate Moments novels take you away from everyday life and let you share the magic of love. Adventure, glamour, drama, even suspense—these are the passwords that let you into a world where love has a power beyond the ordinary, where the best authors in the field today create stories of love and commitment that will stay with you always.

In coming months look for novels by your favorite authors: Kathleen Creighton, Heather Graham Pozzessere, Nora Roberts and Marilyn Pappano, to name just a few. And whenever you buy books, look for all the Silhouette Intimate Moments, love stories *for* today's woman *by* today's woman.

Leslie J. Wainger
Senior Editor
Silhouette Books

Kathleen Creighton
Tiger Dawn

Silhouette Intimate Moments

Published by Silhouette Books New York

America's Publisher of Contemporary Romance

SILHOUETTE BOOKS
300 East 42nd St., New York, N.Y. 10017

ISBN: 0-373-07289-9

First Silhouette Books printing June 1989

Books by Kathleen Creighton

Silhouette Intimate Moments

KATHLEEN CREIGHTON

has roots deep in the California soil and still lives in the valley where her mother and grandmother were born. As a child, she enjoyed listening to old timers' tales, and her fascination with the past only deepened as she grew older. Today, she says, she is interested in everything—art, music, gardening, zoology, anthropology and history, but people are at the top of her list. She also has a lifelong passion for writing and recently began to combine her two loves into romance novels.

For Leslie Wainger,
who turns my words into books
and seldom gets any of the credit;
with heartfelt thanks for your patience
and friendship.

ACKNOWLEDGMENTS

I owe the inspiration for this story to the National Geographic Society and the World Wildlife Fund, and to their sponsorship of orangutan research and rehabilitation, specifically the work of Biruté Galdikas-Brindamour in Borneo and the Bohorok Rehabilitation Center on the island of Sumatra.

Thanks also to Muhamed Alie, of the Indonesian Tourist Promotion Center in Los Angeles, who filled in the gaps; and to his friend from West Sumatra, who danced for me and made the music come alive.

Chapter 1

Dawn had come, and the People of the Forest were stirring. As the first rays of the tropical sun began to filter through the canopy, they left their solitary nests and made their way to the feeding tree on the riverbank. The young ones, rolling and tumbling with the exuberance of adolescence, were first to arrive; the mother, with her infant clinging to her side, came later. She felt no need to hurry, for the great old fig tree was heavily laden with fruit. There would be plenty for all, including those rowdy cousins, the siamangs, and even the leaf monkeys, the hornbills and the wild pigs would have their share. So one by one they came, as was their solitary nature, and settled down to breakfast in placid serenity, while the rising sun struck gold into their rusty coats.

A series of staccato explosions shattered the morning. The fig tree erupted into screeching, chattering, hooting pandemonium as its occupants fled from unknown catastrophe.

In fear and confusion great apes and smaller creatures alike hurled themselves toward the safety of nearby trees.

All but one.

As the last reverberations were dying, a red-gold body tumbled down in graceful slow motion, crashing through branches, bringing with it a shower of broken twigs and ripe fruit, to land with a thud on the muddy riverbank.

An eerie silence settled over the forest. In that silence, three men emerged from the dense vegetation on the opposite bank of the river and waded across the shallow stream, holding their rifles high above their heads.

One of the men dropped to his knee beside the body. "Dead," he grunted, and rose, squinting up into the tree.

Another man pointed. "There!" The third man propped his rifle against the tree and began to climb.

The first man, the American, lit a cigarette and tossed the match into the river. "Looks good," he said through the smoke. "Not too big, not too small." He glanced at the small dark man beside him. "How old would you say?"

His comrade shrugged. "Hard to say. Less than a year, maybe."

The American shaded his eyes and craned up into the tree. "Male or female?"

The reply came drifting down: "Male."

"Huh. Female would have been better." The American watched dispassionately while his comrade made his way down from the tree with his precious burden. "But what the hell, he'll bring a good enough price." He stretched out a hand to touch the coarse, reddish hair. "Cute little devils, aren't they?" He sounded almost tender. Then he threw down his half-smoked cigarette, picked up the extra rifle and, shouldering it along with his own, grunted, "Let's get out of here."

The three men stepped around the inert body without affording it so much as a glance. They waded back across the river and a few minutes later had disappeared into the forest, leaving a silence broken only by the chuckle of flowing water and the incessant whine of insects.

Gradually, then, the rhythms of the day resumed. The sun rose higher, the brief, tropical rains came again and obliterated all signs that men had been there, and little by little the animals and birds and even the People of the Forest returned to the fig tree.

The baby orangutan lay on her bed of rags, gazing at the world with sad, intelligent eyes.

"Hi baby... come on, sweetie, come to Sarah."

The baby stirred laconically, reaching with one arm toward the calm, soothing voice. Gentle fingers scratched her round little belly and stroked her red-gold hair. Suddenly she clutched the hand and held on—*tightly.*

Sarah Fairchild winced, but the strength in that tiny grip felt good to her.

"Come here, sweetie...atta girl," she crooned. With only a little encouragement, the baby crept into Sarah's arms and curled against her side, snuggling into the warm nest of her body as if she belonged there.

Sarah backed out of the cage and straightened. As she pried those amazingly strong little fingers loose from her arm she gave the man in the khaki uniform who was hovering nearby a determined smile.

"She's in very good condition." She hefted the tiny bundle in the crook of her arm. "I'm glad you called the Foundation so promptly."

The man looked pious. "The work you are doing to help preserve our national treasures is greatly appreciated. Of course, we wish to cooperate with the Foundation's efforts whenever possible."

Sarah nodded and refrained from looking at the inhabitants of the other cages in the compound: white-handed gibbons, siamangs, pig-tailed macaques. The man in khaki was a high-ranking official in the city government and, she was sure, well acquainted with the laws against keeping, capturing, buying or selling certain primates.

"The little one is an orphan," her host went on, mournfully. "Tragically, her mother was dead when my men found her."

Again Sarah kept her face expressionless and nodded without comment. She was quite certain that the baby's mother *was* dead, murdered by the same men who "found" the baby and then sold her on the black market. But it wasn't her job to scold, accuse or condemn; it was the Foundation's policy never to prosecute, except in the case of the poachers themselves. She would never know what twinge of conscience or circumstances had moved this man to turn the infant orangutan over to the Foundation for rehabilitation and eventual return to the wild instead of adding her to his private collection, but there was sincerity in her voice when she said, "The Foundation is very grateful to you. Thank you."

A battered blue Land Rover with the Foundation's logo on the door sat waiting for her, simmering in the intense tropical sun. There were several sturdy crates in the back, but Sarah didn't have the heart to put the baby in one of them. As she settled herself behind the wheel she curved her arm protectively around the tiny orange bundle, even though the baby orangutan was already clinging to Sarah with the same tenacity that would have kept her safe while her mother swung unconcerned through the forest canopy, a hundred feet or more above the ground.

"Poor little sweetie—hey, I guess that's going to be a good name for you, huh? Sweetie?" As she gently stroked the orphan's coarse red-gold hair, the tiny bald head slowly swiveled. Two black currant eyes peered up at her, patient and trusting. Swallowing an all-too-familiar ache in her throat, Sarah reached for the ignition.

True to the placid nature of her species, the baby orangutan exhibited no signs of nervousness or alarm as the Land Rover's engine coughed and fired. With a wave to the smiling official, Sarah pulled out into the traffic on the main road.

An easy one, she thought with an inner sigh of relief. She could only hope the next one might go as well.

The prospect wasn't encouraging. From the voice on the telephone this morning she'd drawn a pretty clear mental picture of the man she'd be dealing with at her next stop. Ordinarily she liked deep voices, but this one had rough edges, and a touch of a Texas drawl. Dan Cisco, that was his name. He'd be a hard man, she decided—he'd have to be, to supervise a drilling crew in the middle of an Indonesian jungle—and if he had any sensitivity in him at all, he'd have learned to bury it beneath layers and layers of machismo. He'd be big and brawny, the fleshy, ex-jock type inclined toward, if not already sporting, a beer belly. His tone and manner would be patronizing, while his eyes would peel her clothing from her body, slowly, one article at a time.

Ugh. Sarah made a face and uttered a wordless sound of distaste. Under the very best of circumstances she'd always found those overly macho types intimidating. And all she had to do with this one was convince him to turn over his crew's pet orangutan to a bunch of bleeding heart zoologists—free of charge!

She was already on the outskirts of town, and traffic thinned rapidly as she headed toward the highlands and the all but impenetrable rain forests of the reserve. Steam rose from the blacktop ribbon that stretched ahead of her between endless green walls of plantation trees, a reminder of a midmorning shower that had done nothing to allay the heat and humidity.

As she drove, Sarah paid very little attention to either, or to the fact that her tank top was soaking wet with perspiration. She had learned to combat the climate as the natives did—quite simply, by ''keeping her cool.'' She had learned to be patient, to move slowly and economically, so as to generate no unnecessary body heat, and because she knew only too well that passion agitates the body as well as the soul, she tried always to keep her thoughts serene and her emotions under strict control.

Which for her, admittedly, was easier said than done, since it was so strongly against her nature. She'd come a long way, though, in the last few years; working with the placid and peace-loving orangutans had taught her a lot about governing her own passions. Too bad she hadn't learned the lessons sooner, she thought as she slowed to read the large sign bearing the logo of an internationally known oil company. How different her life might have been.

The twinges of regret were mild and brief, poignant reminders of another time, another world and a Sarah that didn't exist anymore. Whatever accidents of fate had brought her to where she was now, she was pleased with her life. She loved and believed in what she was doing. This, she thought, curving her arm protectively around the baby orangutan as she turned onto the well-traveled gravel road—*this* was something worth doing.

The road swept past plantation groves and rice fields, then wound upward through foothills that had once been heavily forested but were now blotched with logger's scars as if by the ravages of a terrible disease. As she came down onto a plateau she began to see the oil rigs, sometimes singly, more often in clusters of two or three, occupying small clearings hacked out of the dense vegetation. Like pockmarks, Sarah thought, although at least the oil crew seemed to have avoided the wholesale destruction associated with the loggers.

Not far from the oil company's headquarters she came upon a crew of Indonesian workmen clearing space for yet another drilling site. She had to stop and wait while a bull-dozer maneuvered on the narrow road for a better position from which to attack a tangle of lush undergrowth. The workmen waited, too, leaning against the trunks of trees a hundred feet tall, their chain saws stilled for the moment as they regarded her with frank curiosity. They all wore hard hats and either blue denim jeans or khaki pants and thick-soled boots for protection against snakes, scorpions and parasites. Some wore white sleeveless undershirts, most worked shirtless, but all had the same type of body—whip-cord tough, nut-brown, gleaming with a patina of sweat so that they seemed more like varnished hardwood than human flesh.

Patience, Sarah coached herself as she sat sweltering in the Land Rover waiting for the bulldozer to get out of the way to let her pass. Stay mellow. But it wasn't easy, with a thousand insects whining in her ears and a dozen pairs of male eyes watching her with varying degrees of interest, ranging from mild curiosity to frank lust. She was suddenly very aware of her bare arms and throat, and of the cotton knit fabric clinging damply to her breasts.

Just then one of the workmen came leaping and sliding down the slope, holding up his hand as a signal to the dozer operator.

Beautiful. The thought came to Sarah unheralded as she watched the man clear the last embankment and stride out into the middle of the road. Though it had been years since she'd been forced to give up her dreams of becoming a dancer, she still noticed the way people moved, and this man made something in her thrill and quicken, made certain nerves quiver and muscles tighten. Not only did he have a beautiful, well-proportioned body, but every movement he made was graceful—graceful in the way of a wild animal—

unconscious, unaffected, completely natural. And while she knew it was probably a cliché to think of a graceful human being as feline, the one image that came instantly to her mind and refused to go away was that of a great jungle predator. Not a tiger, but something more slender, more agile. Perhaps a panther.

He was motioning to her now, having directed the dozer to move just far enough to one side of the road to let her pass. He must be the one in charge of this crew, Sarah thought as she put the Land Rover in gear and began to edge forward into the narrow space he'd allotted her. He wasn't a big man, though taller than most Indonesians, but there was an air of command in the way he held his head, something about the lines of his neck and shoulders, the set of his jaw. There was self-assurance in the way he stood, with feet apart and hands on his hips, and arrogance in the way he waved her on, as if he owned the road and it was only by his grace that she was granted passage.

His hair was long and clung to his sweat-glazed neck in dark wet commas. As she came closer to him Sarah could see that it was dark brown rather than black. Mixed blood, she thought, which would also explain his height and the rocky contours of his jaw.

The rest of his face was shaded by his hard hat, so she didn't see his eyes until she was directly opposite him. When she did, she felt a little current pass through her body, as if she'd received a low-voltage electrical charge.

Amazingly, the man's eyes were blue.

But it wasn't that unexpected color that made Sarah swallow her thank-you and drive on with eyes straight ahead, or, when she was safely out of sight, to pause to wipe sweat-slippery hands on her tensed thighs, as if she'd just had a narrow brush with catastrophe. What had her feeling confused and upset out of all proportion to the importance of the incident was the *look* in those eyes.

She thought she must have surprised him; he hadn't expected her to make that direct contact. Because the look she'd caught in his eyes had been one of naked desire, primitive and unmistakable. She had an idea it was the kind of thing a man wouldn't willingly let a woman see, except perhaps in the heat of passion, beyond its point of no return, when he wouldn't need to fear alarming her or revealing his own frailties.

But it was only there for a moment. Then, like a chameleon changing color before her eyes, it became something else entirely, something that in a way was even more shocking because it was so inexplicable. Contempt.

She'd jerked away from the contact then as if she'd been stung, but the memory of those cold blue eyes stayed on.

A small movement at her side was like a pebble dropped into a pond's reflection, shattering the image, banishing the memory. The baby orangutan was nuzzling her breast, looking instinctively for food. Silly, she thought as she gently but firmly redirected the baby's searching muzzle and sharp little teeth, meaning herself, not the orangutan. What did it matter what one man—an oil-crew roughneck— thought of her? She was here for only one reason. That was all she needed to concern herself with at the moment.

She had an idea it was going to be quite enough.

The oil company's field headquarters were in a large cleared compound and consisted of modern office buildings, heavy-equipment storage barns made of corrugated aluminum, tennis courts and comfortable residences shaded by flowering trees. It was all very pleasant and suburban, if you overlooked the oil pumps bobbing slowly up and down like giant grasshoppers, the piles of drilling pipe, the tangle of hoses and equipment. The drainage ditches and holding ponds she drove past were stagnant and coated with a rainbow petroleum film, and the stench of crude oil hung in the air like ground fog. It was something you got used to, Sarah supposed, but she had to fight an almost reflexive reaction against allowing that hot, fetid air into her lungs.

She parked the Land Rover in a paved parking area in front of what she assumed, by the flower beds and flagpole in front of it, to be the main administration building. Once again she decided against leaving the baby orangutan in one of the travel crates; there was no shade in the parking lot, and besides, there is probably nothing in the world so endearing as a baby orangutan. If anything in the world could soften a hard man's heart . . .

Taking a deep breath and cuddling Sweetie close for courage, Sarah walked down the wide sweep of concrete and pushed through the double glass doors. She found herself in an air-conditioned reception area that could have been the front offices of any large company in San Jose, California, her hometown. There were mounted photographs on the walls, large blowups of old pictures showing scenes of the oil company's earliest explorations, in the days when these islands were known as the Dutch East Indies and the local tribesmen still occasionally ate their enemies alive. There was a tank full of tropical fish on the counter and a smiling girl in a crisp cotton dress behind it. Sarah began to feel grubby and conspicuous in her sneakers and jeans and downright chilly in the damp tank top. She wished she'd had a chance to at least wash her hands and face and comb her hair before facing Mr. Cisco.

"May I help you?" the girl behind the counter asked in pleasantly accented English. Sarah stepped closer, and the girl's professional smile became instead a softly exhaled "Oh . . ." She stood up and leaned across the counter to get a better look at the baby orang. Sweetie obliged by reaching toward her with a languidly exploratory hand. The girl touched the tiny fingers, then shot Sarah a look of wonder and inquiry. "Is it all right? Can I pet him?"

Sarah hesitated. Apes are susceptible to all the viruses and ailments that afflict humans, but the girl looked healthy and Sarah thought it unlikely one little pat would do any harm. It wouldn't do to become an overprotective mother. So she nodded encouragingly and said, "*Her* name is Sweetie."

The receptionist shyly stroked the sparse orange hair on the baby's head. The expression on her face was besotted. Sarah understood just how she felt. She knew it was likely that, although she was apparently Indonesian, the girl had never been so close to an orangutan in her life.

"I've never seen one," the girl whispered, confirming the guess. "Except in the zoo, and in pictures. She's so cute. Oh, I wish I could hold her! Do you think—ow!" She laughed uncertainly and jerked her hand away as Sweetie gave it an experimental nibble.

"She's hungry," Sarah explained, gingerly easing Sweetie's grip on her own much-too-accessible breast before offering the receptionist her hand. "I just picked her up about an hour ago. Hi, I'm Sarah. I spoke to someone on the telephone, about picking up an orangutan that's being kept as a pet? The man's name was Dan Cisco. I believe he's expecting me."

"Oh." The receptionist looked doubtful. "I don't know anything about an orangutan. Maybe the work crew? Hmm. I'm afraid Mr. Cisco isn't here right now. He's out in the field. You say he is expecting you?"

Sarah nodded and thought peevishly, Great, just great. She couldn't help being out-of-sorts. She was critically in need of a bathroom, a good wash and a clean shirt, and the baby orangutan required food. She still had a long drive ahead of her and a tricky river crossing to make before dark, and what she didn't need was to be stood up by an inconsiderate jerk of an oil executive. Damn!

The receptionist was smiling reassuringly. "Well, I'm sure if Mr. Cisco is expecting you, he will be here very soon. If you would like to wait?"

Stay cool. Sarah firmly squelched her impatience and nodded, glancing at her watch. "Umm, okay. Listen, is there a restroom I could use?"

"Oh, sure." The receptionist pointed. "Down the hall and to the left." She tickled Sweetie's hairy arm and crooned, "Bye-bye, little one."

Sarah felt better after washing her face, neck and arms with wet paper towels, but after giving herself a critical once-over in the mirror she decided there wasn't much she could do with the rest. She'd given up on mascara and lipstick long ago; the heat and humidity made any kind of makeup more of a liability than an asset. Her blond hair was short, its simple cut designed for coolness and convenience rather than style. It did accentuate her long, dancer's neck, and she supposed that with the right clothes and under the right circumstances it could even be coaxed into elegance, but at the moment, the most she could say for it was that it looked neat and tidy.

She sighed and looked down at Sweetie, who was watching her new "mother's" activities with a kind of passive curiosity. Once again Sarah found a sense of perspective in those black-button eyes. After all, she told herself, she was a scientist, with a Ph.D. in zoology. She didn't need blond hair, long eyelashes and feminine curves to charm some brawny male chauvinist into doing what was right; all she needed was dignity, composure and common sense.

Meanwhile, Sweetie was hungry, and there was formula and fruit in the Land Rover. Sarah decided to take advantage of the wait to see if she could get the baby orangutan to eat.

She stopped into the lobby to tell the receptionist where she was going. "I'll only be a minute," she emphasized. "If

Mr. Cisco comes in, please tell him I'll be right back, okay?"

"Yes, of course, I will tell him. Oh—" The girl's face blossomed into a smile. "Here he is now."

The front doors opened with a sound much like a sigh. Sarah felt a breath of warm, moist air on the back of her neck and turned, half in relief, half in dread. Then, for an instant, she felt nothing, nothing at all. Her mind was a complete blank.

Once, only a few weeks after she'd arrived at the rehabilitation center, while loping full tilt along a forest path with her attention focused on the treetop canopy, she'd rounded a bend and come literally face-to-face with a rhinoceros. She'd suffered the same kind of mental short circuit then that she was experiencing now. And when her mind had begun functioning again, a similar confusing jumble of thoughts and emotions: surprise, of course, at encountering the unexpected; awe and a sense of wonder at being within touching distance of a creature even more rare and more gravely endangered than the orangutan; fear and full awareness that the creature could harm her. Finally, blank uncertainty. Oh, Lord, what did she do now?

"I'm Dan Cisco," the voice with traces of Texas said.

He'd taken off the hard hat and put on a shirt, a short-sleeved khaki work shirt left open at the throat. Sarah could see beads of moisture shimmering on the smooth, walnut skin. In spite of that and the fact that his hair still clung damply to his neck, he did not smell of sweat. She wondered if he was late because he'd stopped to take a shower before coming to meet her.

The hand he offered her was cool and dry. She had to gird herself, gather all of her courage in order to meet his gaze, expecting the same look she'd flinched away from as if from a physical blow only a short while ago. But his eyes were impassive now, their expression partly shielded behind straight, black lashes. Had she imagined it all, then, both the contempt and the desire?

For just a moment, with her hand in his hard, cold grasp, she wondered whether he was capable of either emotion, whether he was capable of sweating; whether, in fact, his body was human flesh at all.

Just for a moment. Then his hand grew warm in its intimate contact with hers. She felt heat and energy radiating from his body, like steam from hot asphalt after a midday shower. Feeling slightly suffocated, she disengaged her hand and, in a gesture that was instinctively protective, placed it over the baby orangutan's head.

Cool. Stay cool.

"Mr. Cisco," Sarah said, inclining her head politely, "I believe we spoke on the phone. I'm Dr. Fairchild."

Chapter 2

Dr. Fairchild," Dan murmured, returning the nod with rigid formality, shielding his thoughts and feelings.

Dr. Sarah Fairchild, I know exactly who and what you are.

He'd known the moment he'd laid eyes on her. Just another golden girl. She had the look, that unmistakable aura of money and privilege that was part breeding, part good health and the rest self-confidence. Oh yeah, he told himself, she had it all—the classic bone structure, sun-streaked blond hair, flawless skin and straight white teeth, strong, healthy body. Most of all, though, she had that certain way of moving, a tilt to the head and a gleam in the eyes that said to a man, "Look out, are you sure you're good enough for me?"

Dan had no use for her kind of woman. Though, to be honest, he acknowledged, remembering the double-barreled blast of pure lust that had hit him back there in the road, he could think of one use he wouldn't mind putting her to.

Even now, as she stood there looking at him with the butter-wouldn't-melt-in-her-mouth self-assurance, showing her perfect teeth in a plastic smile, he was thinking about that perfect, expensive mouth hot and open under his, lips swollen and glazed from his kisses. He thought about his hands, his work-hardened, callused hands, caressing her soft, pampered skin, raking through her neat blond hair; and *her* hands, her long slender fingers digging into his flesh as he buried himself in her.

But even as he felt his loins grow hot and his pulse quicken at the fantasy, he laughed at himself. Because aside from the fact that he was a healthy male with a healthy libido and she was an attractive female, he knew that her kind wasn't for him. She had her world and he had his, and no one had better reason than he did to know that the two didn't mesh. As a hundred small but unforgettable cruelties reminded him, he wanted nothing to do with golden girls.

But, oh, he thought, how sweet it would be to conquer this one, to break that cool facade, to make her want him, hunger for him, cry out his name in the throes of her passion!

And then he laughed at himself and felt a little ashamed, too, because he thought he'd healed those wounds and outgrown the need for childish revenge.

"We spoke on the phone?" she prompted again, unnecessarily. She was looking less confident, now, Dan noticed with a small measure of satisfaction; there was a little frown of uncertainty between her eyes, and she was holding the baby orangutan in her arms as if she thought he might snatch it away from her.

For a moment, then, he wondered what he'd said or done to put her off, those bitter rejections sang in his memory like hungry mosquitos. How many times in his childhood had he asked himself that question, not understanding then that he didn't have to do anything at all. That he *was* was enough—dark, alien, *different*.

But that was the past, and Dan brushed away the memories the way he'd swipe at a cloud of mosquitos. Hell, he thought sourly, she probably just wasn't used to dealing with a hard-workin' man, one who occasionally got his hands dirty, one with a few rough edges. He almost wished he hadn't gone to the trouble to shower and change clothes before coming to meet her; it might have done her good to smell a little honest sweat.

No sweat on her body, that's for sure, he noticed, dropping his gaze to assess the flawless drape of tanned skin over her collarbone. He caught the swift in-and-out movement of her chest and the slight breathiness in her voice and smiled inwardly, knowing she was more aware of his scrutiny than she wanted to be, and maybe, just maybe, unsettled by it.

"I was wondering whether you had spoken to your men, yet? About turning the orangutan they've been keeping as a pet over to us for rehab—" Her breath hissed sharply through her teeth.

Dan's gaze shifted downward a little bit more, just in time to catch the reflexive movement of that protective hand of hers to cover her breast. He also noticed the other breast was round and firm and fully erect, the nipple poking enticingly against the material of her tank top.

"Looks like you've kinda got your hands full already," he drawled in amusement, letting his eyes travel slowly upward again, tracking the flood of embarrassment across her skin.

She cleared her throat, visibly fighting for composure. "Umm, she's . . . hungry. I haven't had a chance to feed her yet. I was just about to, when . . ." Her still husky voice trailed off. She took a breath. "Would you mind if I try to get her to eat while we talk? I have some formula in my car."

Dan wasn't sure what happened then. While she was talking he must have let his eyes wander too close to hers, because before he knew what was happening, she'd snagged him. And then, instead of resisting that intent golden gaze, he just let her reel him in. Looking back on it later, he thought that was probably his first big mistake. He hadn't expected her eyes to have so much warmth in them, warmth that hit him in the chest like a slug of neat whiskey and spread like wildfire through his veins.

It struck him that even her eyes were golden—light brown, topaz, hazel—call them whatever you wanted, he felt their heat like a bonfire in his belly. Yes, he would watch them while he stroked her elegant body to melting, trembling readiness, watch them darken, soften, grow slumberous with desire.

"Don't know that we have that much to talk about," he said bluntly as he held the door for her. "Haven't had a chance to talk to my men yet. The orang's out at the drilling site, so far as I know. I'll drive you out there, you can take a look at him, see if you still want him."

"Oh, I want him," she murmured as she slipped past him.

Dan just grunted. After the overly air-conditioned indoors, the heat outside was like a slap in the face with a wet dishrag. Which, he suddenly remembered, was something Annie used to say about the climate in Galveston. Weird, to be thinking of her now, after all these years!

"Keys." He held out his hand. She looked at him, hesitated, then dug the keys to the Land Rover out of her pants pocket and dropped them into his palm. The metal was warm from the contact with her body. He closed his fingers around the keys slowly, almost caressingly, watching her with heavy-lidded appraisal for signs that she, too, was aware of the vicarious intimacy.

Hell, no. He should have known better. Oh, she was cool, so cool, he thought, looking down at her sleek blond head, her pristine profile. He might have managed to rattle her a little bit there for a minute, with some help from that baby orang's sharp teeth, but she was back in control now. Her kind would always have to be in control, of course. *God*, how he'd love to make her lose it, just once!

The Land Rover was like an oven. Dan adjusted the driver's seat to fit his long legs, started the engine, then fiddled his fingers irritably on the steering wheel while she rummaged around among the boxes and bags in the back. He was just taking his cigarettes and lighter from his shirt pocket when she finally climbed into the passenger's seat. He saw her glance at the cigarettes, but she didn't say anything, so he lit one and tossed the pack and lighter onto the dashboard.

"Mr. Cisco," she said as he threw the Land Rover in gear and pulled out of the parking lot, keeping her voice low and oh, so refined, "I want you to know how very much I appreciate you taking the time to help me."

He glanced at her and met a gaze that was as direct and candid as sunflowers. It made him feel vaguely ashamed. He took the cigarette from his lips and muttered, "Dan."

"I beg your pardon."

"Call me Dan."

"Oh." She hesitated, then coughed and said, "Dan," as if it were a word in a foreign language. "I guess you probably think this is a lot of trouble to go to, just to save one wild animal." She didn't sound argumentative, just sad.

"Hadn't thought about it one way or the other." But he couldn't resist looking at her again. She'd shifted the baby orang in her lap and was trying to get it to eat some stuff that looked like pablum. There was something about her—the angle of her head, maybe, or the soft set of her mouth. "That looks like baby food," he said abruptly, before the warmth in his chest could crystalize into liking.

Her laugh was a surprise; it came bubbling up from inside her like a natural spring. "That's because it is. I'm not sure what she's used to eating. Her owner sort of left that up to his servants. So I just thought I'd try some things and see what she likes. Okay, Sweetie, what do you think, huh? Is that good?"

She was crooning, the way a mother talks to her child, tickling the orang's belly, trying to get it to take some of the glop from her fingers. The baby cooperated just enough to get a good bit of the stuff smeared on her face. Then she hid her face against Sarah's side and tried to climb up her chest.

Obviously unperturbed by the smears on her shirt, Sarah murmured, "Oops, guess not. Well, let's try the bottle, shall we?"

"Messy job," Dan observed dryly.

Out of the corner of his eye he saw her head turn, and he felt her eyes on him, another of those direct looks he was beginning to find so disconcerting. Sounding faintly amused, she said, "Zoology isn't for the squeamish, Dan."

He glanced at her, then quickly back to the road. No, it wasn't, come to think of it. He smoked in silence, frowning while he thought about that and a few other things, as well. Dr. Sarah Fairchild was beginning to confuse him.

He wasn't ready to change his mind about her. She was a golden girl, no doubt about it; he was too familiar with the breed to be mistaken. What he mostly felt for her was pure, unadulterated lust, no doubt about that, either. And that was fine. He'd never been disconcerted by his natural sexual impulses; in fact, following them had led him into some memorable experiences. But this new element that was creeping into the picture had him muddled, as though he'd walked into a sucker punch.

He was beginning to like her.

He sure liked watching her. And why not? She was a good-looking woman, with a nice, firm sexy body. Except that the feeling he got, watching her with that baby orang, feeding it milk with her fingers, trying to get it to take a bottle, was a nice warm feeling that didn't have anything to do with sex.

Just then the Land Rover lurched in and out of a chuck-hole he'd been too busy watching her to avoid, and because both of her hands were occupied, she was thrown hard sideways against the door. She gave a little yelp, but instead of putting out her arms to brace herself, she wrapped them around the baby orangutan. Dan swore under his breath and threw out his arm, pinning her back against the seat while he wrestled the steering wheel one-handed.

When he had things under control again he jammed on the brakes and rasped, "Are you okay?"

She nodded, but with a wide-eyed, frightened look that made him realize he still had his arm across her chest and was leaning against it pretty heavily. It occurred to him to wonder if she might be afraid of him, not an unreasonable assumption, seeing as how he was a man she didn't know from Adam and they were alone together with the jungle rising up on either side of the road like green walls and the heat and jungle sounds settling down on them like a blanket. He was so close to her he could see a trickle of sweat on her temple and a fine mist of it under her eyes. He could feel her heart bumping against his forearm. When he saw her lips move and her throat convulse with a nervous swallow, he suddenly knew that if she was afraid, it wasn't what he wanted.

"I'm sorry," he said, letting go of a breath he didn't know he'd been holding. "These damn Sumatran roads. Guess I'd better pay attention."

"That's okay." She gave a shaken-sounding laugh as a tiny brown hand snaked around the bottle of baby formula she was holding. "I know how you feel. They're so cute, it's hard not to watch them."

Dan grunted noncommittally as he crashed the Land Rover's gears. Just as well she didn't know it wasn't the orangutan he'd been watching.

It wasn't much farther to the drilling site, and Dan managed not to hit any more bumps. By employing all her self-discipline, Sarah was able to forget about the feel of his arm across her chest—hard as a tree limb, but vibrant, pulsing with strength and life—and her own heart, knocking like a hammer against it. She forced herself to concentrate on getting the baby orangutan to eat, and by the time they pulled to a jerking stop in front of the field-office trailer, she had Sweetie drinking from the bottle as if she'd been born to it.

She caught the look Dan gave her when she got out of the car with the baby orangutan on her hip and sensed that for some reason he wasn't happy about it. His attitude toward Sweetie puzzled her. It wasn't anything he'd said—in fact, he hadn't said much at all, about the orang or anything else. Obviously, Dan Cisco wasn't much of a talker. It was the way he'd kept looking at her all the time she was trying to get Sweetie to eat that bothered her—with that dark impassivity, like a curtain drawn across his thoughts.

She couldn't read his face, that was the trouble! There was something exotic about his face, something fascinating, something disquieting. She wondered what clash of cultures had produced a bone structure with so much strength and character in it and so little of gentleness and joy; a mouth so sensual and yet so hard. She wondered what those keen, intelligent eyes had seen that he had learned to shield them behind a steel-blue mask that revealed no hint of what he was thinking or feeling. She couldn't tell whether he was protecting a soft spot with that stony facade or whether it was his heart that was stone.

The door of the trailer opened, and a man wearing the standard uniform of hard hat, work shirt and heavy boots came clumping down the steps to greet Dan in the brief, casual way of an old, if not always comfortable, association. Sarah was immediately struck by the contrast between them. Here was the big, brawny ex-jock she'd been expecting, with the macho swagger and ready grin, big hands and thick forearms covered with freckles and reddish-blond hair, eyes with a frankly appreciative twinkle. Beside such brash simplicity, Dan seemed even more exotic, more catlike and inscrutable.

"Tank Guthrie," Dan muttered, introducing her with a minimum of courtesy. "Dr. Fairchild."

Sarah's hand was swallowed up in a warm and lingering grasp. "Well, hello there." The accent was Southwestern, more pronounced than Dan's. "Am I gonna have to call you 'Doc,' or have you got a first name?"

With a gurgle of laughter Sarah gently but firmly reclaimed her hand. "It's Sarah. Nice meeting you, Tank." She wasn't usually susceptible to that kind of blatant flirtation, but after the past half hour spent with Dan Cisco and all his enigmas and undercurrents, it was almost a relief to banter with someone so upfront and uncomplicated.

"She wants to see that orang your men've been keeping," Dan said. He'd been watching the exchange between Tank and Sarah through half-closed eyes, the tilt of his mouth wry and cynical. Even when she looked away from him, she was intensely aware of him, standing there with his arms folded on his chest, legs apart, rocking slightly, up and back on the balls of his feet, with lazy and casual grace.

Tank's eyebrows shot up. "Old Beau?" He looked at Sweetie, who was sleeping soundly now, curled in a ball against Sarah's side, and made a clicking sound of disappointment. "Shoot, and I thought they'd hired you as the new company sawbones. You sure are a lot prettier than old Doc Sako, I'll tell you that. Listen, sweetheart—" his voice became a seductive rumble "—I don't care if you are a vet,

you can check me out any time.'' He sighed regretfully and
reached out to briefly touch Sweetie's head. "Oh, well. So,
how come you want to see old Beau? Somethin' wrong with
him?''

"I'm not a vet,'' Sarah explained, chuckling indulgently.
"I'm a zoologist. I don't know if there's anything wrong
with the orangutan or not. I'm ... kind of hoping I can talk
your men into letting me have him.''

"Hell, I think they'd be glad to sell him. They're always
lookin' to make a few extra bucks—who isn't?—and if you
ask me, that ape is more trouble than he's worth. It's like
havin' a kid around all the time, you know? And he's gettin' too big to handle, too. They mostly keep him on a chain,
I think, just to keep him from gettin' in the way. Well,
shoot, let's go ask 'em how much they'd take for him. I'll
be willing to bet—''

"I don't want to buy him,'' Sarah interrupted. "I'm
afraid it's against our policy to offer money.''

"She's from the Wildlife Foundation,'' Dan put in,
somewhat unexpectedly.

Sarah threw him a look as she explained to Tank Guthrie
about the work of the Orangutan Rehabilitation Project,
but as usual, found his eyes as impenetrable as mirrors.

"What I want to do,'' she finished, taking a deep breath
like a diver preparing for the plunge, "is try to persuade
your men to give Beau to us, so we can reeducate him and
eventually return him to the wild.''

Tank took off his hard hat and scratched his head. "Well
now, I don't know,'' he said doubtfully. "That's a pretty
valuable animal.''

"It's also an *illegal* animal,'' Sarah quietly pointed out,
looking him in the eye. She wouldn't tell him, unless he
asked her straight out, that it was the Foundation's policy
to neither pay nor prosecute.

Tank let go of a gust of laughter and shook his head. "Lady, you do drive a hard bargain." His expression became one of earnest sincerity. "Hey, listen now, I don't want any trouble."

Sarah smiled sweetly at him. "Oh, goodness, neither do I." The unmistakable Texas twang that had crept into her speech was unintentional; she had always been a natural mimic. It brought a sound from behind her that sounded suspiciously like laughter, but when she looked at Dan, he seemed as impassive as ever.

He gave an impatient cough and growled, "Tank, if you don't mind, just show her the goddamn animal. It's too hot to stand here and dicker."

Tank was apparently used to Dan's bluntness because he just put his hard hat back on, grinned good-naturedly and said, "Sure, Doc, right this way."

As they were slogging through the inevitable mud and the jumble of drilling equipment, though, he shook his head and said doubtfully, "I don't know, Doc, my men are pretty fond of old Beau. He's been around awhile."

"But you did say he was getting to be a nuisance," Sarah reminded him. "And the older he gets, the worse it's going to be. In fact, he'll probably be dangerous. Why don't you suggest to your men that they get a less troublesome pet? Like a dog, maybe."

Tank gave a loud bark of laughter. Sarah glanced at Dan and found him smiling. The effect was so unexpectedly devastating that she stumbled and would probably have gone down in the mud if he hadn't grabbed her elbow to steady her. "What in the world did I say?" she asked breathlessly, taking a moment to collect herself while Tank went striding on ahead, his big shoulders shaking.

With his hand still touching her elbow, Dan looked at her in silence. His smile became sardonic. "You really don't know much about this place or its people, do you?"

"No," she admitted, "I guess I don't. I don't get away from the reserve very often, except for things like this. I'd like to, but there's just Marina and me—and the rangers—and we can't be spared. I don't understand. What—"

As he tightened his grip on her elbow and turned to walk on, she caught the mocking gleam in his eyes, a chilling reminder of the look she'd seen there earlier. "Most of the men here are Bataks," he said, and she knew that the touch of disdain in his drawl was for her, not the culture of which he spoke. "They don't eat people anymore, but they do eat dogs."

Sarah looked at him in horror and gasped, "Oh...yuck!" His only response was another snort of humorless laughter. She looked away again, feeling resentful and defensive, not knowing exactly what it was she was defensive about, knowing only that for some unknown reason this man, this stranger, disapproved of her. She wondered why she cared.

The orangutan she'd come to see was chained to a length of drainpipe that lay across a ditch near the edge of the clearing. He was smaller than Dan had expected him to be, with a name like Beau. Dan didn't know a lot about apes, but he guessed this one had to be just a youngster. Maybe he'd come by the name because of the expression on his face. Like a little old man with a lot of sad memories.

He was sitting on the pipe, right about in the middle of the ditch. He didn't seem very interested when they walked up, but just went on picking at something in the general vicinity of his navel.

"Well," Tank said, "there's your monkey. Howdy, Beau."

The orang's head swiveled slowly toward them. His little black eyes solemnly examined them, one by one, but he didn't budge.

Tank looked at Dan and grinned. "I don't know, Doc. He doesn't seem to want to come over here and visit. I guess you're just gonna have to see what you need to from here."

Sarah had moved up to the edge of the ditch and was looking intently at the animal. Dan thought he knew what she was going to do next—ask either him or Tank to go out on that pipe and get him so she could take a closer look.

He was wrong. What she did was suddenly turn around and plunk the baby orang she was holding into Dan's arms, mutter, "Hold her a minute, would you please?" and drop down astride the pipe.

Well. It took one hell of a lot to throw Dan, but finding himself all of a sudden with his hands full of sleeping baby orangutan had him as close to losing his composure as he was ever likely to be. A lot of things about it surprised him: that Sarah had given the baby to him instead of Tank, whom she'd been so chummy with and who was standing closer to her; the way the little rascal just cuddled into the curve of his elbow and went right on sleeping, as if she were in a cradle. The most surprising thing of all, though, was what an insignificant and comforting weight she made. He could see now why Sarah didn't seem to mind carting her around everywhere she went.

He caught Tank grinning at him. Dan coughed once, gave Tank a look that dared him to say a word and turned his attention deliberately back to the doc.

She was hitching herself along the pipe toward the orangutan, talking softly to him all the while. Beau just sat and watched her come. When she got within an arm's length of him, she reached out and touched one of his leathery brown hands, almost as if she were offering to shake hands.

Beau hitched himself closer to her and grabbed a handful of her hair. Dan's muscles tensed, and he caught his breath; he could see her wince, and he knew it must have hurt her. But she just went on talking softly to the orang while she pried his fingers loose, petting and scratching him with her other hand. And then Beau crawled right into her arms and latched on to her the way Dan had seen wild young ones do with their mothers.

"Well, he seems healthy," she called back to them over her shoulder, "and he obviously hasn't been mistreated or he wouldn't be so quick to come to me."

Tank asked her if she needed a hand, but she just smiled at him, murmured, "No, thanks, I'm fine," and started back along the pipe. When she got to the ditch bank she shifted the orangutan's weight slightly, braced her feet on the pipe, gathered herself and stood up in a single, fluid motion that reminded Dan of something, he couldn't quite think what.

He could barely think at all, in fact, because he was watching the play of muscles in her back and buttocks, thighs and calves, fascinated by the way they bunched and pushed against the fabric that covered them. She was in great shape, he'd say that for her; to be able to stand in one motion like that was something to begin with, and that ape had to weigh at least thirty pounds. Though he didn't want to, he kept imagining what she'd look like without clothes, wondering what it would be like to feel that long supple body sliding sinuously against his, to have those strong legs locked around him, with nothing separating them from him but sweat.

"He's in good shape," she was saying to Tank, turning on the charm full blast. "Not too old, either—I'd say about four or five. That's a good age for training. You see, what we'd do is teach him to be a wild orangutan again. When we're sure he's capable of surviving in the jungle, we'd take him deep into the reserve and set him free. Look at this—" She gave the collar around Beau's shaggy neck an angry tug. "He shouldn't have to wear this! He belongs up there!" As she pointed toward the treetops, Dan caught the shine of emotion in her eyes, like the flash of sunlight on distant water.

Tank looked uncomfortable. "Well now, Doc, you know if it was up to me, I'd give him to you in a minute." He reached out to pet the orangutan, but Beau suddenly screeched, turned his face against Sarah's shoulder and covered his eyes with his hand.

Startled, Tank jerked his hand back and used it instead to rub the back of his own neck. "Yeah, but . . ." He glanced over at Dan. Dan shook his head, telling him to keep his mouth shut. Tank picked up his cue and shrugged. "Like I told you," he said smoothly, "ol' Beau isn't mine to give away. I'll have to ask my men how they feel about it. Honey, I'll do my best, but that's all I can do."

Sarah sighed and said heavily, "I understand. I appreciate your help. Thanks." She turned to Dan. "Will you help convince them? Please?"

Her voice was quiet. She hadn't bothered to turn on the high-voltage charm for him, Dan noticed, but instead just looked at him with that straight, steady gaze of hers. He wondered why it affected him the way it did, like staring into flames.

He said, "I can try. No guarantees."

She took a deep breath. "Well. I guess I'd better go, then. There doesn't seem to be anything more I can do right now." She glanced at Beau, who was poking through her hair, apparently fascinated by its pale color. Dan saw her throat move as she gently but firmly untangled the orang's fingers. "You'll let me know?"

He nodded. "I'll do that."

Sarah returned the nod, but still hesitated. Dan felt her reluctance to part with the animal in her arms like a resistance in his own muscles. Then she said huskily, "Okay, Beau, you stay here now, that's a good boy." Tightening her

mouth, she peeled the orangutan off of her and swung him
back down onto the pipe.

When she started to walk away, Beau snaked out a long
arm and caught her by the ankle. She said firmly, "No,
Beau. Stay here." She pried his fingers off her ankle and
moved quickly beyond the reach of his chain. The animal
threw himself on the ground and slapped himself on the
head and screeched blue murder until they were out of sight.

"Looks like a kid throwing a tantrum," Dan said.

"That's exactly what it was. Sometimes it's scary—" she
nodded toward the baby still sleeping soundly in the crook
of Dan's elbow "—how much they seem like us." After a
moment she said, "But they aren't, you know. They don't
belong with us. They belong in the forest. That's what their
name means, you know—People of the Forest."

She was speaking in a low voice, for him alone, while
Tank plodded on ahead of them. He answered her the same
way, but dryly. "I know. I'm not completely ignorant." He
could feel her turn to look at him, but he kept his eyes aimed
straight ahead. He didn't care for the feeling he got when he
looked into those golden eyes of hers. It was like going down
a stretch of whitewater without a steering oar.

They walked awhile in silence, then, while the baby
orangutan slept on in the nest of his arm and body. The doc
didn't seem in a hurry to take her back, and somewhat to his
surprise, Dan wasn't in any hurry to get rid of her. He told
himself it was because he didn't want to wake her up, that
she was less trouble asleep. Still, when they got back to the
Land Rover it was with definite reluctance that he turned to
Sarah and prepared to hand his tiny burden over to her.

She put a hand on his arm, stopping him. "Why don't
you just keep her until we get back to headquarters? I can
drive—if you wouldn't mind?"

For a moment or two Dan didn't say anything. He wasn't
sure why. He was a little suspicious about her motives for

wanting to drive back; he could hardly blame her, after that bump he'd given her on the way up here. With any other woman he'd have responded with a little light flirtation, a teasing remark: "What's the matter, don't you trust my driving?" But somehow with this one, teasing seemed impossible and flirting something akin to playing with matches in a dynamite factory. Every word, every gesture, every look seemed weighted with significance. It was beginning to make him feel edgy.

So he thought about it and then shook his head and said gruffly, "No point in you driving all the way back to headquarters. It's an hour out of your way. I've got some things to do here anyway. I'll hitch a ride back with Tank."

"Well," she said, "if you're sure."

He imagined she was probably relieved, though he couldn't tell from her tone of voice or the expression on her face. His own was sardonic. "No, it's okay. Thanks, anyway. So, I guess you'd better—" He coughed and shifted his body, turning the sleeping baby orangutan toward Sarah, not quite sure how to proceed with the transfer. "Uh, how do you want to do this? Kind of a shame to wake her up."

She laughed softly and stepped closer to him. All his muscles tensed and hardened, bracing for her touch. With every nerve in him he felt her hand slip into the space between the baby and his side, felt the other hand brush his arm. He was aware of her with every sense: of her hair sliding across her cheek, so close to him he could count the individual strands, in every shade of blond there was, from silver to honey brown; of its sweet, flowery scent, the warm pressure of her hand trapped against him and the husky murmur of her voice. He closed his eyes and concentrated on making his breathing slow and steady.

She moved away from him finally, with Sweetie coming languidly to life in the curve of her left arm, and Dan could let his breath out and relax again. As she pushed her hair back from her forehead with her free hand, he realized all at once that she wasn't looking as cool and unflappable as before. She looked as if she'd been wrestling with a python. She looked, in fact, pretty much the way he felt.

It occurred to him that not much more than an hour ago it would have given him a lot of satisfaction to see her like this. Now, he wasn't sure what in the hell he felt.

After a moment's awkward silence, she wiped her hand on her jeans and offered it to him. As he shook it he realized that even her hand felt different to him now.

She said, "You'll let me know, then? About Beau?"

He nodded. "I'll do that." Then, surprising himself, "Why don't you leave me one of those crates? If I do get him sprung, I'll see that he gets to the reserve."

There wasn't anything plastic about the smile she gave him. The warmth in her face and the light in her eyes gave "golden girl" a whole new meaning.

"Hey, that would be great! Do you know how to get to the station? You have to cross the river—there's a ferry, but it's—"

"I'll manage," he said sharply. "Don't worry about it."

"Okay...well, thanks." She turned away to shake hands with Tank, who tipped his hard hat and said gravely, "Doc, honey, you come back any time, you hear?"

Dan moved and stood a little distance away, watching her say her goodbyes and thank-yous, watching her smile and chat and flirt as if she'd been carrying on with Tank for a while and then some. She never did that with *him*, he noticed, but then, he didn't have Tank's way with women. Well, if what she went for was that kind of easy, down-home country bullshit, she'd sure as hell get plenty of it from Tank. She'd better be careful, though, because Tank's brand of charm was like blue sky reflected in a mud puddle—all on the surface. If she stepped in it she was liable to find herself up to her pretty ankles in something she hadn't bargained for.

He wondered why he cared.

She climbed into the Land Rover, backed around, waved and drove off. Tank came strolling over, grinning.

"Now that is one hell of a good-lookin' woman."

Dan's reply was wordless and noncommittal. He pretended preoccupation, patting his pockets, looking for his cigarettes and lighter. When he remembered where he'd left them he swore a short, sibilant oath and said, "Got a cigarette? Mine just took off down the road."

Tank pulled a pack from his shirt pocket, tapped a couple of cigarettes loose and offered the pack to Dan first before taking one for himself. He lit his and passed the lighter over. "You owe me one."

Dan's chuckle was more irony than amusement. "The hell I do." Tank was notorious for bumming—cigarettes, lights, after-shave, you name it.

They smoked in silence for a moment, squinting in the direction of the departed Land Rover. Then Tank dropped his half-finished cigarette into the mud and threw Dan a narrow, sideways look.

"You coulda sprung that ape. You've got the authority."

Dan gave an indifferent shrug. "Maybe."

"No maybe—I caught your high sign. So why didn't you? Sure woulda made that pretty lady happy—and grateful."

"Well, I guess I don't think it's worth getting on the wrong side of my men just to get on the good side of a woman," Dan said evenly as he ground his cigarette out with the toe of his boot. His words brought a hoot of laughter from Tank.

"Now see, old friend, that's where I disagree with you. Anything's worth it, if it makes this stinkin' place easier to stomach, that's my feelin'. And speakin' of which, I hear you aren't going to have to put up with this hellhole for very much longer. Hey, congratulations, man. I sure do envy you.''

They were on the way up the steps of the field-office trailer. Dan threw Tank a quick, startled look and said, ''What for?''

''Come on, the word is you've been offered a desk job back in the States. Which kind of accounts for your attitude, come to think of it, since, if I remember right, tall, slim blondes are a dime a dozen where you're goin'.''

Without comment, Dan pushed open the door to the trailer and held it. As Tank squeezed past him, he shot Dan a look and said, ''You are gonna take it, aren't you?''

''I don't know. I'm thinking about it.''

''What's there to think about? Man would have to be crazy not to jump at a chance like that.''

Dan shrugged and said, ''Maybe.'' The whole job-offer thing made him uncomfortable, and he sure wasn't going to discuss it in much detail with Tank. But while it wasn't his favorite subject for conversation, it beat the hell out of the one they'd just left.

Because his reasons for not turning that orangutan over to the doc on the spot weren't anything he wanted to discuss with Tank, either. He didn't even want to discuss it with himself.

The fact was, Dan had only one reason for hanging on to old Beau awhile longer. In spite of all his reservations and mixed feelings, in spite of the fact that he'd just sent her away because he needed breathing room, in spite of the old ghosts she'd raised, he wanted an excuse to see Sarah Fairchild again.

The rest of the trip back to the reserve was uneventful; Sarah only had to winch the Land Rover out of the mud once and, after a second bottle, Sweetie slept most of the way. Even so, it was sundown by the time she got to the end of the road.

Jungle sounds and smells settled down around her like fog as she turned off the engine and began to gather her things together for the mile walk to the river crossing. She would only carry Sweetie and her backpack with her; the rangers, Joka and Salim, would come back for the rest of the supplies.

The river was shallow enough to wade at that point, but very swift and slippery, and the ferry consisted only of a dugout canoe attached to a rope stretched from one bank to the other. As she maneuvered herself and the unwieldy boat across the stream, Sarah couldn't help but smile, remembering how nervous she'd been the first few times she'd made the crossing. Now it seemed to her simpler—and much less dangerous—than crossing a San Jose street in rush-hour traffic.

Twilight threatened as she passed the deserted ranger post and plunged into the well-traveled path from the river to the rehab station, but the coming of darkness didn't concern her; the jungle held no terrors for her, and she knew every inch of the path. She didn't know why she should feel a stirring on the back of her neck—a formless disquiet, like the fear that assails children on the way home after dark and sends them hurtling those last few yards to light and safety in a breathless, heart-thumping panic.

Sarah didn't quite quicken her step, but she was relieved to see the thatched roof and lighted windows of the main cabin through the trees just the same. Everything was fine, of course. It was peaceful and as quiet as it ever gets in the rain forest. Marina Witt, the Dutch zoologist who was her partner on the rehabilitation project, was just coming down the slope from the feeding platform behind the main house. Everything was fine. It was good to be home.

Sarah waved and called, "Mari! Come see what I've got."

Marina stopped abruptly, letting the sacks of bananas she was carrying drop to the ground. "Sarah! Oh, thank God—"

Something in her voice and the way she came, picking up speed until she was almost running, made Sarah go cold with fear. "Mari?" she cried hoarsely as the girl threw her arms around her, shaking with sobs. "What is it? What's happened?"

Marina tossed her long dark braid over her shoulder and stepped back, wiping her cheeks with both hands. "Oh, Sarah—"

Sarah pulled the baby orangutan closer to her body. "For God's sake, tell me."

"Oh, Sarah," Marina sobbed, "it's so terrible. Sukey's been murdered!"

Chapter 3

Poachers?'' Sarah forced the word past stiff, cold lips, and its echoes whispered around her in the twilight.

Marina nodded, brushing again at her wet cheeks. "Salim found her this afternoon, down by the river. You know that big fig tree?"

"What about her baby?" Sarah asked woodenly, but she already knew the answer. Marina clamped one hand over her mouth and confirmed the worst with a shake of her head. Sarah closed her eyes. The sob she'd been trying to hold back shuddered through her.

"They shot her," Marina said, crying, too. "While she was feeding in that big tree by the river. Salim said he looked and looked, but he couldn't find her baby anywhere, so I guess they got him. Oh, Sarah, what are we going to do? They are becoming so bold! To take one of our own, right off the reserve—"

Sarah's throat felt like concrete. She heard herself ask calmly, "Where are Joka and Salim now?"

Marina drew a deep breath and held it for a moment, fighting for control. "After they brought Sukey's body back here, they went to see if they could find anything—evidence, clues, I don't know what. They haven't come back yet." She sniffed and added flatly, "They took guns."

There was a long silence, and then Sarah swiped at the tears on her cheeks and said matter-of-factly, "There are supplies in the car. They'll have to be brought in. We can't leave them out there all night."

"And you've brought us this new little one." Marina's voice was liquid and soft as she took Sweetie from Sarah's arms. "We'll have to make a place for her in quarantine."

"Yes." Sarah took a deep breath and gave her backpack a hitch. "I've been calling her Sweetie. She's in good shape, I think. Anyway, she's been taking milk from the bottle."

Together, then, they continued on toward the house, walking slowly, discussing Sweetie's care and feeding in neutral tones, each of them using the demands of work, of the routine, the necessary, the mundane, to keep grief at bay.

After all, Sarah reminded herself for the second time that day, they were zoologists. She knew that in her job, as in any job involving animals, especially wild animals, tragedies were inevitable. They were scientists. The animals they worked with weren't pets, they were wild, and life in the jungle was fragile and precarious. This wasn't the first time they'd experienced the loss of a project orangutan, and it wasn't the first time they'd encountered poachers' work. Nor was it likely to be the last.

Oh, but Sukey had been special. A new flood of anger and grief rushed stinging to her eyes as she remembered that when she'd first arrived at the station, Sukey had been a beautiful young female just coming into maturity. She'd been one of the first captive orangutans to be successfully rehabilitated; it had been just a little over a year ago that she'd been "graduated." She'd kept coming back to the feeding platform now and then, so, to a certain extent, Sarah and Marina had been able to keep track of her. They'd rejoiced when she'd turned up pregnant, the result of a brief association with a wild male. They'd been ecstatic when she'd given birth to a healthy infant and showed every sign of being a good, attentive mother, because it had proved to them, as nothing else could, that Sukey's rehabilitation was complete. After spending most of her life in a cage, she was at last living wild and free in the forest, where she belonged.

Now she was dead, shot down in cold blood by a poacher, for no other reason except that it was the only way he could get her baby away from her. And the worst of it was, the odds were the baby would die, too, of neglect or from some human-transmitted disease.

When Sarah thought about that, the tears spilled over again. She couldn't help it; it was just so damned unfair. Death was a fact of life, especially in the jungle. But not this! *Not this.*

"I want them dead," Marina said. "I want to kill them myself."

It was evening, and she and Sarah were sitting at the kitchen table in the station's main cabin. While Marina fed Sweetie, Sarah sipped black coffee from a tin mug. She wasn't hungry, although except for some fruit she'd had with her in the Land Rover, she hadn't eaten anything since the huge American-style breakfast in the motel that morning.

She wasn't hungry because she was too full of rage. She looked at Marina across the rough, orangutan-proof table and saw her own feelings mirrored in her friend's pale, Dresden shepherdess face: pain, anger, revulsion. She decided that there could be no species of vermin so despicable, so irredeemably wicked, as these men who would, without a qualm, slaughter a most inoffensive, peaceful and critically endangered creature, solely in order to steal its young. They were the lowest and most loathsome form of life on the planet!

"Thank God for this little one." Marina sighed, nodding at the baby orangutan in her lap. After a moment she gave a short laugh and added, "It is ironic, isn't it?"

Sarah knew what she meant, and her answering laugh was harsh and bitter. "Yeah, we lose one and we get one back, all in the same day. Does that mean we break even?"

"No," Marina whispered, looking at her with swimming eyes. "There's still Sukey."

Sarah sat silently for a moment, then rubbed her own eyes and said, "Well, it won't replace Sukey, but we may be getting another rehab candidate in a day or two." Very briefly, then, she told Marina about old Beau, carefully avoiding any mention of the enigmatic and disturbing Mr. Cisco. She didn't want to think about him right now. She had a feeling she would probably do quite a lot of thinking about him, sooner or later, and maybe some talking, too. Maybe talking with a friend would help her figure the man out, help her understand why she'd responded to him the way she had. But not now. Not tonight.

"You had a good trip, then. I'm glad." Marina suddenly shuddered. "You know, we have been observing that tree. All week, every day, one of us was there. Until the last two days, because you were away and there was so much to do, and no one could spare the time...."

"I know. I thought of that." Sarah drained the last of her coffee and carried the cup to the small stainless-steel sink.

"I wonder," Marina said slowly, "if one of us had been there, would they have shot us, too?"

Sarah shook her head, frowning. "No, I've been thinking about that. I think they want to avoid confrontation. It's almost as if they knew that no one would be there today. But how could they know?'' She shivered and rubbed at the goose bumps on her arms, for the tropical night had suddenly turned cold. Even though the bamboo shades had been lowered she felt exposed and vulnerable in the lighted cabin, completely surrounded by dark jungle. She felt an urge to glance nervously over her shoulder, as if something terrifying lurked just beyond the light.

It was a relief to hear the familiar clomp and scrape of boots on the wooden veranda, a firm, unequivocal knock on the door.

The two Indonesian rangers came in, looking tired, muddy and grim. They propped their high-powered rifles carefully against the wall and accepted the mugs of coffee Sarah offered them, but didn't sit down.

"Nothing," said Salim, who was older and had a better command of English than Joka did. "We found nothing. They left no sign, except this." He took something from his shirt pocket and laid it on the table.

The two women looked at it. Sarah said, "A cigarette butt?"

Salim shrugged. "It was on the grass beside the body. Joka found it earlier this afternoon." He drained the last swallows of his coffee and placed the mug on the table. Joka did the same.

"We will bring the supplies from the truck," Salim announced, handing one of the rifles to Joka and taking the battery-powered lantern from its nail by the door. "We will leave you the gun." Just before he went out he turned and said gravely, "It would be best if you do not go alone into the forest, either of you. If you go, Joka or myself must go with you. *Ja?*"

"*Ja.*" Sarah murmured absently. "*Terima kasih.*" Yes. Thank you.

She picked up the cigarette butt and turned it over in her fingers, trying to ignore the cannon leaning against the wall.

It looked as if it would stop an elephant in its tracks; she didn't want to think about what it would do to a man.

"What is it?" Marina asked after the rangers had gone. "Do you think it means anything? That cigarette?"

"I don't know. I was just noticing—it's an American brand. Not a common one, either. It's one of those funny little thin ones."

"So what? You can buy American cigarettes in any store in town."

"In town, yes," Sarah said slowly. "But they're expensive. I doubt that most Indonesians could afford them."

"Poachers could," Marina muttered darkly.

"True." Sarah didn't say any more, but it had just occurred to her that she knew of one place, located conveniently nearby, where there were both Americans and American cigarettes: the oil-company complex.

"I don't see J.J.," Sarah said, observing the general chaos on the feeding platform the next afternoon.

Marina frowned as she absently slapped away a hairy hand bent on stealing one of the bottles of milk from the bucket beside her. "He wasn't here yesterday, either. It's very odd. It isn't like J.J. to miss two meals in a row."

Sarah agreed. Ordinarily it was cause for rejoicing when an orangutan elected to pass up the midafternoon handout; it meant that he was finding better things to eat all by himself in the forest. But J.J. was still too young to be completely independent.

"Luki's here." She nodded toward the potbellied youngster sitting apart from the crowd around the milk pan. "I thought those two were inseparable."

"They are." Marina poured some milk into a tin cup and offered it to Luki, who drank without enthusiasm and then crawled into her lap. Over the shaggy red head, Marina's dark eyes met Sarah's with a look of foreboding. "I wonder if something's happened to J.J."

Neither of them spoke the word that was in both their minds: *Poachers*.

"Someone's coming," Marina said, standing up and shading her eyes.

Salim and Joka were coming up the path from the river, carrying a crate between them. Sarah could only spare them a glance; she had her hands full, scattering green bananas and trying to keep larcenous fingers away from the milk bottles. "Looks like we may have a new rehab candidate. I wonder if it's that one I told you about, from the oil crew."

"What an interesting-looking man," Marina murmured. "I wonder who that is."

Something in her voice made Sarah snatch another quick look. And then another, much longer.

Keeping her voice carefully neutral, she said, "That's the man I spoke to yesterday at the oil-company's headquarters. His name is Dan Cisco." She didn't stand up, for the simple but puzzling reason that her legs had suddenly lost the strength to support her.

"Really? But he's not an American, is he? He doesn't look American."

Sarah managed a dry laugh. "Actually, I think he may be more genuinely American than I am. He looks like he could be part American Indian."

"Really!" Marina's voice had acquired a new note of interest. "How nice of him to bring the orangutan to us personally. Are you coming? I want to go and see our new pupil." She was already on her way down the ladder, her sparkling eyes and dimpled grin casting some doubt as to just who it was she was eager to see. Sarah couldn't blame her; attractive, available men were something of a rarity in their lives at the moment. Life in the jungle was full and rewarding, but that one particular kind of excitement was definitely missing.

"You go ahead, I'll be along in a minute," she mumbled vaguely. "I'll just finish up here."

Abandoned by his foster mother, Luki crawled to Sarah and wrapped his hand around her ankle, almost as if he were offering his sympathy. She reached over to scratch his belly, crooning, "Yes, Luki... what's the matter, huh? Where's J.J. today? Where's your buddy?" But every nerve in her body was humming with tension, tuned to the murmur of conversation drifting up from the compound below.

She felt confused, uneasy, like a wild animal sensing a trap. Why was he here? A busy man, with responsibilities of his own—why would he come personally just to deliver an animal in whom he'd obviously had no particular interest up till now? She seriously doubted that it had anything to do with being "nice." Nice, she thought ruefully, remembering the look of icy disdain he'd given her, wasn't the first adjective that came to mind when she thought of Dan Cisco!

Down below, she heard a familiar male voice join Marina's in laughter. The slam of the main cabin's screen door. Silence.

She wondered what was going on. She wanted to go down to find out. There was nothing to stop her from doing so, but instead she went on sitting there in the hot sun, needlessly distributing bananas to orangutans she no longer really saw.

She was seeing Dan the way she'd seen him for the first time, standing in the road, arrogant as an Aztec chieftain, his body gleaming with sweat, like polished hardwood. She was remembering the way he'd looked at her then—the *first* look.

Oh, she did want to see him again, but the thought of it made her feel the way she'd always felt before a dance recital—heart pounding, stomach in knots, sweating ice water, certain her legs weren't going to hold her.

"Is this a private party, or can anybody come?"

Sarah almost fell off the platform. Stay cool, she counseled herself, and desperately prayed, Please God, don't let me make a fool of myself.

She knew he didn't like her; that look in his eyes had said so. Oh, he'd tried to hide it since, behind that Indian's mask of his, behind conventional politeness, but she knew. She'd heard him laughing with Marina, sounding friendly, open, relaxed. But with her he always seemed taciturn, distant, vaguely disapproving.

And every time Sarah looked at him, her knees melted. It wasn't fair, she thought. It was humiliating.

And now he was standing just below the platform, looking up at her. There was a cynical little half smile on his face. "Sorry," he drawled, "didn't mean to make you jump."

His mocking tone brought pride to her rescue. "You didn't," she assured him. Satisfied that her own voice carried the right note of detachment, she added, "It's quite all right if you want to come up. They won't hurt you. Orangutans are rarely aggressive."

Dan responded to that with an ambiguous chuckle, but he came up the ladder with the effortless grace she remembered so well and settled himself on the planks a few feet away from her. The orangutans paid very little attention to him; they were used to visitors. To Sarah it seemed as though the platform had suddenly shrunk to the size of a kitchen table.

"The party's breaking up anyway, I'm afraid," she said. "The food's gone."

Dan was glancing around him with interest and failed to take the hint. "I brought your new pupil," he remarked, bringing his gaze back to Sarah.

Momentarily unnerved, she stammered, "I know, I saw." Then, after a pause, "Thank you, it was...nice of you to bring him yourself. We're very grateful to you for your help." Like a little girl remembering her manners, she thought, chagrined.

Dan shifted, making himself more comfortable on the rough planks, and drawled, "Well, I sorta wanted to see what you were all about here." He'd been watching the orangutans as they drifted off one by one into the forest, but as he spoke he swiveled his head and gave Sarah a look that made her wonder if he meant it personally.

Then he gave another of those soft chuckles that seemed to hold more irony than amusement. "Kinda surprised me, though. First thing your friend did with poor old Beau is stick him in a cage."

Sarah nodded sympathetically. "Quarantine. We have to do that, otherwise they might expose the wild orang population to all sorts of human diseases."

"Yeah, I know. Your friend told me."

They were almost alone on the platform now, except for a couple of stragglers and, of course, Luki, who seemed happy to stay right where he was, in Sarah's lap. Dan's eyes began to seem to her like scalpels—cold, impersonal, skillfully and purposefully cutting through the layers that protected her innermost thoughts while revealing nothing whatsoever of his. Under their relentless dissection she felt the silence become audible and then jaw-tightening torment, like an insect whining in her ear.

Just when she thought it would become intolerable, Dan leaned over to scratch Luki's belly and asked softly, "Where's the little one? The one you had yesterday. I suppose she's in quarantine, too?"

"Sweetie? Well, she is in quarantine, but she's so small we're keeping her in the cabin. Right now I'm sort of her foster mother."

"Yeah?" Something flared briefly in his eyes, like a match in a windstorm. "Looks like somebody else already has you spoken for."

He went on scratching Luki's belly while the orangutan inspected his hand and arm with lazy curiosity. Sarah found herself staring at the muscles twisting like ropes beneath the smooth brown skin and remembering the weight of that arm across her own chest, pinning her against the car seat. She suddenly wondered what it would feel like to touch it gently with her fingers, her lips....

The dryness in her throat came to stay.

"This is Luki," she said, shifting the orang so that Dan was obliged to withdraw his hand. "Usually he stays in the forest. I don't know what's gotten into him today. I think he misses his sidekick, J.J. They were inseparable."

"Yeah? I didn't know they had attachments like that. Aren't orangutans supposed to be loners?"

Sarah looked at Dan with some surprise. Somehow she'd gotten the impression he didn't know or, for that matter, care very much about orangutans. "They are, especially when they get older. These two are pretty unusual, the way they're always together. That's why I'm beginning to worry. J.J. hasn't shown up for two days, now. And with Luki acting like this, I'm afraid something's happened to him."

"Something?" Dan prompted. "Like what?"

She shrugged, carefully not looking at him. "Accidents happen, even to wild orangs. Pythons...rotten branches...."

"Heard you had some trouble with poachers." His tone held only casual interest. Sarah shot him a look and came up hard against a steady blue gaze.

"The rangers told me," he went on, chuckling ruefully. "Set me back a little when they came to meet me armed to the teeth with elephant guns." And then his voice changed, becoming gentler but, at the same time, more substantial.

It became something to cling to, like a friend's hand in the dark. "Said you'd lost a mother and baby just recently. I'm sorry."

I'm sorry. So simple and straightforward that she believed it. And was so touched by his sympathy she couldn't speak.

"Are you thinking they might have gotten this little one's buddy, too?"

Sarah straightened and squared her shoulders, clutching at self-control with a kind of desperation. In another moment she was going to reveal much more of her emotions than she cared to. She cleared her throat and said carefully, "Yes. But I'll probably never know. If they shot him and he managed to crawl away into the jungle, it isn't very likely we'll ever find him." She stood up, shifting Luki to one hip. "Well. It was very nice of you to come and, umm, bring Beau . . ." And then she stopped, because Dan was just sitting there, looking up at her, holding out his hand.

Could he possibly mean what she thought he did? It seemed so natural, so spontaneous, almost playful—oddly intimate. And none of those things would she ever have associated with this particular man, this man who'd always seemed to her as arrogant, as taciturn, as forbidding as a pagan god. But, yes—as she looked from his outstretched hand to his face, Dan made a small, insistent gesture, and with a gurgle of surprised laughter, Sarah gave him her hand and braced against his weight as he used it to pull himself up.

Heat and wonder washed through her. Why had he done that? She'd seen him move; he certainly didn't need her help to get up off of his backside!

She felt as if the platform she was standing on had suddenly tilted, throwing her off balance, compelling her toward him. The simple act of releasing his hand, of turning away from him, starting down the ladder, seemed an exhausting struggle against natural forces, forces stronger than she was.

And she knew a moment of panic, like an infant's inborn fear of falling.

"What now?" Dan asked her as they walked down the slope to the main cabin. He indicated the orangutan in her arms.

Sarah didn't answer immediately. She felt him looking at her, but she didn't dare look back. She could still feel that incredible magnetism, the way a sailor feels the pitch and roll of the deck even while standing on solid ground.

What now? God, if she only knew! For a moment she thought that what she wanted most was for Dan Cisco to leave, to go away from her, release her so that she could relax the tension in her muscles and breathe easy again.

Or, she wanted him to give her a reason to stop fighting the pull, to surrender to it and go wherever it took her.

"I'll have to go take Luki back into the jungle," she said finally. "I can't let him develop a dependence on me." She didn't know why she should feel a little sad, all of a sudden. A strange, wistful yearning, like a child wishing on a star for something she knows she can't have.

Dan jerked his thumb in the direction they'd just come from. "Isn't the jungle that way?"

"Uh-huh. I have to find one of the rangers to go with me." She took the risk of giving Dan one quick glance. "After that last raid, they don't want us to go into the forest alone."

They walked two, three, four steps in silence. Then Dan said, "I'll go with you."

Thoughts and impressions filled Sarah's head like a swarm of gnats. The noisiest and most persistent was the one that had come to her last night as she'd held a poacher's cigarette butt in her fingers. Dan was an American, from the oil-company compound. But there were other images, too: a pair of cold, contemptuous eyes, an Aztec mask, a sensuous mouth with no hint of a smile, hands cupped around a cigarette, a hard arm slamming her back against the car seat. And still others: those same blue eyes and a brief glimpse of something bright and joyful in them, like a candle in a dark window. A soft-tough voice, and a hand gently scratching a young orang's round belly.

No, she thought. No, not Dan.

Still, as she stopped walking and faced Dan, she felt a little chill of excitement that told her she was about to do something foolish and possibly dangerous. Ignoring it, she took a deep breath and said, "All right."

Dan hoped he wasn't making the biggest mistake of his life. As he followed Sarah through towering bamboo and head-high ferns he was asking himself what the hell he was doing here. He felt at home in jungles; he'd had his share of run-ins with snakes, scorpions and most of the other disasters that go with the territory. He thought he knew what to expect, what to look out for. But this woman was something else, a whole new kind of jungle. He had a feeling she could do him some serious damage, if he wasn't careful.

He knew that what he ought to do was turn around, go back home and leave her alone. Getting mixed up with a woman like her was the surest way he knew of to get hurt. In the long run, nothing good could ever come of it.

Ah, but in the short run. He knew he hadn't been this attracted to a woman in a long time, for sure not since Annie'd walked out of his life for the last time. Sarah haunted his dreams, waking and sleeping. He'd risen this morning knowing he had to see her again, even if it made him seven different kinds of a fool for doing so.

Maybe there was something in heredity after all, Dan thought wryly. Heredity, destiny, whatever it was, he sure did seem bent on following in his father's footsteps. Except that he wasn't about to make his father's mistakes; no sir,

he'd learned that lesson well. He'd be fine, as long as he remembered the rules: If you're going to get involved with
someone from a different world, do it for fun. Just don't
ever fall in love.

Which, as he told himself, he was in no danger of doing.
What he felt for Sarah Fairchild was physical chemistry,
nothing more. And it was his personal feeling that chemistry as potent as this should always be pursued, as long as it
was mutual and he wasn't poaching on another man's territory.

Poaching. Unfortunate choice of metaphor, he thought,
considering the circumstances. But it brought him back to
the here and now, to the soggy green reality of the rain forest, to the echoing shrieks, squawks, thumps and whines and
the rich brown smells of growth and decay that gave the
moist air texture, like steam rising from a caldron.

Back to Sarah, walking ahead of him down the forest
path, pale light filtering through the canopy, casting eerie,
mottled shadows that blurred her elegant lines and dulled
her sunshine colors. She seemed to be changing before his
eyes, like a chameleon; to lose even form and substance until she appeared to him as ephemeral as those moving shadows. He knew the Old Religions believed that spirits lived in
all things—plants, animals, inanimate objects. She could
almost have been an embodiment of one of them—a forest
spirit come to life.

He quickened his step and moved up beside her. The
direction his thoughts had taken both surprised and annoyed him. He didn't believe in spirits, old or new, and the
only Sarah Fairchild he was interested in was warm flesh and
blood. All of a sudden he had a need to verify that, a need
as compelling as a sneeze.

When he put his hand on the back of her neck, she jerked
her head around and gave him a surprised look. Surprised
and maybe a little apprehensive. He remembered, then, the

way she'd seemed so startled when he'd flung his arm across her in the car, the way she'd hesitated when he'd volunteered to escort her into the jungle. He wasn't sure exactly what it was she was afraid of, so he smiled at her in what he hoped was a reassuring way, gave her neck a friendly little squeeze and let his hand fall away.

"Well," she said a moment later, sounding out of breath, "I guess this is far enough. All right, Luki, you be a good boy, now. Go build yourself a nice nest." She peeled the orangutan off her and transferred him to a trailing creeper as big around as her arm.

Luki didn't seem to mind; he just hung there, casually holding on to the creeper with one hand and one foot, watching them with his little black eyes—until they turned and started back down the path toward the station. Then he dropped to the ground and scuttled after them like a giant, hairy orange spider, screeching his head off.

"Oh, dear." Sarah sighed as Luki shinnied up her legs and wrapped his arms around her neck. "I guess this is going to be a little more difficult than I thought."

Patiently, she put the orangutan back onto a vine. And again he seemed happy enough about it—until they started back toward camp.

Sarah was firm. "No, Luki, behave yourself. You have to stay here. It's where you belong. You just haven't figured that out yet."

Luki was determined. As Sarah pried the orangutan's fingers off her wrist for the third time, she said soberly to Dan, "Something must really have upset Luki to make him regress like this. I'm more convinced than ever that something's happened to J.J."

Her voice was matter-of-fact, but there was a set look about her mouth and chin and something in the way she held her shoulders that made Dan want to touch her again, this time to offer comfort. It was an unfamiliar feeling, and it made him awkward and irritable because he wasn't sure he even knew how to comfort a woman. At least, according to Annie, he'd never been much good at it.

"He seems happy enough in the tree," he pointed out as they stood watching Luki dangle one-armed from a branch.

"As long as we stick around. I know. He doesn't want me to leave. I guess he's decided I'm his mother, so this is where I belong, too." Sarah looked at Dan and smiled ruefully. "I'm open to suggestions."

Dan was silent for a few moments, because he knew he was about to tell her something he almost never talked about, and he didn't quite know why. Finally he cleared his throat and, still looking up into the leafy canopy, drawled, "When I was a kid, I used to hate kindergarten. My mother'd take me to school, and I'd throw a big fit, so what she'd do was hang around until I got busy doing something, and then she'd split when I wasn't looking." He glanced sideways at Sarah and grinned. "Guess I wasn't too bright, because it always seemed to work."

She winced and said, "Ouch. I'm not sure I agree with that method, but in this case, I'm tempted to give it a shot. Okay." She turned around, leaned back against a tree, folded her arms and smiled at him, unexpectedly and with a touch of mischief. "So, we ignore him, is that it? All right, let's see. Conversation. Now where was it you went to kindergarten?"

He'd been afraid of this. Give a woman a scrap, and she wanted your whole life story. "Massachusetts," he said briefly.

Her eyebrows shot up. "Massachusetts?"

She looked as if she didn't know whether he was kidding or not. Anyway, she was too well-bred to call him a liar. He didn't feel like explaining it all to her, so he just shrugged and said, "Small town—you never heard of it. You?"

"San Jose. In California. Any brothers and sisters?"

"Nope. You?" Verbal Ping-Pong. That was fine with him, he figured he could keep batting the ball back to her all afternoon, if that was what she wanted to play.

"Two sisters, one older, one younger. Both married. The younger one's a musician—writes songs, teaches, makes a little money playing in a rock band. She's married to an artist. They haven't got a bean—live on a boat in Sausalito. The older one's married to an orthopedist. They have piles of money. She paints and raises horses."

"Hmm, interesting," Dan murmured, leaning against another tree. "Artists, musicians, all creative types. Makes me curious. What are you, the black sheep?" He was feeling more relaxed now that she seemed content to talk about her own background and leave his alone. So it surprised him a little when a small but unmistakable spasm of pain knocked her smile off center.

"Being a zoologist wasn't my first choice." She pushed away from the tree and peered up into its branches, looking for Luki.

Dan didn't take the hint. "Yeah? What was?"

"I wanted to be a dancer."

A dancer. The way she'd stood up on that drain pipe, yesterday at the drilling site, that way she had of holding her head—not arrogance, then, but training. "What happened?" he asked softly.

"I fell." She said it without emotion, as if it were something she'd repeated so many times it had become rote. "I was practicing a difficult combination, and I landed wrong. I broke my leg in three places. End of career." She gave a little shrug that said, *"C'est la vie,"* and dismissed the subject. This time Dan let it go, although he had a feeling there was more to it than that. He also made a vow to himself that he was going to hear the rest of her story some day.

"What do you think?" she said out of the side of her mouth, jerking her head in Luki's direction. "Do we make a break for it?" It was a pretty fair Bogie impression.

Dan shook his head. "Little stinker's still watching us like a hawk."

"Damn. Maybe we can fake him out." She began strolling casually down the path, but in the direction of deep jungle rather than the camp. With a soft chuckle, Dan pushed away from his tree and fell in beside her. Overhead, Luki was moving, too, at the orangutan's deceptively languid pace, swishing and crashing through the foliage, pausing every now and then to make sure they were still in sight.

Strolling along with Sarah beside him, stepping back now and then to let her go first when encroaching ferns narrowed the path, holding a trailing creeper out of her way, Dan found himself thinking about what she'd just told him. About the dancing and the broken dreams. Even the Golden Ones, it seemed, occasionally got dealt a joker. It made him feel a little bit ashamed of himself, judging her the way he'd been doing. He wished he could tell her he was sorry, that he sympathized.

Before he knew he was going to, he'd plucked a flower, a trailing orchid, and handed it to her.

She stopped, stock-still, in the middle of the path. She looked at the flower and then at him, and he saw confusion in her eyes.

He couldn't think of anything to say to explain himself. Well, hell, he'd meant it—he didn't know how he'd meant it. It had been an impulse, and he was as confused about it as she was. So he just shrugged, tossed it off—no big deal.

Apparently it didn't seem like that to her. She said "Thank you," in a shy, breathless voice, then laughed kind of self-consciously and tucked the flower behind her ear. But she was nervous, her fingers were clumsy, and as she turned to walk on, the flower came loose and tumbled to the mossy ground.

She uttered a soft cry and grabbed for it, but Dan grunted, "I'll get it," and forestalling her, bent over to pick it up. Then, instead of giving it back to her, he made a low, murmuring sound and put his hand on her shoulder. She opened her mouth to say something, but he shook his head, silencing her. Bewildered eyes gazed up at him, mirroring him. His heart beat strong and steady against his ribs as he took her head between his hands and deftly wove the orchid's stem through the soft hair behind her ear.

Soft. Her hair, feathering over his fingers, her cheeks, like sun-warmed peaches in the palms of his hands. So soft.

Her eyelids fluttered and dropped, and her lashes brushed the tips of his thumbs, as delicately as a moth's wings. He moved his thumbs back and forth across her cheeks and whispered, "Look at me."

The effort it took for her to open her eyes and focus on him brought stress lines to her forehead, but Dan found the answer he needed in their sultry depths. He lowered his head and then paused, every nerve in his body tuned to her response. He saw her eyelids quiver and her lashes fall again like curtains over her eyes; he felt heat course through her skin and heard the whisper of her indrawn breath. He pushed his fingertips into her hair, tunneled them through its softness and pressed gently, guiding her head to the angle he wanted. Then he lowered his head some more, and with his lips all but touching hers, paused again.

He felt something—her hand—touch his waist; he felt her lips tremble and part beneath his. Then, finally, he sighed, slipped his hand around to cradle the back of her neck and kissed her.

Now it was the world that paused. Sound and motion ceased; time stopped. It seemed as if the whole world waited for that kiss. And since he had all the time in the world, Dan brought her to him as slowly as he'd brought himself to her, letting her feel it, all of it—the warmth, the trembling, the swelling, the blossoming.

The hand at his waist curled, clutched and then relaxed. He felt her fingers splay along his side, their moist warmth penetrate his shirt. His own fingers spread wide over her scalp, moving in gentle rhythms, matching other rhythms so subtle they seemed only part of the natural movements of their bodies, and no more theirs to control than their heartbeats.

Dan didn't know how long it might have gone on between them, deepening, growing. As far as he was concerned, there wasn't any reason why he shouldn't let things go along to whatever conclusion came naturally. But he'd forgotten one thing.

He'd forgotten all about Luki.

Chapter 4

Just as the kiss was about to shift gears, take on a new dimension, Luki came crashing out of a nearby tree like an overripe fruit. It was enough to make Sarah stiffen and pull away from Dan, though he'd have been happy to ignore the damned orangutan and just go right on doing what they were doing.

"I guess we'd better give it up," she said as she gathered Luki into her arms. Her voice sounded shaky, and above the orang's head her eyes were glowing like topazes. Tiger eyes.

Dan swore under his breath. He didn't think she'd even thought about there being two ways to take that remark. He was feeling some unexpected pangs of frustration. Shoot, he thought disgustedly, that orangutan was worse than a chaperon. He'd dated divorced ladies with little kids who'd given him less trouble!

He felt her hand on his arm, just the lightest of touches. "Dan..."

He looked at her and waited, but whatever it was she'd wanted to say to him seemed to have hung up in her throat. He thought he knew how she felt. He didn't know what to say to her, either.

Well, what could he say? Something glib and casual? Hey, that was nice, let's do it again sometime.

But he didn't feel glib, and he didn't feel casual, and that wasn't what he wanted to say.

Sarah shook her head, trying to clear away the confusion that had settled over her. She searched Dan's face with the intensity of one looking for familiar landmarks in the fog, but his eyes were shrouded, revealing nothing. Nothing to indicate he'd felt what she'd felt—the upheaval inside, the aftershocks, which were still trembling through her body and soul.

Please, God, she prayed, her standard plea, don't let me make a fool of myself—again.

Aloud, she cleared her throat and said, "Nothing." And she turned and started back the way they'd come.

Before she'd gone two steps, Luki hopped out of her arms and scuttled off in the opposite direction.

Bemused and distracted, Sarah muttered, "Now what?" A few yards down the path, Luki had stopped and was looking back at them. Sarah threw Dan a rueful smile and said, "Well, I guess that takes care of that!" He replied with a shrug of agreement, and once again, they turned and headed home.

Once again Luki came after them, scrabbling crabwise along the ground, screaming at them like a child left behind in a grocery store.

Sarah heaved a vexed sigh and pressed a hand to her forehead, striving for calm. The patience she'd learned over the past years was evaporating fast, and Dan's nearness and the aftereffects of his kiss weren't helping. "I don't understand this at all," she said in a voice that had developed a precarious note. "I've never seen an orangutan behave like this."

Reluctantly, not knowing what else to do, she picked Luki up, but as soon as she took a step toward the station compound, he jumped out of her arms and bolted in the other direction.

Dan coughed and rubbed the back of his neck.

Sarah threw him a resentful glance and snapped, "What?" She felt like a parent with a misbehaving child—half defensive, half embarrassed.

"Well," he drawled, "I may be way out of line here, but..." Now it was he who seemed uncomfortable. "Do you think he could be trying to tell us something?"

Sarah burst out laughing.

Dan shifted with endearing awkwardness. "Well, hell, didn't you ever watch old Lassie movies? I figure an orang's at least as smart as a dog."

"Smarter," Sarah said slowly, not laughing. Dan wasn't wearing his mask now. The expression on his face was quizzical—a little half smile that didn't match the watchful look in his eyes. It was a look she couldn't quite define; it touched her in ways she couldn't explain.

"Much smarter," she murmured, looking thoughtfully at Luki. As an experiment, she took a step toward him. He moved away from her, maintaining a few yards distance. She stopped. Luki stopped, too, and looked back at her. Then he extended one long arm toward her in an almost human gesture of appeal.

Something—a little frisson of unease—rippled through Sarah, raising goose bumps on her arms.

"Luki," she said cautiously, still not quite believing it, "what is it? Is it J.J.? Where's J.J., Luki? Can you show me?" This time, instead of picking him up in her arms, she held out her hand. When Luki's long fingers closed on her wrist, her heart began to pound. Muttering "I don't believe this," she followed the orangutan into the jungle.

A few hundred feet farther on, Luki suddenly let go of her hand and disappeared into the shadows among the roots of a huge banyan tree. Again Sarah looked at Dan, thinking of all the unpleasant things that could be lurking in those cracks and crannies.

He must have been thinking of them, too, because he touched her arm, muttered, "Stay here," and started to move past her.

"No." Sarah swallowed hard and whispered, "I'll go."

He didn't argue, but his eyes held hers with a curious intensity as he muttered, "Watch where you put your hands and feet."

She nodded, and with hammering heart, stepped gingerly into the mossy undergrowth.

A moment later, she forgot caution and dropped to her knees with a soft cry.

"Sarah?" Dan's voice had a hard edge of alarm. "Hey, Doc, are you okay?"

"It's all right," she said, not even trying to hide the fact that she was crying. "I'm all right. I've found J.J."

He wasn't dead, although she thought at first he must be; he made such a pitiful pile in his nest of bruised and crumpled ferns. But when Luki crawled to him, he swiveled his head slowly and looked at Sarah with eyes that were flat and dull. Luki touched J.J.'s rough red coat with his knuckles, then sat back on his haunches and uttered one forlorn squeal. J.J. didn't make a sound, not even when Sarah lifted him gently into her arms.

She felt Dan's hand on her shoulder; she hadn't heard him come up behind her. She sniffed and mumbled, "He's alive. I can't imagine how he managed to survive a night on the ground. It's just luck that some predator didn't find him."

In response to the pressure of Dan's hand she turned, but reluctantly, self-conscious about her tears now. With her hands full of J.J., she had nothing to hide behind, nothing with which to wipe away the evidence of her vulnerability. She felt, at the very least, unprofessional, but it was more than that. She felt so terribly exposed, emotionally naked before this disturbing and enigmatic stranger who looked at her one minute with lust and next with contempt; this man she barely knew, who, though seeming to possess no more gentleness and compassion than a drill bit, had kissed her with the sensitivity of a poet.

"He's hurt," Dan said, stating the obvious in a flat voice, touching the animal's blood-caked hair. "Gunshot?"

Sarah shook her head. "I don't know, I can't tell. He's lost a lot of blood, and I don't know how long since he's had anything to eat or drink. He's so weak and dehydrated—he hardly weighs anything—" Her voice broke. She gave an embarrassed laugh and added in a whisper, "I'm sorry."

He shifted and mumbled, "Hey, it's okay," seeming almost as ill-at-ease with her tears as she.

"It's just that . . . he's only a baby. In human years. . . ."

"I know. I understand."

His voice was like a rusty file, but something in it made her believe him. She took a deep breath, fighting for control. "Well, I guess the first thing is to get him back to camp. I can get a better idea what the damage is. I don't know..." Her voice trailed off. She wasn't a vet. This was out of her league, and she knew it. She had a pretty good idea that it was going to take a miracle to save the little orangutan. She sniffed, feeling perilously close to another flood of those helpless and humiliating tears.

"Here." Dan shifted abruptly, taking her by the arms and moving her ahead of him in the cramped space between the banyan's roots. With a crooked smile and a more than usually pronounced Texas accent he drawled, "You better go first. I'm not absolutely sure, but with all that comin' and goin', I think I'm probably lost.''

Lost? Sarah didn't believe it, not for a minute, but that disarming and wholly uncharacteristic admission of fallibility was just what she needed to make her pull herself together. If he'd done it on purpose, it was an incredibly sensitive and intuitive thing to do. She threw him one quick, speculative look as she began to pick her way through the vegetation, but his face gave no answers.

''What about the other one?'' he asked, hesitating.

''Luki?'' Sarah paused to look back. He was sitting in J.J.'s nest, looking forlorn and abandoned. She knew he was probably capable of taking care of himself in the forest; it was, after all, the reason they were all here in the first place. But if the poachers were still around . . .

Before she could say anything, Dan muttered something under his breath and ducked back under the banyan's roots. When he emerged, he had Luki clinging to his chest and a look on his face that would have sent the first Spanish conquerors fleeing back to their boats. Sarah wisely gulped back comment, but there was a new warmth in her chest as she turned once more and plunged headfirst into the ferns.

Why is it, Dan asked himself on the way back to the camp, that every time I see this woman, I wind up with my arms full of orangutan? He didn't even like animals much. He'd never had a pet; there hadn't been much place for dogs and cats in the mausoleum he'd grown up in. He hadn't had any experience to speak of with small children, either, and as far as he could see, these orangs came somewhere in between. What in the world was he getting himself into?

Trouble. Even now, the slender figure gliding ahead of him along the narrow path seemed more like a fairy-tale princess lost in an enchanted forest than a zoologist with a wounded animal in her arms. Rays of sunlight touched her hair like greedy fingers reaching for a gilded crown. Golden Girl.

He remembered what she'd said about wanting to be a dancer. And he remembered the way her face had looked, wet with tears. Again he thought, with deep-down rustlings of unease, this woman means trouble.

The Dutch girl—Marina, that was her name—came out to meet them as they emerged from the jungle. Now, she was a nice girl, Dan thought, pretty in a quiet way, with that long dark hair, nice brown eyes and a few freckles scattered across her cheeks and nose. Much more his type, and friendly, too. He let his eyes rest for a moment on her soft, feminine curves, measuring and testing his own responses. A pity, he decided, with a little inward sigh of regret. She'd be good company—warm and uncomplicated and probably a lot of fun. And he was a damn fool. Like his father before him.

He stood at a little distance, holding a very subdued Luki in his arms and watching the two women exclaim and explain and fuss over the injured orangutan. And he knew there was no question about which of the two fired his blood and stirred his senses. Somewhat fatalistically, he reflected that there was just no such thing as good judgment when chemistry was involved. He knew the golden-haired, golden-eyed woman wasn't for him, but, God help him, he wanted her anyway.

"There is so much blood," Marina was saying breathlessly. "It's all caked and dried. If we get him inside, maybe we can see where he's hurt."

"I don't know whether there's anything we can do for him," Sarah said with a hopeless sniff. "He needs a doctor. X rays. Blood or fluids—I don't know. Oh, God, Mari, maybe it would have been better if I'd never found him!"

"Don't say that! We just have to find him a vet, that's all."

"Where? The closest vet is in town, and to find one with any experience with orangs, we'd probably have to go to Medan, or Jakarta, to the zoo. J.J.'s not going to last that long." The last sentence was barely audible.

Watching Sarah's face as she gently stroked the rough red coat, watching the way her lips tightened and her throat moved, did something to Dan's insides. Almost before he knew he was going to, he stepped forward, cleared his throat and drawled, "Can't get you a vet. How would a real doctor do?"

The two women stared at him. Marina, looking bewildered, said, "A real doctor?"

Dan shrugged. "Yeah, a doctor. For people. There's one at AMINCO headquarters. I can drive you, if you think it'd help."

There was a good possibility Doc Sako was going to kill him, Dan thought, but at that moment all he could see was the look on Sarah's face, and he figured it was worth it.

Both girls were talking at once, so damn grateful it made him feel like a fraud. There wasn't much altruism in his offer. He knew that a moment later when Sarah turned to Marina and said, "You take J.J. I'll stay."

Marina opened her mouth to begin a half-hearted argument. "It's your turn," Sarah pointed out as she transferred the injured orangutan to Marina's arms. "I just got back from an overnighter, and besides, there's Sweetie and old Beau. You go."

She wasn't looking at him, so he couldn't see her face. Her voice was calm; there was nothing in it to tell him whether she felt what he felt—that sharp jab of disappointment. Nothing to tell him whether she was glad not to be going with him, or sorry. As there'd been nothing to tell him whether she'd liked being kissed by him, or not. She was cool, so cool and controlled, he thought. She'd show emotion for a wounded ape but not for him.

So he would be as cool as she was. Hiding his disappointment behind an imperturbable mask, he took Marina's elbow, smiled and said, "Well, let's go, then. Got everything you need?"

"Just my backpack—"

Sarah said, "I'll get it," and ran up the steps to the cabin. The screen door slammed. A moment or two later it slammed again, and she was back with a yellow backpack and two bottles of water, which she thrust into Dan's hands. She still wasn't looking at him, though there was a bit of color in her cheeks now and a sheen of perspiration on her throat. Which would be from exertion rather than emotion, Dan would bet.

"Maybe you can get him to drink something," she said to Marina.

The Dutch girl nodded, but looked uncertain. "Are you sure you will be all right? Here, alone . . ."

"I have the gun," Sarah said firmly, "and the rangers are just down the road, I'll be fine. Don't worry about us here, just get J.J. to a doctor, okay?"

The last word was whispered as she touched the orangutan's rusty coat. When she turned to take Luki from Dan, just for a moment her eyes found his. And just for a moment, he thought he saw fire in their golden depths. In the next second, though, they were opaque as polished metal, giving him back his own reflection and nothing more.

The set of her head—so elegant, so fine—the lines of her neck and shoulders, the austerity of her jaw. So must the Queen of Spain have looked, Dan thought, half admiring, half resentful, sending her captains off to search for the Cities of Gold.

Sarah walked with them a little way, talking with Marina, giving and receiving last minute instructions and assurances, farewells and hugs. They left her at the edge of the clearing, just beyond reach of the lengthening shadows.

Before the jungle closed in on him, Dan looked back to see her still standing there motionless, looking after them. When he turned again to follow Marina down the path to the river crossing he was frowning, but it wasn't until much later that he realized what it was about the image that bothered him.

Standing there like that, she hadn't looked anything at all like a queen. She hadn't looked cool or confident or in control. She'd looked small, and alone, and unprotected.

He was right about Marina, Dan discovered on the long drive back to AMINCO. She was good company and easy to talk to. She'd be a good friend, he thought with another of those twinges of regret, but that was all.

It was easy to get her talking about herself. He'd had a lot of practice at that kind of thing and was good at it. He found out that, although she'd been born and educated in the Netherlands, Marina's parents were native-born Indonesians, descendants of colonial Dutch planters.

"Funny," he said during the next lull in her narrative, with the easy familiarity that had come between them, "you don't look Dutch."

"No?" Her dark eyes twinkled back at him. "Why not?"

"Ah, well, you know, blond hair, blue eyes." He glanced sideways at her and grinned. "Those little white caps with the flaps."

"And wooden shoes?" She laughed and explained, "Actually, I'm what is sometimes called 'black' Dutch. Some of my ancestors were Spanish conquerors."

"Huh!" Dan said. "No kiddin'?" His grin became wry. "So were mine."

"Really? You are Spanish, then? Sarah said she thought you might be—" She stopped, just a little too late.

Or too soon. Dan told himself he'd be damned if he'd ask what Sarah'd said about him, he'd sound like a kid in junior high school! But it gave him an odd feeling just the same, knowing he'd been the subject of her conversation, and the object of her thoughts.

"Mexican," he said shortly, intending to leave it there. He was surprised to hear himself explaining, "Well, half, anyway. My father was Mexican. My mother was from New England."

"New England! What an unusual combination." Marina's voice was full of friendly curiosity.

She was nice, she was interested, and he felt comfortable with her, so instead of shutting off the subject, as he ordinarily would have done, he chuckled and said, "Yeah, I guess it is."

"How did it happen?"

How did it happen? It was a question he'd asked himself a thousand times, once upon a time, trying to fathom the collision of cultures that had produced him. A collision, it had seemed to him then, of almost cosmic proportions, a union so unlikely it must surely constitute a genuine miracle, perhaps even evidence of divine intervention.

Then, close on the heels of that question had come two others: Who the hell am I? Where do I belong? It had been a long hard road to the answers, and along the way he'd stopped believing in both miracles and divine intervention. He knew now that he was whoever he made of himself and that he belonged wherever he chose to be.

"How'd it happen?" He gave a short laugh with no humor in it and drawled, "The usual way, I imagine."

Marina stammered a little as she said, "I didn't mean—"

"I know," Dan interrupted softly. And because he liked her and felt ashamed of himself, he told her about the beautiful young student from an old New England family, descendant of pilgrims and Puritans, who went to Mexico one summer on an archaeological dig. He told her about the young Mexican college professor in charge of the dig and how he fell in love with the golden-haired *notreamericana* caught in the spell of the jungle and the Aztec ruins.

"How very romantic." Marina sighed.

"Yeah," Dan said, without bitterness or irony, because it had been. But he'd learned that romance and chemistry—and even love—aren't enough. So he told her the rest of the story, about how the young American student had found herself pregnant in a country where her options in those circumstances were limited. How she had chosen to stay in Mexico and marry her lover rather than go home in disgrace to her rigid, judgmental family. How she had tried and failed to adapt to the alien culture and eventually returned to her own people with her five-year-old half-Mexican son.

"What a terrible thing to do," Marina said in her softly accented voice. "Such a little boy...."

Dan shrugged. He hadn't blamed his mother for doing what she'd had to do. She'd loved him, and in every way she could, had tried to make it easier for him. "It was a long time ago," he said neutrally. "I stuck it out for my mother's sake, until I was through high school. The day after I graduated I was on a bus back to Mexico. Back to my father's people."

"And?"

This time Dan's laugh held irony, but no bitterness. It had been a long time ago, and ultimately the struggle, the pain and the loneliness had made him strong. "And I didn't fit in there any better. So I hit the road again—figured I'd better go see where I did fit. Eventually I found my way to the oil fields of Texas." He shrugged, as if to say, "And here I am."

Marina said quietly, "You are a long way from Texas."

He looked at her, and it came as a small shock to him to see dark eyes gazing back at him, a dark braid falling over her shoulder. He knew then that he'd been thinking of a pair of golden eyes, a neat cap of sun-streaked hair. And he knew that he hadn't told his story for Marina at all. He'd told it for Sarah.

"Ah, yes, there it is," Dr. Soekardja said. "Just where the X rays said it would be."

As the murmur of voices from behind the curtain broke into intelligible words, Dan glanced up from the pamphlet on intestinal parasites he'd been reading to pass the time. Doc Sako's chuckle had a satisfied sound, so things must be going okay for J.J. He hadn't been sure there, for a while. There'd been times, on the road, when both he and Marina had been afraid the trip would turn out to be a waste of time.

He stood up and began to move restlessly around the room. Hospitals and doctors' offices weren't his favorite places, though he'd had close acquaintance with more than a few in his younger, wilder days. They made him feel claustrophobic, as if he weren't supposed to touch anything. Pretty much, come to think of it, like the house he'd grown up in.

He took his cigarettes out of his pocket, shook one out, then put it back. Damn. Of course, he couldn't smoke in here. He'd about decided to step outside for a quick one when he heard Marina's soft exclamation, followed by a metallic clang.

"Such a big bullet for such a small target," Doc Sako's soft voice commented. "I am amazed that it hasn't done more damage. He is a very lucky little fellow, this one." Dan heard Marina's murmur of agreement, and then the doctor again. "Who did this? Poachers, I assume?"

Dan couldn't hear Marina's reply, but she must have nodded because the doctor's response was a sound replete with both sadness and disgust. "It's too bad," he said. "Too bad."

The silence that followed was busy and intent. Dan was just about to head outside for his smoke when Marina's voice suddenly came through clearly. "The rangers think they may be Americans."

Dan stopped with his hand on the door, listening.

"Oh?" Dr. Soekardja's tone was interested but not much surprised. "Why do they think that?"

There was another metallic clatter that partly obliterated Marina's reply. "... a cigarette. Sarah says it's an American brand, not a very common one." She sighed. "It isn't much, but I suppose it is something."

Dan looked at the pack of cigarettes in his hand, then pushed open the infirmary door and stepped outside. He was leaning against the front of the building in the shade, squinting thoughtfully through his own smoke, when Tank drove by in one of the company pickup trucks, saw Dan's Jeep and stopped.

"Hey," Tank called through the truck's open window, by way of a greeting.

Dan waved his cigarette, then tossed it to the ground and pushed reluctantly away from the wall.

"How'd it go with old Beau?" Tank asked him as he got out of the truck. He slammed the door and ambled over to him, grinning. "How'd it go with the pretty doc? She glad to see you?"

Dan shrugged. He wasn't in the mood for Tank's good-buddy routine right now, so he offered him a cigarette, figuring that was as good a way as any to sidetrack him.

It worked. As he was handing back the pack, Tank jerked his head toward the infirmary and asked, "What are you doing here?" then answered his own question with a raw remark.

Dan grinned good-naturedly. "Naw," he drawled, "brought back a casualty. Gunshot wound."

Tank's eyebrows shot up. "No kiddin'? Who—"

"One of their project orangs. Looks like a poacher must have got him."

"Yeah?" Tank made a clicking sound with his tongue. "Geez, that's too bad. That's a real shame." He did a double take then, and started to laugh. "You mean you brought an orangutan to Doc Sako? Shoot, I wish I'd been there to see that!"

Dan said mildly, "Didn't seem to mind. Didn't bat an eye, in fact."

"So, what's the verdict? He going to make it?"

Before Dan could say anything, the two people with the answer to that question came out of the infirmary. Dan could almost feel Tank snap to attention when he saw Marina. Well, damn, she was a pretty lady, nice figure, tall— about an inch taller than Doc Sako, as a matter of fact— with that long hair and those big, dark eyes. Right now those eyes had a definite sparkle to them, and there was some pink in her cheeks, too. What was it about old Tank? he wondered. Whatever the man's mysterious appeal for the ladies, it sure escaped him.

"I don't know," he said dryly, "let's find out." Turning to Marina, he asked gruffly, "So, how is the little guy?"

Marina and Doc Sako were both smiling, so he had an idea what the answer was going to be, even before she answered, "He is very weak, but Dr. Soekardja thinks he is going to be fine." She looked at the doctor then, as if for reassurance. "He took the bullet out of his shoulder."

Doc Sako nodded his confirmation. "I would be happier if we could have given him some blood," he said with a little smile, "but it seems we are a little short on orangutan blood at the moment."

"Type O?" Tank said, and everybody laughed. He stepped forward, then, and took Marina's hand. "Hi, I'm Tank Guthrie. I'm a friend of ol' Dan's. And you..."

"This is Marina," Dan supplied reluctantly. "She works at the rehab station with Sarah."

"You work with the doc? Hey, nice lady." Tank was still holding Marina's hand, and she was staring at him with her mouth half-open, almost, Dan thought, as if she were dumbstruck. He could see Tank's thumb moving, stroking along the tendons on the back of her hand as he went on talking in that melted-honey Texas croon of his. "I'm sure sorry to hear about your casualty. Listen, if there's anything I can do to help, you just call on old Tank, you hear?"

"Well..." Marina glanced at Doc Sako, then looked at Dan. "Dr. Soekardja says J.J. should stay here at least twenty-four hours, and I am the only one who would know how to take care of him. But I am very worried about Sarah. I don't like it that she is alone there, with the poachers becoming so bold. The rangers are so far away, and there are all the orangutans in the quarantine cages—"

Tank gave her a great big smile and expanded his already impressive chest. "Say no more, darlin', don't you worry about a thing, I'll—"

Dan clapped a hand on his shoulder and tightened it. "Already got it covered," he said in a quiet voice that Tank had heard before. And remembered, Dan saw by the way he gave him a quick, hard look and shut up. "Don't worry," he said softly to Marina. "I'll go keep her company."

Marina nodded, seeming relieved.

"Well, then," Tank said smoothly, making a quick recovery, "since you're going to be stuck here tonight, why don't you let me take you to dinner?"

"What?" Marina faltered, "do you mean...here?"

Tank chuckled. "Sure. We got a pretty nice cafeteria, a rec hall with a jukebox and a dance floor."

"But, I'm not dressed—"

"Honey, you're the prettiest thing to hit this place in a long time, just as you stand. Don't you worry about that."

"Well..." Marina glanced at Doc Sako, who gave her his gentle half smile and nodded. She took a deep breath, then laughed and said, "All right, that would be very nice. Thank you."

Tank beamed. "Hey, great. That's great. I'll pick you up in, say, couple hours? Where, here?"

"Yes," Marina said. "I will be here."

Since Tank was leaving, Dan said his goodbyes, too. On the way to the cars, Tank said in an undertone, "You really goin' all the way back up there tonight?"

Dan nodded. "Uh-huh."

"You kiddin' me? That's a two-hour drive, and you got an hour's daylight left."

"I know the way."

Tank hooted softly and elbowed him in the ribs. "Hope she's worth it. Hey—" he waved and climbed, grinning, into his pickup "—don't do anything I wouldn't do, okay?" He jerked his head meaningfully toward the infirmary, where Marina was just turning to follow Doc Sako back inside, uttered a low whistle and drove off.

Dan stayed where he was for a few minutes, staring after Tank with narrowed eyes. Something was bothering him, and he couldn't decide what it was. He thought maybe it was that he liked Marina and he didn't feel good about leaving her to Tank Guthrie. He considered whether he ought to drop a word or two of warning, or at least a hint that she might be getting into more than she'd bargained for, but then he remembered the way she'd sparkled and blushed, talking to old Tank, and he thought maybe she'd just as soon he minded his own business. She wasn't a kid, he told himself, and he wasn't her big brother.

Besides, he reminded himself grimly as he climbed into his Jeep, he had something else to worry about right now. Namely, one slender, golden-haired woman, all alone in a godforsaken outpost with the nearest company a quarter of a mile away down a dark jungle trail.

He lit himself another cigarette, took it out of his mouth and looked at it for a long time. Then he stuck it back between his lips, threw the Jeep into gear and roared out of the compound, bouncing and bucking through potholes and mud puddles as he headed north, toward the reserve.

Dan made good time, but even so, the night was deep and dark by the time he reached the river. That didn't bother him; he was used to the thick, impenetrable blackness of jungle nights. The only thing he dreaded running into in the dark was a python, which was the main reason he carried a large, powerful flashlight and a small, powerful handgun in the Jeep's glove compartment.

He parked beside the only other car in the clearing, a pickup truck with the Wildlife Foundation logo on it. He wondered where the Land Rover was that Sarah had driven the day before. It bothered him that it wasn't there, so when he started down the path to the crossing, he had the flashlight in his hand and the gun tucked securely under his belt.

The ferry canoe was on his side of the river, further evidence that at least one of the rangers had gone somewhere and wasn't back yet. Dan didn't like it. As he maneuvered himself across the swift, shallow current he could feel his heart beating faster, feel the little electrical impulses running through all his muscles, whispering, Danger. Watch your step. Be alert. He had good instincts, and they'd never failed him; he was on guard, every sense tuned, every nerve poised. Normally under those circumstances he should have felt a cold, deadly calm, and a strange, indefinable exhilaration. But he didn't. What he was, was scared. This was something different, something he'd never experienced before. For the first time in his life, he was afraid for somebody else rather than himself. It wasn't a good feeling.

The ranger station was dark and looked deserted. Dan called out, "Hello, anybody home?" but there was no answer. He swore softly as he moved past it and plunged headlong into the jungle, following the path leading to the rehab station. He moved as rapidly as he dared, the beam from his flashlight slashing the darkness, the soft ground muffling his footsteps. Around him in the jungle a hush fell as the forest creatures, recognizing a predator, waited silently for the danger to pass.

His heart pounded against his ribs. His throat felt dry. Driven by a terrible sense of urgency, almost against his own will, he began to run, silently, on cat feet.

At the edge of the clearing, in sight of the main house, Dan stopped and turned off the flashlight, letting his night vision adjust to the darkness. He could barely make out the lines of the cabin, using his memory of its location as a point of reference. No lights shone from its windows, and that seemed ominous to him. Barely an hour past dusk, surely Sarah wouldn't already have gone to bed, would she?

He started forward, then froze as a rustling sound came from the quarantine cages, off to the left. He listened, straining his senses to their limits, but the noise wasn't repeated. The jungle was quiet—too quiet. Dan eased the gun from his belt and, crouching low, sprinted across the silent compound.

The house, like all dwellings in the Indonesian jungles, was elevated on stout wooden pylons. As Dan paused to listen below the front porch, something scuttled away from him under the stairs, something too small to be of concern—a lizard, perhaps, or a rodent. Above him, the house, like the jungle, seemed unnaturally quiet. His own heartbeat echoed in his ears like a bass drum in a cave.

Where in holy heaven was everybody? Where was Sarah? It seemed inconceivable that she could have gone with the rangers, leaving the camp and the caged orangutans to the mercy of poachers. What was going on in the silent house, just above his head? Was Sarah peacefully sleeping under a cascading veil of mosquito netting or huddled in terror with a poacher's hand over her mouth and a gun to her head? There were other possibilities, too, ones with Dan didn't want to think about.

He thought maybe he ought to call out, the way he had down at the ranger station, but then he thought, no, that would give away his position. He laughed at himself a little, told himself he was being crazy, a paranoid fool, a little boy seeing monsters in the dark. But dammit, he knew something wasn't right. His instincts were telling him there was danger here, and he'd be a fool to ignore them; they'd saved his bacon more than once. Helluva lot better to be safe than sorry. He was going to find out what was going on in there before he made his own presence known.

So he eased the gun out of his belt and, with its comforting weight in one hand and the flashlight in the other, mounted the wooden steps, slowly, testing each one. At the top of the steps he angled away from the door and flattened against the wall. Listening.

There. He'd heard something. Faint, but unmistakable. Someone was there, on the other side of the wall, listening as hard as he was. He'd bet his life on it.

Slowly, carefully, he slid his hand along the wall, feeling for the window. And touched a void. The window was open. Now Dan knew beyond any doubt that something was wrong. Who in his right mind would leave a window unscreened at night, in the jungle, in the tropics? His mind clear and calm, all his muscles poised for action, he adjusted his grip on both gun and flashlight and then moved his foot slightly, deliberately making noise.

In reply there came a sound that chilled his blood: the sliding click of a bolt-action rifle.

Chapter 5

Dan's flashlight beam stabbed through the dark window, and for a frozen second he just stood there, staring down the barrel of a Winchester .70. Then instinct took charge. He dropped to the floor, and the night exploded.

The blast left him temporarily deafened. As the flashlight rolled away across the porch, its light went out, and in the silent darkness he bounded up and dove headfirst through the open window. He hit the floor rolling, came up against something solid and, lashing out with both feet, was gratified to hear a muffled exclamation. He hooked his legs around the solid object and gave it a sharp jerk. There was a thud and simultaneous "Oof!"

Then with one catlike twist of his torso, Dan was on top of the writhing body, pinning it down with his own weight. Something—a part of the rifle—struck him a glancing blow across his cheekbone. With unexpected ease, he captured a pair of straining wrists and forced them up and back, increasing pressure until the rifle dropped from nerveless fingers and the wrists lay limp in his grasp.

They felt slender as vines.

For a moment or two longer Dan held his breath, counting two sets of heartbeats. Then as reaction took him, he let it expire in a rush and dropped his head onto his forearm, swearing softly.

The wrists in his hands jerked.

"Goddamn it, woman," he ground out between clenched teeth, "you almost killed me." He didn't know when he'd been so angry or so scared. He felt cold clear through and weak as a newborn kitten.

"Dan?" It was a squeak, halfway between horror and relief. "Is that—"

"Yeah, it's me. No thanks to you. What the hell do you think you're doing? You damn near shot me!"

"Me? I didn't expect— What are you doing here?"

"What difference does it make? Listen, lady, don't you think you could look before you pull the trigger?"

"How could I? You had your flashlight right in my—"

"Where in the hell did you get that gun? That thing's big enough to stop a rhino! Do you know what that woulda done to me? Do you?"

"Stop yelling at me!" He wasn't yelling at her, unless it was possible to yell in whispers. Anyway, she was answering him in kind, in a hoarse rasp that seemed to tear at her throat. "What were you doing, creeping up on me like that? Why didn't you knock?"

"Because I thought something was wrong, that's why! Where were all the goddamn lights? Why were you sitting here in the dark with a—"

"Because I was scared, that's why!"

Dan stared down into a pool of darkness, hearing the echoes of her fear, wishing with everything in him that he could see her face. He could feel her chest moving rapidly up and down, pushing against his, feel the planes and hollows of her body, the hard edges of ribs and pelvis, the softness of belly and breasts, the firm resilience of thighs, all heated, moist, trembling. He felt his anger subside and a surge of heat replace the chill in his bones.

He swore softly and rolled off of her. They lay on the floor, then, side by side on their backs in the dark, breathing hard, like lovers in the aftermath of violent passion.

Passion. Dan felt a rather painful impulse to laugh. It wasn't the kind of passion he'd had in mind, but at least he knew now beyond any shadow of doubt that she was capable of it. And that she was nowhere near as cool as she seemed. The imprint of her body seemed to have been seared onto his; his whole front tingled with nerve-memories so powerful and immediate he could feel her in his arms still. Solid, warm, real.

Her voice was real, too. She said in a stricken whisper, "Oh, God, I almost shot you."

"Yeah."

Sarah felt his silent laughter like a small earthquake and wondered about the note of bitter irony in it.

She knew she ought to say something more, but she couldn't. She kept swallowing, fighting down the cold-metal taste of horror that still hung like persistent nausea in the back of her throat. As much as she tried not to, she kept seeing Dan the way he might have been if it hadn't been for those cat-quick reflexes of his.

He does move like a panther, she thought, and she shivered, not with revulsion, but with something else entirely. She thought of the way he'd come through the window, so swiftly, so surely, even in the dark. She remembered the wiry strength of his body....

"I'm sorry," Dan said unexpectedly, on an exhalation that made the words almost a sigh. And then, awkwardly, "Did I hurt you?"

"No," Sarah said, swallowing again. "I'm all right."

There was another little silence, and then, "Are you sure you're all right? You don't sound all right."

"I'm fine." But she had clamped her teeth together to keep them from chattering. She wasn't fine, and she knew exactly what she needed to make herself feel better. Oh, yes, she knew what she wanted, but it was so preposterous she thought it might be a symptom of impending insanity. What she wanted was for Dan to reach out his arm and draw her close, to cradle her head in that special hollow just below his shoulder, to wrap her in his arms and whisper comforting words that would drive away the lingering cobwebs of fear. It had to be insanity—jungle fever, she thought with a half-hysterical urge to giggle—to want such a thing as tenderness from this man. A man with the strength and reflexes of a predator, a man who could hide his feelings behind features as cold and forbidding as an Aztec mask.

What did she know of this man? How could she know what he might be capable of?

With that thought blowing like a cold breeze through her consciousness, she finally bestirred herself and sat up. "Dan?"

"Yeah?"

In a rush of bravery, she blurted, "What are you doing here? Why did you come back?"

Then, as a new possibility struck her she instinctively put out a hand as if warding off an obstacle in the dark. And touched moist, heated skin. She gasped, jerking her fingers back and folding them protectively against her palm. "Oh, God, is it J.J.? What's the matter? Is it Marina? Is she all right?"

"Marina's fine." Dan's voice came from the darkness in surprisingly gentle reassurance. "I think J.J.'s going to make it. They're both staying with Doc Sako tonight." He hardly made any sound at all, but Sarah could tell by the change in the direction of his voice that he was sitting up, now, too. There was a faint grunt, the briefest of exhalations, and then, "I just came to see how you were." Sarah's heart betrayed her with a joyful surge. "Marina was worried about you."

"Oh," she said, deflating. "I see."

She got to her feet and groped for the lantern on the table. Its soft light was kind, illuminating without blinding. The tiny sound that escaped her was one of surprise, for Dan was standing, too, and again she hadn't heard him.

He was holding the rifle. By the lantern's light Sarah silently watched him while he sighted along the barrel, cracked the chamber, closed it again, hefted its weight. He looked at her and remarked, "Quite a weapon."

Sarah nodded. Her hand went unbidden to her shoulder, where she was just becoming aware of a dull, throbbing ache.

Dan's eyes followed her gesture. He gave a snort of dry laughter. "Yeah, quite a kick, too, I'll bet. Where'd you get a thing like this, anyway?"

"Ouch—one of the rangers left it."

"Uh-huh. You ever shoot one of these things before?"

Sarah looked at the gun with revulsion. "No. Of course not. I couldn't. I could never shoot anything. I mean, I didn't think—" She broke it off.

After a chilly little silence Dan said softly, "For somebody who has never killed anything, you were sure quick to pull the trigger when you thought it was a man standing there."

In self-defense, knowing how lame it sounded, Sarah cried "It was an accident!" How often, she wondered, had those words been spoken in shock and grief, too late?

It was an accident. And just like that are lives irrevocably changed. Her head began to throb with memories of blinding pain, to ring with the echoes of disaster. It was the sound she remembered most vividly, she realized, the sound of her own bones snapping, like rifle shots.

She heard herself babbling. "I didn't intend to shoot, I was just going to say something—tell you to stop or I'd shoot, I suppose—and then you turned that flashlight into my eyes, and it startled me. M-my finger was on the trigger, and I guess I must have jerked it—"

"Here—sit." It was an order, barked in her ear. She felt hard hands on her shoulders. Pain slashed through her—real, not remembered. Her breath hissed involuntarily through her teeth. As she sank into a chair she heard Dan swearing, softly and with feeling. "What is it?" he asked when he'd run out of steam. "Your shoulder?"

With her eyes closed, fighting nausea, she nodded. Hands touched her shoulder, gently, this time. "Here, let me have a look. You'll be damn lucky if you haven't broken it."

Muttering under his breath, he began with deft fingers to unbutton her shirt.

Sarah sat very still, watching him, his face in sharp focus, so close to hers, eyelashes like brushes shuttering his eyes. She noticed little things: that for one so dark, he had very little beard; that his ears, half hidden by his hair, were small and lay close to his head. She became unnaturally conscious of her own breathing, her heartbeat, the tingle of air on the surface of her skin. The pain-filled memories retreated, slipping back into the dark envelope of her mind marked Over and Done With.

She realized then that she was searching his face for . . . something. Anything. Some flicker of emotion. She knew he had emotions, strong ones—she'd heard them in his voice, felt them in his body, just moments ago, in the dark. Safe in the dark. But now, with the lantern light turning his dusky skin to gold, his broad cheekbones, arrogant nose and chiseled mouth seemed more than ever like a mask. An Az-

tec chieftain's mask of gold, the likes of which had once se-
duced a conquering army into a futile search for El Dorado.

Sarah gave her head a shake, as she would to fight off
drowsiness. Disquieting pagan images scattered like dry
leaves as Dan murmured softly, "It's okay."

She realized then that he had drawn her shirt down over
her shoulder, baring it to his searching eyes and probing
fingers, and that he'd taken her head shake for protest
against that invasion of modesty. Oddly, she felt no inclination to protest, in spite of the fact that she was normally
a fairly modest person. She pondered that fact in bemused
silence, sitting bolt upright and stiff as a post, her eyes
clinging to Dan's face as he examined her shoulder. Her
throat was dry, but she dared not swallow; if she could have
stilled the beating of her heart, she would have done so.

His fingers were gentle, unhurried, their touch as sensitive and sure as a sculptor's—or a lover's. And she could
not—she could not—stop her body from responding to that
touch or her mind from imagining it on her body's most re-
sponsive places.

"Move your arm," Dan commanded. His gaze and all his
concentration were focused on her shoulder and nothing
more. She was being foolish, as usual. "Okay...that hurt?"

She nodded, and Dan's eyes flickered to her face. Hard
eyes, unreadable.

"Nothing broken," he said briefly, straightening.
"You're gonna have one hell of a bruise there tomorrow,
though. Probably help if you put some ice on it." He moved
away from her, his face remote.

Sarah pulled her shirt back over her shoulder and began,
with shaking fingers, to button it. "Thank you, I'm sure I'll
be fine." There was an awkward little silence filled with the
noises of the jungle night. "Can I . . . would you like something to eat or drink before you start back? Coffee?"

Now at last he did look at her, a measuring, almost wary look, while he stretched and then rubbed the back of his neck. "Hadn't planned to go back."

Sarah tried to speak, but no sound emerged. She cleared her throat carefully and tried again. "Oh. Well, sure. I guess it is pretty late. Of course, you're welcome to stay, if you think... Umm, there's Marina's cot, or you could stay at the ranger's—"

"Cot's fine," Dan said shortly, interrupting her. "And I will take that coffee, if you have it."

"Okay, sure. Is instant—"

"Fine."

His words were clipped, his voice harsh. He must still be angry, Sarah thought, and why not? He hadn't thought much of her in the first place, and then she'd almost shot him.

She was glad to have something to do. The simple, oft-repeated tasks of turning on the propane burner, adjusting the flame, filling the teakettle from the supply of bottled water, selecting two mugs, opening the jar and finding a spoon, became complicated procedures that required all her concentration. She measured coffee crystals with the dedicated precision of a clinical chemist.

Dan sat in one of the wooden chairs, tipped it back and watched her in brooding silence. When Sarah asked him if he took milk or sugar, he shook his head and grunted, "Black." He waited, then fired a question at her back.

"Where are the rangers?"

The question surprised her, coming out of the uneasy silence. She said, "What?"

"The rangers. The Land Rover was gone and the station looked deserted when I came by. Just struck me as kind of odd." There was a pause, and she felt the thump of his chair's legs hitting the plank floor. Then his presence, warm and substantial was beside her.

Sarah frowned at the spoonful of sugar she was holding, emptied it carefully into her cup, then looked around desperately for something else to do with her hands. She wished he'd go back and sit down, his nearness made her feel hot and cold at the same time, as if she had a fever. Her shoulder had begun to throb again, too. Fighting a compulsion to rub it, she closed her eyes and, in her imagination, felt Dan's gentle, exploring fingers once again.

"Today," he said in his softest drawl, leaning against the counter and folding his arms on his chest, "they didn't want you going into the jungle without an escort, and tonight they go and leave you here all alone. How come?"

The teakettle went off like an air-raid siren. Sarah released her breath in a rush and spoke over her shoulder as she went to answer its call. "Salim had to take Sukey's body to someplace in Medan to be held for evidence. Police or Parks Department headquarters, I'm not sure which. He won't be back until late tomorrow. Then, just before dark, Joka got a call on the radio. Apparently a logging-crew helicopter had reported seeing what looked like a campfire up in the northern section of the reserve, about five or six miles upriver from here. Joka told me he thought it might be the poachers and he was going to go and investigate. He left me the gun and told me to stay inside...."

Her voice trailed off as she picked up the two cups and carried them to the table, silenced by her feelings of futility. He'd never understand—a man as hard and strong as he was. How could she tell him what it had felt like to her, alone in that silent cabin with the darkness closing in all around and that awful presentiment of danger stirring the fine hairs on her skin like the touch of an unseen hand? She'd sound like a hysterical child seeing monsters in the closet!

She sat down and waited for Dan to do the same, blowing on her coffee, wrapping her hands around it as if for warmth though the night was as sultry as a sauna.

Dan took out a pack of cigarettes and asked her if she minded if he smoked. Sarah shook her head. She tried not to notice the brand, and she tried not to feel relief when it was a common, ordinary one and not the long slim kind with that little gold band around the filter.

No, of course not, she said to herself, feeling foolish. Not Dan.

Almost as if he were following the path of her thoughts, Dan took the cigarette from his lips and stared at it, then regarded her narrow-eyed through its smoke while one corner of his mouth tilted wryly upward. Unexpectedly, he smiled—a full smile that softened his mouth and warmed his eyes and carved charming grooves in his cheeks. Under its influence, Sarah felt her fears and tensions melt away, like dew in the morning sunshine.

"And you got scared," he said, gently mocking.

Unoffended, Sarah smiled back. "Yeah, I did." Then, for the first time feeling at ease with him, she shook her head and said, "I can't explain it—I tried to tell myself I was imagining things, but I really felt there was something out there. I felt—" she paused and leaned toward him over her coffee cup "—have you ever heard a tiger? Do you know how it gets in the jungle when there's one around?" Dan nodded, but Sarah didn't wait for it. She rushed on, her voice low and intent. "I've only heard it once. We'd camped overnight at a release point. It woke me—you know that coughing noise they make? It took me a moment to realize what it was, and then I froze, and so did everything else. The forest was . . . it was more than silent. It was like it was listening. There's so much tension, so much fear, that you can hear it, but not with your ears. Do you know—"

"I know," Dan said softly.

"Well, that's how I felt, like I were being stalked. I knew something was out there and that these walls wouldn't be any protection from it at all. Then I heard a noise."

"And instead of a tiger..." Dan murmured, smiling.

Sarah didn't say anything. The analogy that sprang to her mind was vivid and disturbing. The way he'd come through that window, his body lean and lithe—and lethal. She got up to put the screen on the window.

Dan leaned back in his chair and stretched out his legs. Sprawled there, completely at ease, he watched her with curtained eyes. She felt their touch like roving hands on her back, buttocks and thighs.

"Ow!" she cried involuntarily, and dropped the screen on her foot. She'd forgotten about her sore shoulder.

And he was there, instantly, silently, his hands settling onto her shoulders, his body heat surrounding her. Though the night was warm, she didn't feel suffocated or crowded, but rather, comforted, as if a lover had given her his coat on a cold winter day.

"Here." His voice rumbled from his chest like a lion's purr. "I'll get that."

Sarah nodded without saying anything, fighting against the pull of his body, her heart beating as if it were a physical battle instead of an emotional one. Her breath caught slightly as his hands tightened on her arms. But he was only shifting her to one side, out of his way.

The screen in place, Dan swept the room with his gaze and remarked, "Nice house. Tight. I'd expected a lot less."

Sarah wiped sweat-slippery hands on her thighs and laughed ruefully. "It has to be tight to be orangutan-proof. You should have seen the place we had before this—a nice little hut, thatched roof, open sides. The orangutans demolished it."

"No kiddin'?" He was interested, relaxed, smiling, and as before, Sarah responded to his smile and relaxed herself.

"In no time flat," she affirmed with a chuckle. "Nothing was safe. They shredded our underwear for bedding, ate the toothpaste, soap, shoes, flashlight batteries—"

"Flashlight batteries! Thought they were poisonous."

"So I've always believed! I'll never forget the time we came home and found Sukey sitting in the middle of the table, looking like the cat that ate the canary. I knew she'd been up to something. Well, she started spitting out size D batteries—three of them, one at a time. When I thought sure that was all, she grinned at me and spit out another one! Marina and I couldn't believe it—it was like one of those circus acts, you know? Where clowns just keep coming out of a Volkswagen or a phone booth? We thought we'd die laughing!"

"Sukey. Wasn't that the one you said the poachers—"

"Yes. She was our first..." Sarah looked away, struggling for control. "Damn."

"You really do get attached to them, don't you?"

His voice was gentle again. Sarah shrugged, and managed to smile. "Well, we try not to, but you just can't help it sometimes. They have such individual personalities, you know? Some are just...special."

"Like Luki?"

"Yes, and J.J. We've had those two since they were babies."

"Speaking of babies," Dan said, looking around, "where's the little one? The one you had the other day?"

"Sweetie? Oh, she's down in quarantine, keeping Luki company. He was so upset about J.J., he was making a real nuisance of himself. And there just wasn't room for both of them in my bed." She coughed, and after a moment began to clear away the coffee cups. She wished Dan would say something; echoes of the word *bed* seemed to bounce around the room like a runaway Ping-Pong ball.

As she always did when she felt uncomfortable, to her
own profound dismay, Sarah began to babble. "It really was
nice of you to come all the way up here, just to see if I—if
we were okay. Marina was worried because of the poachers—we both were—but it's still a lot to ask. I hope she
didn't—Marina can be very persuasive, sometimes."

"She's a nice lady," Dan interjected, looking amused.

"Oh, I know. I love her to death, just like a sister. We
really do get along well, which is a good thing, since we
spend so much time together and in such close proximity. I
mean, look at this—our living quarters don't exactly give us
a lot of privacy." She stopped and, leaning against the sink,
surveyed the two narrow cots, side by side under their veils
of mosquito netting. Dan's gaze followed hers, but he didn't
comment, and after a moment, she struggled on. "Umm,
the cots aren't very comfortable, not exactly the Hilton,
but . . ."

"I've slept on worse," Dan drawled, strolling over to take
a closer look. Sarah stayed where she was, fidgeting.

"The, umm, latrine's outside—so's the shower. There's
bottled water if you want to brush your teeth—do you have
a toothbrush? I might be able to find one, if you—"

"That's fine." No hint of a drawl now; the words were
clipped, like punctuation marks. Sarah swallowed and fell
silent. Heat surged beneath her skin. And then, suddenly,
Dan turned, thumbs hooked in his belt, a wry half smile on
his lips, and asked, "Doc, am I makin' you nervous?"

"Nervous?" She shook her head, then closed her eyes and
released her breath on a little ripple of laughter. "Yes. . . ."

He moved toward her with that silent, fluid grace. Heat
billowed into her belly, her chest, her throat.

"Because I kissed you?" He was standing close, looking
down at her through a veil of lashes. That mouth, so sensitive, so sardonic—she could feel it, taste it on her own. Heat
exploded into her face, her lips tingled.

She licked them and mumbled, ''Well, since you mention it . . .''

''No need to worry.'' His voice was flat. ''I won't lay a finger on you, I guarantee it.''

''Oh,'' Sarah said, the heat inside her turning to sludge. ''Well, of course. I know you wouldn't—I mean, I trust you—''

His smile grew more wry, and his lashes lifted briefly, revealing a gleam that may have been amusement or something else. ''Well, now, I wouldn't go that far, if I were you.''

How soft his voice was, yet it drowned all other sound.

''I kissed you today, that's a fact, and the only reason I'm not kissing you right now is that it has a way of leadin' to one thing and another.'' He jerked his head toward the beds. ''And I don't relish the idea of makin' love on one of those things.'' At her shocked gasp, quickly stifled, his smile slipped and then disappeared altogether. In a voice so quiet she wasn't exactly sure she heard him right, he said, ''Not with you, Doc. Not the first time.''

Inside the cabin silence fell, and the jungle chorus rushed to fill it. Seconds passed, measured in heartbeats. Then Dan said in a normal voice, ''Got a flashlight?''

Sarah blinked. ''What?''

''A flashlight. I think I lost mine out there somewhere when I came through the window. If you've got one I can borrow, I think I'll go find that latrine you mentioned.''

''Oh,'' Sarah mumbled. ''Sure. Right here.'' Moving on autopilot, she opened a drawer, found the flashlight and handed it to him. He took it from her, muttered his thanks and was gone.

Without him, the night seemed huge and lonely, the cabin a small, empty space in which she rattled around like a pebble in a can, making noise to no purpose whatsoever. She tried to think what she needed to do to get ready for bed.

Bed! With Dan sleeping in the next cot? She'd never felt less like sleeping; every nerve and sense was humming, louder than the night chorus.

She must have heard him wrong. He couldn't have meant it, not that way. It was the sort of thing men say, sometimes—arrogant, macho stuff. Except that Dan wasn't like that. It seemed so out-of-character for him, like that flash of desire she'd seen in his eyes—unmistakable at the moment, and yet so quickly gone that in the next moment she thought she must have imagined it. What kind of man was he, anyway?

She was thinking so hard and wound so tightly that when Dan came in carrying both the flashlight she'd given him and the one he'd lost, she jumped a foot.

"Still nervous?" he asked dryly.

She shook her head in pointless denial. "No. Just a little edgy, I guess."

His smile was sardonic, but he let her get away with it. Nodding toward the window, he said, "It's okay, I checked it out. Nothing out there that shouldn't be. It's safe for you to go."

"Thank you," Sarah said stiffly, taking the flashlight he handed her, even though she knew the way blindfolded.

When she came back, Dan was lying on Marina's cot with his head propped on one arm, smoking. He'd thrown back the mosquito netting but not the bedclothes and taken off his shirt and shoes. The lantern light gave his smooth chest a glossy sheen, but not of gold or polished wood or anything so lifeless and cold. It made Sarah think of warm satin, like the well-groomed hide of a healthy animal. It made her want to touch.

He didn't say anything, and neither did she. What was there to say? The tension in the cabin was so thick it seemed to have substance. It filled all the space, leaving no room for words.

Sarah brushed her teeth in a frowning perplexity, wondering how she was going to manage to undress for bed in that one-room cabin, without even a curtain for privacy. And, after working all day with animals in the tropical sun and humidity, she didn't relish the idea of sleeping in her clothes!

Finally, having run out of things to do at the sink, she turned around, braced herself and blurted, "Umm, would you mind closing your eyes?"

Dan raised himself on one elbow and leaned over to extinguish his cigarette. When he straightened up again he had an expression on his face that made Sarah wonder if he was trying not to laugh. "Well now, Doc, I could do that," he said with a telltale trace of huskiness in his voice, "but since I'm not a saint, I'd probably just peek, and even if I didn't, you'd worry about it."

Sarah made a little sound of helplessness and vexation.

Dan looked at her with laughter in his eyes and said softly, "Why don't you just turn out the light?"

Chapter 6

All things considered, Dan thought it was probably one of the weirdest nights he'd ever spent, lying there on that virgin cot under a veil of mosquito netting, close enough to reach out and touch one of the most attractive women he'd ever seen. A woman he'd imagined himself making love to in every way possible. A woman who just a short while ago had tried to blow his head off.

And damn near succeeded. When he thought about it, his heart gave a random skip. It had been a closer one than he wanted to think about.

He didn't find it hard to channel his thoughts elsewhere. She kept pulling at them, and he'd just as well try to resist gravity.

She baffled him. He'd been so sure he had her pegged, but the more he saw of her the more she seemed to keep changing, while her real self—her heart and soul—eluded him. Like one of those candy jawbreakers he used to spend his pennies on when he was a kid; you couldn't crack 'em, no matter how hard you tried. If you did try, you'd only hurt yourself—break a tooth. The only way to get to the center was to work your way slowly through all the different layers, colors, flavors.

The flavors of Dr. Sarah Fairchild. Golden Girl. Woman who weeps for orangutans.

A woman who possessed the elegance of dancers and duchesses, yet seemed happy living in a jungle hut, wearing khaki instead of mink, smelling of insect repellent instead of Chanel No 5.

A woman with a body like a wood nymph's, slender and supple as a vine except for a natural feminine fullness of hip, a dancer's strength of thigh and a sweet and subtle curve of breast, pale as ivory in moonlight.

Which Dan knew about because, although he wasn't about to tell Sarah so, he had excellent night vision. He'd made that suggestion about the lights out of compassion for Sarah, which was something to think about, all by itself. His compassion hadn't extended as far as closing his eyes, though, which should have made him feel guilty, but didn't. What the hell, no one had ever accused him of being a gentleman or a saint.

A saint he sure wasn't. Lord knew, he wanted Sarah about as badly as he'd ever wanted any woman in his life. Watching her undress for bed and even thinking about it now made him distinctly uncomfortable, part of the reason he was still lying here listening to his own heartbeat, and the whine of mosquitos, lizards scuttling up the walls, moths—those damned Indonesian moths as big as his palm—flap-flapping against the screens, confused by the dying of the light.

He stirred cautiously, trying to find relief for the pressure in his loins and finally eased himself over onto his belly. He kept his head turned away from Sarah and took care to steady his breathing so she wouldn't guess he was as wakeful as she was. Oh, yeah, he knew she wasn't asleep; she was too still, her breathing quick and shallow, as if, Dan thought, she were trying not to. As if she feared even that movement of her body might betray her.

Too late, Doc.

Dan knew when a woman was receptive to him, and Sarah Fairchild was his for the taking. He knew it, as surely as he knew he'd regret it for the rest of his life if he took advantage of that fact now, tonight. He couldn't have said why, not in words, but he knew it wasn't the way he wanted it. Things were changing between them, he could feel it. But it wasn't right, not yet.

It really was funny, he thought as he stared at the pattern of moon and starlight through the shutters casting elongated shadows on the rough plank walls. Not funny—crazy. He'd wanted Sarah Fairchild from the first minute he'd laid eyes on her. Since then it seemed as if he'd spent half his time lusting after her body and the other half warning himself to stay away from her. Warnings that had about as much effect on him as they would on those damned moths battering themselves to pieces on the screens.

In the bleakness of a sleepless night it finally came to him that he couldn't stay away from this woman, even knowing that she had the power to destroy him, any more than the moth can resist the call of the flame. Any more than those poor peyote-crazed fools in the old legends his father had told him of could keep themselves from leaping joyfully into the mouth of the volcano.

Any more than his father had been able to resist his mother.

Sarah's favorite time of day had always been that hour or so just before dawn, the closest it ever gets to silence in the rain forest, when the night creatures are returning to nests and burrows and the day creatures haven't yet begun to stir. In that relative stillness, she lay awake listening to the soft breathing sounds of the man in the cot next to her. A reassuring sound. Sleep was a great leveler of men, even one as disturbing and enigmatic as Dan Cisco. Asleep, even the most powerful and charismatic man is vulnerable.

Vulnerable. What an unlikely word to describe a man who could dodge a rifle bullet and then overpower and disarm his assailant in three seconds flat! But the mind plays strange games in the silent, lonely hours.

She saw Dan's face, not the pagan mask with its unyielding mouth and unreadable eyes, but as he'd looked that first day when she'd impulsively given Sweetie to him to hold. And again, yesterday in the jungle, when he'd gone back to pick up Luki—the surprise and then the softening, and then that defensive, almost belligerent look, as if daring anyone to notice.

She felt again the tempered steel strength of his hands and then the cool surprise of flower petals, the gentle rasp of his fingertips against her scalp. His mouth, so unexpectedly, unbelievably tender. And her response, like nothing she'd ever felt before. Pinpoint prickles, like a shower of stardust on her skin.

She heard his words again, every one of them, telling her about his childhood—telling her so little! His words were like salted peanuts to her, only creating in her an appetite for more. She wanted to know how an oil roughneck named Cisco, complete with Texas accent, happened to grow up in New England and why he'd hated kindergarten. She wanted to know what made his eyes so hard and his hands so gentle.

Vulnerable? Dan Cisco?

Sarah lay on her side listening to the sounds of his breathing, waiting impatiently for the dawn, hoping it might bring an answer. But when the darkness had thinned to a pearly gray, she saw that he was on his side, too, with his face turned away from her. She lay back finally, stared up into the mosquito net and released a long slow breath of frustration.

Even asleep, it seemed, he was shielding himself from her.

Somewhere out in the forest a gibbon called; the first streaks of sunlight were hitting the canopy. The day shift would soon be in full voice, and down in the quarantine cages Luki and Sweetie and old Beau would be crawling out of their nests of leaves and branches, demanding to be fed.

Sarah was in a quandary. Staying in bed had become intolerable. She needed to go to the bathroom, her body felt stiff, achy, hot, and the sheet clung to her bare legs like cobwebs. On the other hand, getting up seemed complicated, even risky. What if, at some point in the proceedings, Dan woke up and rolled over? She couldn't very well turn out the sunlight!

Inevitably, though, the demands of her body overcame her qualms, and she eased her bare feet out from under the cover, groping for the terry cloth robe that hung on a hook just outside the veil of mosquito netting. She threw a nervous glance toward the other bed as she drew the robe on over her panties and the Baryshnikov T-shirt she'd slept in. Her hands shook as she knotted the belt around her waist. But Dan didn't stir, and gradually her heartbeat returned to normal.

Still, it was with the stealth and caution of a cat burglar that Sarah tiptoed around the cabin, stuffing shampoo, soap, her toothbrush, clean underwear and a washcloth into her robe pockets. Then she picked up a baby bottle and a can of formula, stepped into her sneakers and, without bothering to tie their laces, slipped out into the morning.

After the dim and quiet of the shuttered cabin, the jungle was an assault on her senses. The early-morning light was like nothing else imaginable—intense, but not brilliant, like viewing the world through green-tinted glasses. The air was not hot yet, its touch still soft and gentle on the

skin. The smell was a tantalizing mix of exotic and evoca-
tive—green grass and mossy riverbanks, windborne scent of
pine and spices and, underlying everything, the all-pervasive
odors of the jungle, of flowers and of decay. Of life and
death. A witch's brew of smells, intoxicating as a love po-
tion.

And today she felt intoxicated, suddenly too happy to
dwell on tragedy or near tragedy, too drunk on life to think
of death. Life! It was all around her; the jungle teaming with
it. The very air she breathed seemed busy, crowded with insect whine and birdsong and gibbon's call, with meander-
ing butterflies and darting lizards and the emerald flash of
sunlight on a hummingbird's wing. The rising sun was warm
on the back of her neck, the grass was soft and wet underfoot, and down in the quarantine cages were three of the
most precious and threatened creatures on earth—and they
were entrusted to her. There was an attractive and enigmatic man asleep in her cabin, a man who'd kissed her and
suggested he'd like to do so again. Life was exciting, and in
spite of Sukey and J.J. and the ever present threat of
poachers, Sarah had never been so happy.

The orangutans were waiting for her, three pairs of black-
currant eyes peering through the wire mesh, giving her the
look of patient acceptance that always tugged at her heart.
Ordinarily, Sarah would have spent some time with them
before going into the forest to observe the wild orangs,
especially Sweetie, who was still young enough to need
constant body contact and cuddling. In the absence of her
own mother and Sarah's attentions, she'd adopted Luki as
a surrogate and was clinging to his back like a fuzzy orange
octopus. Once Sweetie and old Beau had cleared quarantine, she'd take them with her into the jungle, to teach them
to climb and forage as a mother would. This morning,
though, after she fed them, cuddled Sweetie and rough-
housed with Luki and surrendered her toothbrush to old

Beau's inquisitive fingers, she reluctantly returned them to their cages and climbed up the hill to the shower.

There was no sign of life from the cabin as she passed. Dan was still asleep. Yet she felt his presence so intensely, she could almost see him, see his hard eyes watching her. Somehow, because he was in it, the cabin seemed different to her, as if she'd never seen it before. The path she followed seemed unfamiliar, although she'd walked it a thousand times. The shower—the watertank on its platform of bamboo, the canvas vanes to catch and funnel rainwater into the tank—seemed an outlandish, alien contraption, though she'd helped to build it with her own hands.

The idea to attach a hose and shower nozzle to the water tank's spigot had been Marina's, conceived shortly after the day she'd laid her shampoo and towel on the riverbank and then watched them go floating off down the river on the back of a medium-sized crocodile!

It was Sarah, though, who'd suggested the bamboo screen that gave the arrangement at least a modicum of privacy. After the river, it had seemed a luxury. Now, with every nerve attuned to the nearness of an intriguing stranger, it seemed to her flimsy and crude—all but transparent. As she undressed behind the screen she kept throwing uneasy glances over it, while her nipples hardened and her skin shivered with awareness.

Silly, she told herself. She reached up to lift the hose from its hook and couldn't hold back a sharp cry at the unexpected pain. She'd forgotten her bruised shoulder.

Alone in the cabin, Dan had finally gotten out of bed groaning and stretching, swearing disgustedly at the unaccustomed stiffness in his muscles. He added a softly profane exclamation at the discovery of a spot of tenderness on his cheekbone where Sarah's rifle butt had struck him. Not exactly the usual kind of damage he'd expect from a night with a pretty lady, he reflected ruefully as he rolled up the shades and drew in a deep breath of jungle morning.

Not exactly his usual kind of lady.

He was standing there, frowning at nothing, fingering his bruise and wondering what he was going to do about the lady, when he heard her cry out. It came from the rise behind the cabin, one small cry of distress, quickly stifled. Dan didn't stop to ponder it; he hurled himself out the door and off of the porch and hit the ground running.

He hadn't taken very many steps before two things penetrated his consciousness: for one, he wasn't wearing shoes; and for another, Sarah obviously wasn't in danger after all. Both of those observations should have convinced him that an unobtrusive retreat was in order, but instead, he found himself continuing, at a much more sedate pace, on up the hill toward the water tank.

At first all he could see of Sarah above the screen of bamboo that enclosed the legs of the tank's platform was the top of her head, wet and sleek as an otter's, and one slender, golden arm, holding a shower nozzle. As he got closer, her neck came into view, and then her shoulders. She was oblivious to his presence; her eyes were shut tight, the water sluicing over her face and ears. He wasn't sure why he stopped there, but he did, and for a moment or two just stood and watched her.

Dan thought he knew why she'd cried out; that bruised shoulder of hers must be pretty sore, and the shower's arrangement would make it tough even for someone with two good arms. She was trying to get some shampoo on her hair, and every time she lifted her right arm he could see her jaw tighten and her lips stretch in a grimace of pain. And every time she did that, he could feel his own jaws clench and his muscles tense with the impulse to do something about it.

He thought for quite a while about what he was going to do, because he had a pretty good idea what her reaction would be. He thought about it while he watched little rivers of water trickle down over the vulnerable bumps in her spine, and when he couldn't stand it anymore, cleared his throat and said, "Need another hand?"

What followed that was about what he'd expected. Sarah dropped the shower hose, said, "Ulp!" or something similar, and went down after it. Dan heard the hose snaking around, a muffled exclamation, and then a white cap of shampoo lather and a pair of startled golden eyes appeared above the bamboo screen.

"What are you doing here?" Her last word was a squeak of alarm, as Dan moved one step closer to the screen. Her head bobbed uncertainly, threatening to disappear again.

"Heard you holler," Dan said, trying to look nonthreatening. "Thought you needed help."

"Well, I don't." She sniffed. Dan extended a finger and lifted a large glob of suds that was sliding toward the end of her nose.

"That wasn't the way it looked to me," he said softly, controlling an urge to laugh.

"I'm taking a shower!" Her tone was about midway between appeal and outrage. The laughter bubbled up inside Dan, making his lips quiver.

"Yeah, I can see that," he said solemnly. "Looked to me like you were shorthanded."

"Wait—you can't—" Her eyes widened in panic as he moved closer. He stopped and looked at her for a moment with his head tilted to one side.

"Come on, Doc, what do you think I'm going to do? I've had all night to jump your bones, if that's what I wanted." His smile slipped sideways; better she didn't know how badly he'd wanted to do just that. "Hand me that hose and come over here. Hurry up, now, before you get soap in your eyes."

He had her eyes and he held them, lifting all the force of his will into it. After a long hesitation her eyelids quivered and dropped. "Atta girl," he said softly. "Give me that thing—now turn around." He held the sprayer in one hand and put the other on the back of her neck. It felt rigid, cool and slippery, like wet marble. "That's right." Instinctively, he gentled his voice, making it soothing, reassuring. "Tip your head back now, I've got you."

He pressed gently, manipulating the delicate muscles of her neck until they became pliable and the weight of her head settled tentatively into his hand. With tepid water sluicing over his hand, he pushed his fingers into the lather, rubbing in slow circles, following the contours of her head. It felt unbelievably fragile to him, like finest porcelain.

Water drops spangled her forehead and eyelids. She put up her hand to shield her face and accidentally brushed his fingers. He hesitated, and so did she. Instead of jerking away from the contact, she became very still. And so did he. He stood there with water running unnoticed over his feet, looking at their hands—his dark, rough, square, hers long and fine and golden tan. His own shook slightly; he wondered if she noticed it.

"All done," he said harshly, giving her head a little lift of warning before taking away the support of his hand. She straightened and turned to face him, looking like a sleep-walker just coming to consciousness.

Her eyes touched him like sunshine. And like the sunlight, they gave him more than warmth. He felt drugged.

Suddenly he felt her knuckles, like pebbles against his palms and, looking down, found that she was holding on to the top edge of the screen, and that he'd covered her hands with his. He had no recollection of it. He stared back at her, full of the awareness that only a few strips of bamboo separated her naked body from him.

Fresh, wet skin, hair sleek and dripping; pearly drops shivering on her shoulders and pooling in the hollows of her throat; eyelashes clinging in dark spikes. Lips parted and wet—her mouth looked to him like a tall cool drink does to a thirsty man. He wanted to take that moisture from her mouth, take it with his lips, his tongue, drink it in, drink her in, knowing that to do so would only make him thirst all the more.

Her tongue took a water drop from the corner of her mouth. He leaned toward her, tightening his hands on hers.

The sky chose that moment to deliver its daily downpour.

Dan threw one furious glance skyward, and, swearing, began to search for an opening in the screen. When he found the hook-and-eye latch, Sarah gasped, "You're not coming in here!"

"Like hell I'm not!" Then he hesitated, grabbed the terry cloth robe that was draped over the screen and tossed it to her. "Put that on if it bothers you—dammit, these are the only pants I have, and there's nothing I hate worse—" the latch gave, and he opened the screen and slipped inside "—than wet pants!" The hose was still snaking around on the grass; he planted one foot on it while he reached up to turn off the valve on the underside of the watertank. By the time he turned back to Sarah, breathing hard and brushing raindrops from his shoulders, she was knotting the tie on her robe and glaring furiously at him.

"Well," he said, and let his gaze rest softly on her flushed cheeks, "here we are."

Here we are. And where is that? Sarah wondered, glaring to hide the shivery doubts inside. But all around her was the rushing sound of rain, drowning thought. The world had turned to water, and she felt as though she had, too. She felt fluid, formless, weak. Dan was solid, strong, brown as earth. She wanted to put her hands on his shoulders and feel the heat in that smooth, vibrant muscle. She wanted to lay her cheek against his chest and hear the thud of his heart-beat. She wanted his arms around her, his strong-gentle hands on her skin.

But, her doubts cried, I can't trust him! How could she trust a man she didn't understand? How could she under-stand a man whose eyes told her one thing one minute, and the next, something else entirely, and the next, nothing at all!

So she glared, wiped moisture from her face with the sleeve of her robe, jammed her hands into its pockets and said nothing.

Dan's smile was quizzical. "Am I still makin' you nervous?"

Sarah opened her mouth, lifted one shoulder, shook her head. Dan made a little grimace of annoyance and started toward her. Encountering the shower nozzle with his bare foot, he muttered something profane under his breath, picked it up, looked at it for a moment as if he'd never seen it before.

"It goes up there," Sarah said through chattering teeth. "On that hook."

"Oh, right." He disposed of the distraction and turned back to her, his eyes glittering behind a screen of lashes. "Tell me something, Doc." She waited, counting heart-beats. He reached out to touch a strand of wet hair back from her temple, and her involuntary intake of breath brought a sardonic little twist to his lips. "Why do I make you nervous?" He waited, then softened his voice and prodded, "What are you afraid of?"

"I don't know," Sarah whispered, and then corrected herself. "I don't know...you."

He gave a short, hard laugh and let his hand drop away from her. "Well, we sure as hell aren't strangers! Lord, woman, I've kissed you. You tried to shoot me! We've slept together, and now here we are, sharing a shower. Seems to me two people could spend a whole lifetime together and never get as close as we are right now.''

Sarah stood still, listening to the rushing of the rain, the trickling sounds of water collecting on the canvas vanes and running into the tank above their heads. She studied Dan, her gaze moving from the watchful expression on his face to the water drops glistening on his smooth chest to the belly muscles moving in and out just above the waistband of his pants, and on down to his feet, bare as hers and speckled with mud and grass. She felt the rain like a curtain around them, closing them in together.

And to her own great astonishment, she giggled.

Dan tilted his head slightly, asking the question with his eyes rather than words. Sarah lifted her arms and shoulders in a gesture that encompassed it all—themselves, the rain, everything. ''It just struck me,'' she said on the crest of more laughter, ''how silly this is. Two people, taking shelter from the rain—in a *shower*.''

''Yep,'' Dan said, ''that's pretty funny.'' But his smile was wry rather than amused.

''I mean, there it is right out there, nature's own shower, absolutely free, and here we are, going to all this trouble ... Why is that, do you suppose?'' She was babbling again, talking nonsense, sidestepping the issue; she knew it, and so did he. ''Why don't people bathe in the rain?''

''Why?'' Dan glanced out at the rain, then brought his shuttered gaze to rest on the deep slash in the front of her robe. She could feel his gaze. Her skin shivered and then grew hot.

''I suppose,'' he said dryly, ''it's because most people might feel a little bit uncomfortable, dancin' naked in the rain.''

''Excepting children,'' Sarah said with a false and desperate brightness.

"And lovers." His voice was husky, not bright at all.

His eyes made her feel slightly dizzy, like staring into a revolving spiral. She pulled away from them and turned her face again to the rain, hugging herself in her terry cloth robe.

The rain was slackening now; she could see sunshine streaks touching the distant treetops and, off to the north near the mountains, a rainbow. Lovers dancing naked in the rain. The images that came to her mind were wistful and sweet, like a glimpse of Eden.

She felt Dan come close to her, felt the weight of his hands settle onto her shoulders, and she swallowed, trying to think of something clever to say. But when she finally opened her mouth, he spoke first, in a low voice with rough edges.

"What would it take for you to be easy with me?"

When she didn't answer, he moved one hand to the back of her neck; it felt very warm there, not seductive, just comforting. So why was there suddenly a growing, spreading ache in her throat? She didn't understand.

"You said you don't know me. I want you to know me. I want us to know each other. Tell me what you want me to do." His fingers moved, slowly, gently, up and down.

"I don't know." She closed her eyes, fighting a compulsion to swallow. Her heart was beating too fast. He must know it, he must feel her pulse surging against his fingers. Half-fearfully, she turned her head to look at him. "I guess . . . talk to me."

"We'll talk." His fingers were moving still, down into the collar of her robe, up under the wet commas of her hair. His thumb stroked lightly over the ache in her throat. "What else?"

Sarah opened her mouth but said nothing.

"What about this?" She felt the pressure of his thumb on the underside of her chin and, with a whispered sigh, yielded to it. Her eyelids drifted down. "If I kiss you again, will it help?'' There was something wry in his voice, a gentle mockery directed more at himself than at her. ''Or is it gonna make it worse?''

She couldn't have answered if her life had depended on it; her heartbeat was pounding her to pieces, she was suffocating on her own breath!

''You can stop me any time you want to, you know that, don't you?''

His breath warmed her lips like a promise. Stop him? But . . . she wanted . . . did she dare?

''I just want you to feel easy with me, Doc.'' He touched the words to her lips, making them tingle. ''I'm not going to hurt you.''

Chapter 7

Her eyes flew open, glowing like live coals. In that instant, just before he kissed her, Dan understood. Incredible as it seemed to him, someone, sometime, somewhere...

"Doc, I won't ever hurt you," he whispered, and realized with a sense of wonder that they were words he'd never spoken before. Alien feelings were burgeoning inside him. He felt powerful and possessive, fierce and tender at the same time. Although he knew how to take care of himself pretty well, he'd learned the hard way that sometimes it was best if you use your wits, to walk away from a fight, if you could. But at that moment he knew that he'd kill to protect this woman, if it came to that.

All the while he hesitated there, awed by what was happening inside him, her eyes were drowning him in liquid gold. And then tawny lashes fluttered and dropped. He felt her breath sigh across his lips as, with a little whimper of surrender, she lifted her face, blindly seeking him.

Because of the words he'd just spoken, he meant to make it a gentle kiss; a reassuring kiss; a kiss full of restraint and promise. Give her time, he told himself. She'd come to trust him. But somehow, when he touched her mouth with his, their lips seemed to melt and merge. Her mouth opened, and he sank into it as into warm honey, deeper and deeper, unable to stop himself, unable to get enough. He heard her soft, desperate sound again, and answered it with one of his own, a deep-throated rumbling, like a volcano's warning of explosions to come.

He felt her arms lift to his neck and her body come against him, the knotted belt of her robe like a clenched fist between them. Impatient with the obstruction, he pulled away from her and reached for it, at the same time searching her face, asking the question without words.

He saw a faint frown, the tiny shake of her head, but knew that it wasn't the answer she meant to give him. Her true answer was in her famished eyes, in her swollen mouth still glazed with moisture from his kiss, in the hands that rested, trembling, on his shoulders, neither resisting nor restraining him.

As the knot gave and the ends of the sash drew apart, he fought a brief battle with himself: whether to pull aside the edges of her robe slowly, to expose her body to his hungry eyes, to inflame himself further with the vision of his work-roughened hands on her silken skin, as he'd imagined it so many times, or to close his eyes and pull her close and savor the feel of that skin against his. But his fantasies seemed irrelevant to him now, and there would be time later for the slow, sensual explorations, the wonder of discovery. This was now, this was reality—her chest moving with accelerating tempo, her waist, so slender, trembling in his hands.

So he closed his eyes, slipped his hands around her and drew her nakedness against him, and as she came to him she gasped softly, then exhaled in a long, sweet sigh. Her breath merged with his and was extinguished, finally, in his mouth.

And again, he couldn't get enough of her! Nothing would satisfy him, it seemed, but to be inside her, not only in the physical sense, but in every possible way. He wanted to be inside her skin. He wanted to know how her mind worked—what her dreams were, and her nightmares, what jokes she laughed at and whether sad songs made her cry. Most of all, though, he wanted to know the secrets of her heart. He wanted to know who had hurt her and why someone who seemed so self-assured should be afraid of the likes of him.

I don't know you, Sarah had said to him, and he'd replied with glib assurances, promises he hadn't really meant to keep. How could he, when in all his adult life, he'd never let another human being close enough to know him? And now—the irony of it shook him to his core—the greater need to know was his.

He marveled as he ran his callused hands lightly down her back and over the taut swell of her bottom. How slender and soft her body was! As he'd known it would be. Awed, he brought his hands upward along her sides, drawing away from her a little to allow his thumbs to trace the velvety undercurve of her breasts, and heard her breathing quicken and felt her nipples shiver and grow hard at his touch. As he'd known they must.

Here she was in his arms, then—his golden girl, her body supple and moist, her responses flaring white hot—pretty much as he'd imagined her. His fantasies shamed him now. He'd wanted her in sexual thrall to him? It wouldn't take much, he knew, to put her there—he thought of the ways he'd touch her, and the thoughts inflamed him almost beyond reason. He'd wanted her writhing and whimpering and gasping his name. It would be so easy. But he knew it was nothing—nothing—compared to what he wanted from her now.

As if she'd read his thoughts, she broke from him suddenly and stared at him with blurred mouth and shocked eyes. When he smiled gently and gathered her close, she let her breath out in a rush and sagged against him, trembling. Oh, yes, it would be easy, he thought as he stroked her back, her neck, her hair, soothing her, damping down his own desires. Sex was easy. But he knew, even though her skin lay hot against his, searing him from throat to navel, that for what he wanted, they were still miles too far apart.

He was holding her, trying to think of a way to explain it all to her, when he heard Marina's call.

"Sarah? Sa-rah, where are you?"

"Oh." Sarah gave a shaky laugh and turned her face into the hollow of Dan's neck. "Well...damn."

She felt him clear his throat. The vibrations of his words tickled her lips. "Guess you'd better let 'em know you're all right. Under the circumstances, they might think..."

"Yeah." Oh, but she didn't want to move from that place, that warm, safe, wonderful place! It had been so hard to get there, past the barriers of her own fear and uncertainty. Now she was afraid that when he let go of her, when she moved out of that circle of comfort, she would feel the strangeness and doubt again. It was still there, as surely as the cold waits beyond the boundaries of the campfire light.

"Sarah?" There was an edge of concern in Marina's voice now.

Sarah drew in a breath and called, "Up here," as she turned away from Dan, tugging the edges of her robe together. "We're here—in the shower." While she was knotting the sash she looked back at him and found him watching her, his smile slightly askew. Something fluttered inside her, like a newborn butterfly trying its wings. The smile that responded to his felt as fragile and miraculous as that butterfly, too.

Tearing herself away from his eyes and smile was as hard as leaving his arms. Harder. She slipped through the gate in the screen feeling as winded as if she'd been engaged in a tug-of-war. Just in time, too, as Marina came around the corner of the cabin with J.J. in her arms and Tank a few steps behind.

"I've been showing Dan how the shower works," Sarah explained, and was dismayed at the telltale breathiness in her voice. Dan had come to stand beside her, and though she didn't dare look at him, she was aware of him with all her nerves and senses, including some she hadn't known about until that moment.

"We would have been here sooner," Marina said as she approached, shifting J.J. onto one hip. "The rain caught us just at the river, so we decided to wait until it was over." There was a breathy quality to Marina's voice, too, and her cheeks were flushed, though that could have been attributed to her climb up the hill with a twenty-pound orangutan in her arms.

On the other hand, there was a certain smugness in Tank's manner as he nodded at Dan and treated Sarah to his most charming smile. Tank, Sarah was sure, would know exactly what she and Dan had been doing in the shower!

"How is he?" she asked Marina, touching J.J.'s coarse orange coat. The orangutan's head swiveled and turned upward at the sound of her voice. Two round black eyes gazed unwinking at her as she rubbed the whiskers under his chin.

"He is so much better! But still very weak." Marina shifted J.J. carefully so that Sarah could see his bandaged shoulder. "We will have to baby him for a while. We have to give him antibiotics, and Joe—Dr. Soekardja—said to be sure he gets plenty of liquids."

"It won't be the first time we've nursed him back to health," Sarah reminded her. "Remember when we first got him? He was so tiny and sick then, and we thought Luki was too rough with him? Luki is going to be very glad to see this little guy.''

Marina frowned. ''Luki might be a problem, don't you think?''

''Hmm. Well, it will be interesting to see how he reacts to the injury—'' Realizing that the two men were standing there, watching them with arms folded and identical expressions of wry amusement and masculine long-suffering on their faces, Sarah broke off, laughing.

''Scientists,'' Tank remarked indulgently and stepped forward to engulf Sarah's hand in both of his. ''Howdy, Doc. Glad to see you're okay. This sweet lady here was a little bit worried about you, bein' here all alone.''

A small, ambiguous sound from Marina made Sarah glance from her to Tank and back again. Marina still looked flushed. Tank looked complacent.

Then she noticed that Tank's shirt was wet and that both Marina and J.J. were bone-dry. That seemed odd to her, but since she couldn't quite put her finger on why, she didn't comment about it.

''Well,'' she said with a laugh and a shrug, ending what for some reason had become an awkward silence, ''as you can see, we're fine.''

''Sure glad to hear it. Haven't heard any more from those poachers?''

Sarah opened her mouth, but unexpectedly it was Dan who drawled, ''Nah, quiet as a Sunday-school picnic.'' His voice was cool and slightly sardonic, but something in it made Sarah throw him a startled glance. She caught the glitter of his eyes beneath a lazy sweep of lashes and thought of a panther lying in wait on the limb of a jungle tree.

There is animosity there, she thought, shivering with unease because she wasn't sure of its cause or target. She realized she was beginning to be able to read him.

Then she wondered if that were really true or if she could read him now only because he wanted her to.

"Joka got a call," she said, nervously jumping into another of those pregnant pauses that seemed to keep cropping up in the conversation. There were undercurrents here. There were things going on that she didn't understand. It made her uneasy, and, of course, when she was uneasy... "One of the lumber company chopper pilots saw a campfire upriver, and he thought it might be the poachers. Anyway, Joka went to check it out, and he's not back yet, so I don't know..."

"He went alone?" Marina looked alarmed. "When I saw that the Land Rover was gone, I thought—"

"Salim took it," Sarah said, and went on to explain about the ranger's unhappy errand to town with Sukey's body.

Tank shook his head and made sympathetic noises. Dan, Sarah noticed, had adopted a stance she'd seen once before, also in Tank's presence: eyes half closed, smile just a little bit crooked, arms folded, legs apart, rocking up and back.

"You really would have been alone, then, if Dan hadn't been here," Marina said gravely, encircling J.J. with her arms in an unconsciously protective gesture.

With great care to avoid looking at Dan, Sarah muttered, "Well, of course, I had the gun."

Marina looked shocked. "Oh, but you could never shoot anything with it!"

From Dan's direction came a faint but unmistakeable snort, which was almost, but not quite, covered by Tank's chuckle. "If you're talkin' about that cannon I saw down at the house—" he interrupted himself with a low whistle "—that is one helluva lota gun. Way too much for a little lady like yourself to handle. If you did shoot it, it'd likely knock your arm off!"

"I wouldn't bet my life on it if I were you," Dan said in a dry undertone.

"Well, anyway," Marina said to him with a smile, "I'm glad you were here. I know Sarah felt better to have you here for protection. It was nice of you to come all this way. We are so grateful—thank you."

"Don't mention it," Dan mumbled, looking acutely uncomfortable. But Sarah noticed that the smile he gave Marina was warm, and that for the first time since their arrival, his eyes were unshuttered.

"Well," she said brightly, slapping at the mosquitos that had just discovered her unprotected legs, "I don't know about anybody else, but I think I'd like to go in and get dressed. Would anyone care for some breakfast?"

Tank looked interested, but before he could accept the invitation, Dan cut in with that quiet drawl of his. "Thanks, but I think we'd better be getting on back to the ranch. It's a long drive, and there's work to be done—right, old buddy?"

He clapped a hand on Tank's shoulder. Tank gave him a look, then shrugged and turned to Sarah with a grin, seemingly good-natured about being overruled. "Shoot, can't argue with the boss, can I? Thanks for the offer, though, sweetheart. How 'bout a rain check?"

Sarah laughed. "Sure, anytime. Both of you—you have a standing reservation. Just call to confirm."

Tank's eyebrows went up. "You have a telephone here?"

"Oops." Sarah snapped her fingers in mock dismay, and they both laughed.

"There is just the radio at the ranger's station," Marina explained. "No telephones." She was quite serious, not joining in the light banter, not even smiling. It struck Sarah then that Marina seemed uncharacteristically subdued, very unlike her usual effervescent self, and that Dan, too, was being very quiet.

"You know, that is one helluva mean road," Tank said as they were walking down the hill to the cabin. "Looks to me like, if we're goin' to start making regular runs up here, we might have to start usin' the chopper. What do you say, boss man?"

"It's a thought," Dan said laconically. He and Tank were walking together, a few steps behind Sarah and Marina. There was a brief pause, and then Sarah heard Dan ask, "Never been up here before?" His tone was casual enough, but even with her back to him Sarah could see that deadly glint in his eyes—the cat, lying in ambush.

"Nope," Tank said, blithely unaware of undercurrents. "That's because I didn't know what I was missin', a situation to be remedied as soon as possible!" His tone was so blatantly flattering, Sarah couldn't help but laugh. Tank always made her laugh.

She looked sideways at Marina, expecting her to be laughing, too, or smiling, at least. She wasn't, though the flush was back in her cheeks.

Why is it? Sarah asked herself, frowning at her feet as she made her way down the slippery path. Why is it, that the closer two people become, the more difficult it gets? Something was obviously going on between Marina and Tank, but around Tank, Marina was acting strangely awkward and silent. Just as Sarah was nervous and uncomfortable around Dan, with whom there was definitely something going on. On the other hand, Sarah had no trouble at all laughing and joking around with Tank, in whom she had no interest whatsoever, while Marina seemed perfectly at ease with Dan.

Crazy, Sarah thought, frustrated. It just seemed wrong, somehow. Backward.

The two men did allow themselves to be talked into a cup of coffee before starting the long drive back to AMINCO headquarters. Marina, saying she was eager to observe J.J.'s reunion with Luki, left them at the cabin steps and took off for the quarantine cages after volunteering to feed Sweetie while she was at it.

Tank and Dan waited on the veranda, talking in that monosyllabic undertone men seem to use to communicate with each other, while Sarah dressed.

"It's a lot cooler inside," she said with a smile as she rejoined them a few minutes later, wearing jeans and a cotton tank top over her usual layer of insect repellant. She handed Dan his shirt and shoes along with the bottle of repellent. "I thought...you might want..." She stopped, swallowed and felt her cheeks grow warm. Somehow the most ordinary of gestures had acquired a new intimacy. In a country where men worked without shirts as a matter of course, she could barely bring herself to look at Dan's naked chest.

"Thanks." Apparently unperturbed himself, Dan took the bottle from her, laid his clothes down on a chair and unscrewed the top. "Come on, Doc," he murmured, holding out the bottle, "give me a hand. Can't reach my back."

He was smiling his crooked smile, and this time the glitter Sarah saw in his eyes was benign—sunlight on water. She caught her lower lip in her teeth to hold back a tiny gasp of pleasure as he poured a warm pool of the oily liquid into first her palm, then his own.

Oh, Lord, she thought, how do I do this? With Tank standing there, watching, thinking God-knows-what. It has to show, what I'm thinking, what I'm feeling.

His skin was so smooth, so warm, the muscles of his back firm but not unyielding. She could feel the bunch and pull of them as he moved, spreading the pungent oil over his neck and shoulders, chest and belly. She could feel the strength and life in him, flowing into her fingers in electric pulses. She could feel her own blood coursing through her, pounding like storm surf inside her chest, pounding so hard it must surely show.

"Geez, I hate the smell of that stuff," Tank said, sounding disgusted.

Dan grunted. Sarah didn't say anything. At the moment, it smelled like Chanel No 5 to her.

"Can't decide which one I hate worse," Tank went on, "that stuff or the damn bugs. Heat, bugs, snakes and leeches—God, what a country! Where else are you gonna find flowers that smell like dead meat, huh?"

"Oh, I don't know," Sarah murmured, "I've never minded it." Her hands lay motionless now, fingers splayed across the sculpted planes of Dan's back. She'd finished with the repellent long ago, but hadn't wanted to stop the touching.

"Well, I gotta tell you, I don't know how you two ladies stand it, livin' like this, out here in this godforsaken jungle. At least at AMINCO we got air-conditioning and electricity and indoor plumbing!"

"I like it here," Sarah said, taking her hands away and wiping them on her jeans. "Now that I've gotten used to not having those things, I don't miss them. And it can be—" While she was talking, Dan slowly turned around so that she finished what she was saying while looking into his eyes—his unshielded eyes, so intense they stopped her breath and forced her to finish in a whisper, "—incredibly beautiful."

Tank was over by the window, arms folded, squinting out through the screen. He glanced up at Sarah and grinned. "Yeah? Well, you can have it, darlin'. As for me, I can't wait to get back to Texas."

The teakettle's whistle interrupted and crescendoed quickly to a shriek. "Why do you stay here if you hate it?" Sarah asked curiously as she went to take it off of the stove.

Tank shrugged as he straddled a chair. "Shoot, I'll tell you that in one word, honey—money. You get combat pay for servin' time in this hellhole, don't you know that? Just as soon as I got my stake, baby, I'm outa here. I'm not as lucky as ol' Dan here—he's already got his ticket home. Right, ol' buddy?''

Out of the corner of her eye Sarah saw Dan wince, as if Tank had said something that made him uncomfortable. She didn't know whether it was the "old buddy" business or the reference to going home that bothered him, and his frown and noncommittal mutter didn't do anything to enlighten her. But then he took out a pack of cigarettes, and she forgot all about everything else. As he offered one to Tank, then took one for himself and lit it, Sarah carefully measured coffee and hot water into tin mugs, trying not to stare, trying not to pretend she wasn't relieved that the cigarettes were a common brand and not the long, slender kind with a gold band around the filter.

Don't be ridiculous, she told herself. Neither one of these guys could possibly be a poacher. Unthinkable.

The men didn't linger over the coffee. Dan drank his standing up, in fact, putting on his shirt and shoes between swallows, while Turk smoked and engaged Sarah in the kind of lighthearted flirting he was so good at. As always, Sarah enjoyed the laughter, but she couldn't help wishing Tank would go down and keep Marina company at the quarantine cages. In a few minutes, it seemed, Dan was going to leave, without a chance for a private word to her. And there was so much left to say!

All she wanted was a moment, just one moment, to say—oh, she didn't know what she'd say. She didn't know what he'd say or do, but she needed something! Some assurance that what had happened between them was real, that the feelings she was feeling weren't leading her into a fool's paradise—again.

She wasn't going to get that moment. When the last dregs of coffee had been drunk and the last cigarette extinguished, they all walked together down to quarantine, where they found Marina sitting on the grass in front of the cages with Sweetie snuggled in the crook of her arm, J.J. on her lap and a jealous and unhappy Luki attempting to find a place there for himself.

When Luki spotted Dan he must have recognized a former storm harbor, because he immediately abandoned Marina and scrambled up Dan's legs and into his arms. Dan took a step backward and said, "Oof! Hey, what is this?" But he didn't look displeased.

"Cute little fella, ain't he?" Tank said, reaching out a hand to tickle Luki's stomach. Luki screeched at him, and he held up his hands, laughing. "Okay, sorry, little buddy! Didn't mean to get you in an uproar. Hey, isn't that old Beau?"

"It sure is," Sarah said, going over to scratch and pet the long hairy arm that was snaking out of one of the cages. "How are you, boy? Doing okay?"

"What's he doing in a cage? I thought you were supposed to be turning him loose."

"We are—ouch!" Sarah gently but firmly removed old Beau's fingers from her hair, then went on to explain to Tank about the quarantine procedures. "As soon as he's released from quarantine, we'll start taking both him and Sweetie with us into the jungle while we observe the wild orangs. We'll probably have to teach him how to climb, forage for food, make a bed—everything. The baby will have to stay close to us until she's older, but old Beau will probably learn to live outside right from the start."

"Won't he run off?"

Sarah smiled. "If he does, he'll come back when he gets hungry."

"So how do you wean 'em, so to speak?"

"Most of them wean themselves." Sarah glanced at Marina, wondering why she wasn't enthusiastically chiming in as she usually did. But Marina was still being uncharacteristically quiet, so Sarah laughed and continued, "We make sure to give them things to eat that they don't really like, sort of like giving you a steady diet of liver and brussels sprouts. You'd start looking for greener pastures, too!''

"Yeah.'' Tank chuckled. ''I reckon I would at that. So what happens? One day they just up and leave?''

"Some do. But most of the time, when we feel certain they're ready, we take them to some remote part of the reserve and turn them loose. Most of the time, we never see them again.'' She paused. ''Sukey was the exception.''

"Sukey?''

"The one the poachers murdered,'' Marina said abruptly, getting to her feet. Tank jumped to her assistance, then for some reason thought better of it. Marina returned the two young orangutans to their cage and turned, brushing at the soaked seat of her pants. Her eyes were bright and desperate. ''I'm sorry, I—I think I must go and change my clothes. I'm all wet. Please excuse me. Thank you. Thank you both very much for all you have done to help. I'm sorry. I must go—'' After blind and hurried handshakes, she fled.

Tank watched her go, concern making attractive creases at the corners of his eyes. ''Damn—you know, that sure is a shame. I didn't mean to get her upset. Think maybe I oughta go and—''

"Let her be,'' Dan said sharply.

"Well,'' Sarah said, glancing at Dan, ''she's been under a lot of stress the last few days. We all have.''

"Uh-huh. Well, she's sure got my sympathy.'' Tank shook his head and made a sympathetic noise with his tongue. ''She's a sweet lady. You tell her I said so, now, you hear?'' He gave her his warmest smile and engulfed her hand in both of his. ''So long, Doc, you take care.''

There was a moment, then, one of those awkward little gavottes where no one seems to know quite what to say or which direction to step—Tank about to leave and looking questions at Dan; Dan ignoring him, turning instead to put

```
************************************************************
*  You may have already won a lifetime of cash payments *
*  totaling up to $1,000,000.00!  Play our Sweepstakes  *
*  Game--Here's how it works...                          *
************************************************************
```

Each of the first three tickets has a unique Sweepstakes number.
If your Sweepstakes numbers match any of the winning numbers
selected by our computer, you could win the amount shown under
the gold rub-off on that ticket.

Using an eraser, rub off the gold boxes on tickets #1-3 to
reveal how much each ticket could be worth if it is a winning
ticket. You must return the <u>entire</u> card to be eligible. (See
official rules in the back of this book for details.)

At the same time you play your tickets for big cash prizes,
Silhouette also invites you to participate in a special trial of
our Reader Service by accepting one or more FREE book(s) from
Silhouette Intimate Moments.® To request your free book(s), just
rub off the gold box on ticket #4 to reveal how many free
book(s) you will receive.

When you receive your free book(s), we hope you'll enjoy them
and want to see more. So unless we hear from you, every month
we'll send you 4 additional Silhouette Intimate Moments®novels.
Each book is yours to keep for only $2.74* each--21¢ less per
book than the cover price! There are <u>no</u> additional charges for
shipping and handling and of course, you may cancel Reader
Service privileges at any time by marking "cancel" on your
shipping statement or returning an unopened shipment of books to
us at our expense. Either way your shipments will stop. You'll
receive no more books; you'll have no further obligation.

PLUS-you get a FREE MYSTERY GIFT!

If you return your game card with <u>**all four gold boxes**</u> rubbed
off, you will also receive a FREE Mystery Gift. It's your
<u>**immediate reward**</u> for sampling your free book(s), <u>**and**</u> it's yours
to keep no matter what you decide.

P.S.

Remember, the first set of one or more book(s) is FREE. So rub
off the gold box on ticket #4 and return the entire sheet of
tickets today!

*Terms and prices subject to change without notice.
Sales taxes applicable in New York and Iowa.

"GIVE YOUR HEART TO SILHOUETTE" SWEEPSTAKES

DETACH HERE AND RETURN ENTIRE SHEET OF TICKETS NOW!

#1 **$1,000,000.00**
Rub off to reveal potential value if this is a winning ticket: ▶
$35,000

UNIQUE SWEEPSTAKES NUMBER: 6C 860341

#2 **$1,000,000.00**
Rub off to reveal potential value if this is a winning ticket: ▶
$10,000

UNIQUE SWEEPSTAKES NUMBER: 7C 862326

#3 **$1,000,000.00**
Rub off to reveal potential value if this is a winning ticket: ▶
$1,000,000

UNIQUE SWEEPSTAKES NUMBER: 8C 859992

#4 **ONE OR MORE FREE BOOKS**
HOW MANY FREE BOOKS?
Rub off to reveal number of free books you will receive ▶
4

1672765559

Yes! Enter my sweepstakes numbers in the Sweepstakes and let me know if I've won a cash prize. If gold box on ticket #4 is rubbed off, I will also receive one or more Silhouette Intimate Moments® novels as a FREE tryout of the Reader Service, along with a FREE Mystery Gift as explained on the opposite page.   240 CIS YAEH

NAME

ADDRESS   APT.

CITY   STATE   ZIP CODE

Offer not valid to current Silhouette Intimate Moments® subscribers. All orders subject to approval.   PRINTED IN U.S.A.

DON'T FORGET...

... Return this card today with ticket #4 rubbed off, and receive 4 free books and a free mystery gift.

... You will receive books well before they're available in stores and at a discount off cover prices.

... No obligation to buy. You can cancel at any time by writing "cancel" on your statement or returning an unopened shipment to us at our cost.

BUSINESS REPLY CARD

First Class   Permit No. 717   Buffalo, NY

Postage will be paid by addressee

Silhouette Reader Service ™

MILLION DOLLAR SWEEPSTAKES

901 Fuhrmann Blvd.
P.O. Box 1867
Buffalo, N.Y. 14240-9952

NO POSTAGE
NECESSARY
IF MAILED
IN THE
UNITED STATES

Luki back in his cage; Sarah, dangling uncertainly between them, and Marina heading for the house in tears. It might have been funny, if it hadn't been for the undercurrents.

Some communication must have passed between Tank and Dan, because Tank suddenly waved, said, "Okay, then, see you," and took off down the river path. Dan caught Sarah's arm and grated "Stay," as if he thought she'd been planning on following.

He waited in tense silence until the bamboo had swallowed up Tank, then pulled her roughly around to face him. His eyes blazed at her. There was so much emotion in them, so much passion! Dazed, she thought, my God, no wonder he keeps them shielded.

"This isn't finished between us—you know that, don't you?" Without breath or voice, Sarah could only nod. She couldn't tear her eyes from his face. Dark, exotic, his eyes touched her like flames. "We have a lot more talking to do." His head descended, blocking out the light. Her stomach lurched and flip-flopped, driving a sharp gasp from her lungs. His mouth cut off its escape, trapping it in her throat so that it became a moan instead.

"And a lot more of that, too. You can bet on it," he said thickly, and left her there, trembling.

"I wish we had a goat," Marina said crossly when Sarah walked in. She was mixing powdered milk in a bucket, a job she hated.

"Where would we keep it?" Sarah responded absently; they'd had this discussion before, many times. "It would just get eaten by a panther or a python, and then you'd be heartbroken."

"I know. I'm sorry." She sighed. "I didn't mean to get upset...about Sukey. I was just sitting there, you know, holding Sweetie, and I was thinking about Sukey's baby, wondering if he is still alive."

"It's okay," Sarah mumbled, sitting down at the table.

Marina stopped stirring to look at her. "Is something wrong? You sound funny."

"Nothing's wrong." Then she amended, with a shaken laugh, "I feel funny."

"Is it Dan?" Sarah nodded. Marina cried, "Ha!" then added more sedately, "That's good, I like Dan very much. So why do you look so—" she paused, searching for the right word, and finally settled on "—frightened?"

"I'm not frightened," Sarah said, "just surprised. I never expected this to happen to me—" she described a vague circle in the air with her hand "—way out here. I wasn't prepared, do you know what I mean?"

A dimple appeared in one of Marina's freckled cheeks. "Oh yes," she said softly, "I know exactly what you mean."

"It almost seems like a miracle."

"Yes. I think it always does." Her brown eyes were glowing. Sarah decided she'd been right about Tank and Marina after all.

She was dying to ask about it, but before she could, Salim came in to say that he'd brought back supplies and mail from Medan, and since Joka wasn't back from upriver yet, to ask if one of them could help bring things up from the Land Rover. Since Marina was already up to her elbows in powdered milk, Sarah said she'd go.

Following Salim through the bamboo, she thought about Dan, and about miracles.

Marina liked Dan, which was good. But not too much, which was even better, though she couldn't really understand how anyone could prefer Tank to Dan. Tank was charming, but shallow. Still, she had to admit that Tank and Marina seemed suited to each other—both of them always full of laughter and fun. And they would look good together, too, both with freckles, both so tall.

Sarah wasn't sure how she and Dan fit together. He was so dark, she so fair. Night and day. And he was so guarded, while she had always gone through life making a fool of herself, wearing her heart on her sleeve.

Marina was right—she was frightened. And why shouldn't she be? The last time she'd opened her heart to a man, she'd fallen head over heels—literally—and wound up in traction! She could almost—almost—laugh about it now, but making a complete ass of oneself for love was never funny, and she didn't want it to happen again. Ever. This time, she'd be more careful. She'd be sure to look before she leaped—or fell—into love.

That's what she told herself, but of course, it was already too late.

The Land Rover sat sweltering in the sun, with little blue butterflies dipping and fluttering through the heatwaves rising from its mud-spattered hood. While Salim worked in the back, loading the bulkier items onto a handcart, Sarah struggled into a bulging backpack and gathered up the accumulation of mail that had fallen across the seat and onto the floorboards. Feeling under the seat to make sure she hadn't missed anything, her fingers touched something rectangular—not a letter, something smaller, thicker, something that gave slightly with a faint crackling sound. With pounding heart she drew the object from its hiding place.

It was a pack of cigarettes.

Cold settled over her, and along with it, a curious detachment. With hands that didn't seem to belong to her, she tapped one slender cigarette out of the pack and touched the thin gold band around its filter.

Chapter 8

Y ou are having a problem?''

Salim!

Shoving the cigarettes into the middle of the stack of mail, Sarah backed out of the Land Rover and set her teeth in what she desperately hoped might be taken for a smile. "No problem, just a letter from home. I can't wait to get home to read it."

Salim. Why not? Sarah thought, valiantly clutching at the straw. The cigarettes could be his. Neither of the rangers smoked, but he might have seen them in Medan and bought them to compare with the one found with Sukey's body. The cigarettes missing from the pack could have been left as evidence. It even sounded plausible, so why wasn't she asking Salim if they were his? Why hadn't she shown him what she'd found?

Because she knew. She remembered. She remembered dark hands gripping a steering wheel, cupped around a cigarette, tossing the pack onto the dashboard. She remembered the sudden lurch that had thrown her against the door of the Land Rover, the wild jouncing, the swish of something sliding across the dash, the faint plop as it hit the floor. And finally the thing that had driven it all from her mind, Dan's arm, like a band of living steel across her chest, and beneath it her heart, careening as wildly out of control as the car.

That was why she didn't ask the ranger if the pack was his. As for why she was hiding the cigarettes from him, she didn't want to think about that. She couldn't think about that. If she did, the pain inside her would break the bonds of her self-control. She had to control herself until she had a chance to sort it all out. There was an explanation for it. There had to be.

When she got back to the cabin, Marina had already gone up to the feeding station. Sarah methodically unpacked supplies and divided the mail into three neat piles on the table: one for her, one for Marina and one for Foundation business. Then she put the cigarettes under her pillow and went to join Marina, feeling hollow and fragile, like a blown-out eggshell.

Just before sundown, Joka came back from his excursion upriver to report that it had been a wild-goose chase. He had found signs of a camp, but if the poachers had ever been there, they were miles away by the time he had arrived on the scene.

Sarah, when she heard that, slopped the hot coffee she was serving to him onto her hand.

Miles away, she thought, glancing guiltily across the cabin to where two narrow cots stood side by side, barely inches apart. In the bed next to hers!

The cigarettes seemed to be burning a hole through her pillow.

Late that night as she lay awake listening to the chorus of frogs and insects outside and the soft breathing sounds from

Marina's cot, she felt the pack like a hot brand against her head.

"Of course, it is all right that Dan slept in my bed," Marina had said when Sarah told her about it, looking surprised that there should be any questions. "I'm glad he could be comfortable."

But how would she feel, Sarah wondered bleakly, staring into shadows, if she knew that the dark charmer who made himself comfortable in her sheets was also the cold-blooded killer who murdered Sukey and kidnapped and sold her baby?

No! Her mind recoiled, rejecting the terrible thought even as it formed. No. There had to be another explanation. Just because Dan had once smoked the same brand of cigarettes, that didn't make him the poacher. Just because the poacher smoked an American cigarette, that didn't make him an American. Just because American cigarettes were available at AMINCO, that didn't mean the poacher had to come from there. Even if he did, he didn't have to be Dan, or even an American. A lot of people worked for the oil company, people of many different nationalities. Even Indonesian.

Not Dan, she thought, as she had so many times before. There is no evil in Dan. If there were, I'd know.

But would she? She didn't really know Dan; hadn't she just told him so? Both he and Marina had accused her of being afraid. Could it be that she was right to be afraid and that her fear was only her instinct, trying to warn her?

The dregs of night are a terrible time for thinking. Simple problems look like monsters, and grim ones like your worst nightmare. On this night, every newspaper account Sarah had ever read about serial killers—stranglers, knifers, rapists—came slinking out of the shadow to parade before her in hideous detail. The killers' faces were chillingly ordinary, sometimes even handsome, and the comments of the neighbors were always the same, "I just can't believe it—he always seemed so nice! A quiet man—kept to himself a lot." And there was always a woman—even a wife—who had loved him, shared his bed, felt his hands on her body and never dreamed... A woman whose heart had cried *No!* in disbelief and denial, until she was faced with the inescapable truth. Incontrovertible proof.

Once again in that quiet time before dawn, Sarah's tired mind searched for answers. And this time she knew what she had to find. Proof. The cigarettes were only evidence. Somehow she had to get proof, something that would convince her of the truth, one way or the other. She didn't know exactly how to go about that, but she knew where to start. The first thing she had to do was get to know Dan—very well.

Suddenly, there in the thinning darkness, Sarah felt it all again—Dan's hands gripping her arms, his head coming down, his mouth, hard and hot, trapping a cry of pure animal need deep in her throat, her stomach's giddy somersault, her blood boiling, heart pounding, skin shivering with cold fire....

I don't care! she cried, hugging herself in silent anguish. It doesn't matter, she vowed, while tears trickled through her hair and into her pillow. If Dan Cisco was the poacher, she was going to see that he got every bit of the justice he deserved.

"What do you think of Dan?" Sarah asked Marina the next morning as they sat in a leafy glade, watching the activities of a wild female orangutan named Rina and her half-grown son Bob.

Sarah was pleased with herself. She thought it seemed like a natural enough question—Marina already knew she was interested in Dan—and she felt she'd produced it rather well. She'd picked a quiet, lazy time, the kind of time when such things are apt to come up between friends anyway, and she'd injected into it just the right amount of not-so-idle curiosity.

"Hmm?" Marina said, pretending to be distracted and betraying herself with a dimple. "You know what I think of Dan. I like him very much." She dropped her binoculars into her lap and picked up a camera. "You were right—she is definitely weaning him. That explains why Bad John has been making so much noise lately."

Sarah made a dutiful notation in her notebook and then asked without looking up, "Has he said anything at all?"

"Oh, well, I think it's perfectly clear what he's saying, don't you?" Marina said with an irrepressible giggle. "He's telling Rina he wants—"

"Stop that!" Sarah gave the Dutch girl a shove with her foot and threw a scandalized glance over her shoulder, but Salim had apparently checked out the territory and then left them to their research. "You know very well who I'm talking about—Dan. Has he told you anything . . . well, about himself?"

"Like what?"

"Oh, you know. Like for instance, he isn't married, is he?"

Marina looked faintly surprised. "Oh. Well, he didn't tell me *that*."

The inflection wasn't lost on Sarah. She leaned forward eagerly, her notebook forgotten. "He did tell you something! Come on, Mari, please tell me. I'd feel so much better if I just knew a little more about him." That, at least, was not a lie. "He told me he's an only child and that he grew up in New England, of all places. And yet, there's his name and his accent, and, of course, he looks—"

"He's half-Mexican," Marina said, a trifle smugly. "He was born there. He told me his father was a professor at the university in Mexico City and his mother was from a wealthy New England family. They met one summer, at an archaeological dig, and while they were uncovering ancient ruins in the jungle, they fell in love." Marina sighed. "It was very romantic. And very sad."

"Sad? Why?"

"Because it didn't work out. They were very unhappy together."

Sarah drew up her knees and wrapped her arms around them. Her heart was suddenly beating very rapidly. "Really? What happened?"

"Dan told me that when he was five, his parents separated. His mother took him back to New England with her. He hated it."

"Yes," Sarah murmured, remembering, "he told me he hated kindergarten. I wondered why."

"Do you blame him?" Marina bristled. "Poor little boy—he was used to a lot of children, bright colors, sunshine, laughter, playing barefooted in the sand, and suddenly he was in a strange town, in a big, dark house, very cold, very lonely. Can you imagine how it was for him? The children probably laughed at him because he had an accent and stared at him because he looked different. He didn't tell me that, because I think he is very proud, but I can just imagine it."

Oh, God, Sarah thought, looking away to hide the fact that her eyes were filling with tears. So could she. Did he learn it so young, then, how to shield his emotions, how to hide his vulnerability behind a mask of Aztec arrogance and pride?

She swallowed, and in a blurred voice asked, "What then?"

Marina shrugged. "I'm not sure. Eventually Dan went back to Mexico to live with his father, I think, but that didn't work out, either. Oh, my goodness—listen to that!" They both listened in awe to the series of grunts, grumbles and bellows that make up the long mating call of a male orangutan.

"Bad John," Sarah said. "In fine voice, too. It sounds— good grief!" The last howl had barely died before a new call rose in answer to it, from the opposite direction.

"Johnny has a rival!" Marina sang, eagerly gathering up camera and binoculars and loping off through the undergrowth in the direction of the new sound.

Since Rina and Bob had prudently disappeared, Sarah tucked her pencil and notebook into her shirt pocket and followed.

Marina is biased, she told herself doggedly as she ran, throwing up her arms to ward off trailing vines and lashing branches. Because it had occurred to her that the kind of childhood her soft-hearted friend had just described could easily produce a warped streak in a sensitive child.

Still, no matter how hard she tried to block it out, she kept seeing a small, dark boy, stiff-necked and proud, stoically holding back tears. Dammit, this wasn't going the way she'd expected. The last thing she needed was to feel sympathy and compassion for the man she suspected of being a poacher!

A few days later Joka came up to the feeding platform carrying a tranquilizer gun in the crook of his arm. He spoke in Indonesian to Marina, who explained to Sarah that he needed to get the tranquilizer drugs from the propane refrigerator in the cabin.

"They just got a call from AMINCO," she went on, a spark of excitement in her eyes. "There is a big male orangutan in an area they are trying to clear. He wouldn't go away, so they've isolated him in one tree, and now they want us to go and get him."

"Sounds like fun," Sarah said. "You go—you're much better at that than I am. Besides, you speak the language better, and it's probably an Indonesian crew."

"Dan might be there," Marina pointed out, dimpling.

Sarah's heart gave a clumsy hop. She had a flash of memory, of Dan as she'd seen him for the first time, leaping and sliding down a hillside to stand like a warrior prince in the road. "So might Tank," she said, with an effort to appear uninterested.

Marina's dimple disappeared. "You go," she said firmly, "it's your turn."

"I went to the river with Salim."

"That doesn't count. Don't be silly, you know you want to go!"

She should, of course. Marina would think it odd if she didn't. So Sarah forced a laugh and gave in. "Okay, okay, I'll go. Are you sure you'll be all right here alone?"

"Of course, I'm sure. Salim will be here. You go and capture the big fellow—just don't bring him back here to give Bad John more competition. Oh, and say hello to Dan for me!"

Say hello to Dan. And after that, what? Sarah had never been good at hiding her feelings, but she couldn't let Dan know of her suspicions. If he was innocent, he'd probably never forgive her for thinking such terrible things of him. And if he was guilty...

As she was helping Joka assemble the things they'd be needing—crate, nets, tranquilizer gun and tree-climbing equipment—she kept vacillating, sure one minute that Dan would be there, positive the next that he wouldn't. She didn't know which she hoped for more, not until the helicopter landed in a swirl of leaves, grass and butterflies, and the pilot got out and it wasn't Dan. She knew then that, in spite of everything, she'd been longing to see him with a visceral anticipation that was totally beyond her control.

Sort of like having a virus; once you'd contracted it, you couldn't help the way it made you feel.

She didn't see Dan at the drilling site, either. So be it, Sarah thought. It was just as well. She was glad not to have to face him in front of so many people.

Swallowing her disappointment, she set to work immediately, positioning the catch-nets around the base of the tree while Joka prepared to climb it. The plan was for Joka to get above the orangutan and force him to use his only avenue of escape—down the tree trunk to the ground. The orangutan, meanwhile, was expressing his fear and displeasure at all this suspicious activity by raining branches down on them from a hundred feet above their heads.

Everything was ready. Except for the few who would be helping to man the nets, the men from the drilling crew were standing back out of the way, their necks craned, eyes fixed on the swaying topmost branches of the magnificent old hardwood, like children watching a high-wire act at a circus.

There—Joka was finally in position and the big orangutan was moving slowly toward the ground. Sarah watched him as, with ponderous dignity, he reluctantly abandoned his doomed refuge. Her throat tightened. "Hold on. Wait," she murmured to herself, holding up her hand, ready to signal the men with the nets. Patience was essential. A moment too soon and the big fellow would scoot back up the tree; a moment too late and they could lose him.

Suddenly, Dan was there. Her eyes found his as if homing in on a beacon. He was standing alone at the edge of the clearing, smoking a cigarette, watching the drama in the tree. It gave her a terrible jolt to see him there. She didn't know what she'd expected—did she think that since she'd last seen him he'd have grown horns and cloven hooves?—but he looked . . . beautiful.

Steady. Stay cool. The orangutan was on the ground. Just a moment more, let him turn around, now! She brought her hand down; the nets flew. And a few short, busy minutes later, the great red primate lay dazed and blinking among the tree roots, looking like a happy, rotund drunk.

Sarah was kneeling beside him, stroking the russet hair on one massive shoulder and struggling to hold back tears, when she felt someone come to stand behind her. She knew who it was before he spoke.

"Nice job."

She looked up at Dan and nodded, keeping her lips pressed tightly together, knowing that if she spoke one word she would surely cry.

He squatted down and balanced there on his heels, reached out to touch the huge orangutan's coat. Just for a moment his hand lay beside Sarah's—two hands, one big and dark, one small and pale against the vivid orange—and then he withdrew it and laced the fingers of his hands together. He stared down at them, then looked at Sarah, opened his mouth and closed it again. Emotions flitted across his face like figures in a lighted window, not lingering there quite long enough to be identifiable. She saw his throat move as if he'd swallowed something painful, and then he shook his head and looked away.

"We'll find him a good place," he drawled softly, and Sarah knew then that he understood and that some communications don't need any words.

She nodded, and after a moment Dan stood up. Joka and some of the oil men came with the crate, and the next time Sarah looked around, Dan had gone. She saw him a little later, talking to the helicopter pilot, but she was busy supervising the loading of the two-hundred-pound animal into the crate and seeing that the crate was properly secured inside the helicopter. By the time she had a free moment, Dan had disappeared again.

Why not? Sarah thought dismally. Dan was a busy man. The fun was over; he had work to do.

Since there wasn't room in the helicopter for a third passenger, it was decided that Sarah should go with the orangutan to the release point, while Joka and all the equipment hitched a ride back to AMINCO headquarters with the oil crew. As Sarah sat in the helicopter waiting for the pilot, she heard the racket of chain saws begin again in the distance. Already hard at work cutting down the orangutan's last tree, she thought, feeling again that inexpressible sadness. There were so few of them left.

She felt the chopper give with the pilot's weight and turned away quickly to wipe her face on her sleeve, disposing of a few tears along with sweat.

"All set?" the pilot asked briskly as he swung into his seat.

"Yes, I guess—" The air left Sarah's lungs in a rush and she whipped around as if she'd been stung. "Dan! I thought—where's the pilot? What are you doing?"

What he was doing, while her heart was catapulting out of control, was methodically checking dials and flipping switches, turning on the chopper's engine. When it was performing the way he wanted it, he turned, grinning, to shout at her above the racket, "Where to, Doc?"

Inexplicably, she felt herself smiling back at him, felt herself fill up with warmth and light and happiness. As the helicopter rose into the sky, she almost believed that it wasn't the rotors that lifted her but her own effervescence, carrying her away like a hot-air balloon, away from her depression and sadness.

It's Dan, she thought with a new sense of wonder. Just being with him made the world beautiful and right.

The jungle fell away below them, becoming a nubby green blanket carelessly tossed down on a cluttered floor. Mountain peaks rose into clouds and canyons dropped into shadows. Rivers curled and looped through the green in ribbons of blue and gold, reflecting the colors of a late-afternoon sky.

"There," Sarah said presently, pointing to the river that marked the southern-most boundary of the reserve. Dan nodded and altered direction slightly, taking them toward the northwest. They hadn't talked much—there was too much noise for conversation—just pointing out things of interest to each other from time to time: a glimpse of a waterfall cascading between two peaks, a breathtaking gorge, a native village, their own shadow flitting over the treetops like a playful dragonfly.

"It's so beautiful," Sarah said, shouting over the noise. "I never realized."

Dan glanced at her. "You've never seen any of this?"

She shook her head. "No—I told you, I don't get away from the reserve very often, unless it's to town for supplies or to pick up a captive orang."

His eyes were hidden from her behind a pair of sunglasses, but she saw his mouth tighten and then slip into a wry smile. "I used to know someone like you," he said cryptically. Sarah subsided, feeling vaguely hurt, and didn't ask him what he meant.

Dan landed the helicopter in what had once been a dry rice field before the land had been taken up by the reserve. Now it was overgrown with tall grass and fern, one of the few open places within a thousand or so square miles of mountainous jungle. Somehow, between the two of them they managed to wrestle the heavy crate out of the chopper, but after carrying it a few yards, agreed that its two-hundred-pound occupant could make it to the trees on his own.

Although orangutans are rarely aggressive, Sarah knew that the big males can be unpredictable, so she administered the tranquilizer's antidote with Dan standing by, holding the lid to the crate in case it should be needed as a shield or a weapon. Just to be on the safe side, they observed subsequent developments from the chopper.

Little by little, like a drunk emerging into the sunlight with a terrific hangover, the orangutan crept from the box, an arm first, and then the magnificent head with its imposing cheekpads and throat pouch, and finally, the squat, barrel-shaped body covered with long rust-colored hair. "Oh, my achin' head," Dan drawled in an undertone, and Sarah glanced quickly at him and laughed, partly in pleased surprise that they'd shared the same thought.

When the orangutan had moved a few yards away from the crate he turned to look back at the chopper, the great cheekpads swiveling slowly, the close-set black eyes fixing them with a piercing stare. There was so much intelligence in those eyes, Sarah thought. Did he know they meant him well? It seemed an eternity before he finally turned and ambled away into the tall grass.

"Oh, boy!" Sarah let out a breath she'd been holding in a gust of relieved laughter.

"Yeah, he's really something," Dan muttered. All at once he seemed tense, edgy. Then, with a glance at the sky, he added, "Come on, let's get that crate loaded and get out of here. It's getting late."

He wants to be done with this—with me, Sarah thought dismally as she shouldered her end of the carry pole. Apparently he'd changed his mind about wanting to spend time with her, getting to know her, talking and other things....

They were strapped into their seats, getting ready to take off, when Sarah suddenly blurted, "Are you married?"

The out-of-the-blue question took Dan by surprise. He paused with his finger on the starter switch and looked sideways at her. "Now, what in the world makes you ask that?"

Her gaze held steady, though he thought she might have colored a little. "You said I reminded you of someone you once knew. I was wondering who it might be, and then one thought led to another."

He threw back his head and gave a bark of laughter. "Lord, no, I'm not married. I was once—not for long—but you're nothing like my wife." He settled back in his seat, took a deep breath and put his hands on his knees. "If you want me to, I'll tell you about Annie. What do you want to know?"

"You don't—well, anything, I guess." She shrugged, cleared her throat. "Anything you want to tell me."

"There's not a lot to tell," Dan said, a little surprised to realize it himself. "It was a long time ago, and like I said, we weren't married very long. Just shy of two years." It didn't even seem real to him anymore, he realized, like something he'd read about that had happened to a stranger. "She was a nice lady. Pretty." He glanced at Sarah with a little half smile. "She was dark and feisty. I told you—nothing like you."

"What happened?" He saw her throat ripple with a forced swallow.

He thought about it for a moment, then said carefully, "I couldn't give her what she needed. I guess I didn't know how, back then." Sarah didn't say anything for a minute or two. It occurred to Dan that she hadn't asked him if he'd loved Annie. He wondered if that was because it didn't matter or because it mattered too much.

The fact was, he had loved Annie; he'd just never found a way to let her know.

"But you said I reminded you of someone," she said after a while, looking out the window. "If it wasn't your wife, then who was it?"

"Just someone," he said flatly, because he didn't feel like telling her about his mother just then. It wasn't the right time. "Someone I used to know." He flipped on the starter switch. "I'll tell you about her, too, sometime, but right now—" he raised his voice as the chopper's racket escalated "—we have someplace to go!"

They lifted off in a stomach-dropping lurch. Sarah gasped and clutched the edges of her seat, but Dan laughed out loud as he banked into the sun. He felt a strange wildness rising in him, something young and fierce and free. *Like my ancient forefathers,* he thought, laughing at himself again. *Brothers to the eagle and the wind.*

Sarah asked him where they were going. Dan pretended he hadn't heard her, so after a moment she touched his arm and pointed. "Why are we going west? The rehab station is—"

"Yeah, I know." He flashed her a grin. "I guess you could say I'm kidnapping you."

From the look on her face, he wondered if she thought he really meant it. That silent gaze made him uncomfortable, so he took her chin in his hand and turned her face toward the front of the chopper.

"I want to show you something," he shouted, pointing through the windshield. "Look." He was rewarded with a soundless gasp and then an enraptured, "Oh...."

Up ahead, the waters of Lake Toba were just coming into view, lit by the evening sun, and for a moment or two it seemed as if the whole horizon was on fire.

"Ever been here before?" Dan asked as the chopper skimmed across the water.

Sarah shook her head, but didn't take her eyes from the window. He didn't blame her. Below them the lake was a sheet of burnished copper, etched by the crisscrossing wakes of hydrofoils and fishing boats and the rippling fan left by the ferry making its ponderous way from Samosir Island back to the mainland.

He was remembering the first time he'd ever seen this land. It had the kind of beauty that made you hurt inside, that feeling of being so full of wonder you thought you'd have to burst with it. He wasn't sure what he'd hoped to accomplish, bringing Sarah here like this. He only knew he'd wanted to share it with her. Or more accurately, he wanted to know whether she could share it with him. He thought that maybe, if she felt it, too, there was a chance it could work between them in spite of every bit of common sense that told him it couldn't.

He glanced at her, but her flawless profile told him nothing. When he looked away again her image stayed burned in his mind, backlit by the setting sun so that she seemed to have gilded edges.

Sarah didn't say anything when Dan bypassed the mainland resorts, with their picture-postcard palm trees, red tile roofs and rampant bougainvillea, and instead set the helicopter down in a remote part of the island, on a dirt road between rice paddies. She couldn't understand why he was doing any of this or what he wanted from her. There was so much tension in him, an air of expectancy, as if he'd asked a question and was waiting for her answer.

But she didn't know what to say! She was too overwhelmed by the beauty of it all, by the wonder and the joy. She felt confused; so many emotions were tumbling around inside her! Here she was, alone with a man who might be a poacher, a man who had virtually kidnapped her, and all she felt was...*happy*. It didn't make sense. She didn't know where he was taking her or for what purpose, and she felt not the slightest twinge of unease. Just a kind of breathless anticipation.

"Come on," Dan said. "I want you to meet some friends of mine."

He was standing on the ground, holding up his hands to help her out of the helicopter. For some reason it made

Sarah think of that strange moment on the feeding platform, when he'd surprised and unnerved her by holding out
his hand for her to help him up—he had the same wry but
implacable smile on his face. He hadn't needed help then
and she didn't need it now, so what was it that made him do
such a thing? Whimsy? Or was he demonstrating his power
over her, showing her in that small way that he could bend
her to his will, even against the dictates of her own common sense?

Because that was how he made her feel—powerless. When
he looked at her that way, when he touched her... She felt
his hands on her waist, and her stomach turned over. Weak.
Her legs buckled. She clutched at his shoulders for support
and, as he swung her to the ground, just for a moment saw
herself reflected in his sunglasses—tiny twin images, both
strange to her. Vulnerable.

She wanted to ask him for reassurances and explana-
tions, but he laughed and swept her out from under the helicopter's dying rotors. She made up her mind that she was
going to be cool and take whatever came in stride, but when
she saw the group of people hurrying down the road toward them, her heart stumbled and she clutched at Dan's
arm. They don't eat people anymore, he'd said, mocking
her. Right now she wanted to ask him in all seriousness,
"Are you sure?"

They wore sarongs and stoles, many of them of bright
colors, with golden threads woven through, and several
different types of headdresses of the same heavy cloth. The
three elderly men leading the crowd carried long, intri-
cately carved wooden staffs. To Sarah they looked exotic,
magnificent and very fierce.

"It's all right," Dan said, grinning at her. Catching her
hand in a gesture of almost childlike eagerness, he pulled her
with him as he went to meet the welcoming committee.

A few yards away from the couple the three elders halted. Behind them, the rest of the crowd did the same—men, old women with blackened teeth, young women with babies on their hips, children with bright, curious eyes. Dan released Sarah's hand and went forward, holding out his arms and speaking in a dialect she didn't recognize.

The three elders solemnly shook hands and broke into big smiles. The people surged forward then, in the quiet, reserved way of Indonesians, laughing softly, reaching to shake Dan's hand or just to touch him. When he turned to look for Sarah and gestured for her to join him, the crowd suddenly grew quiet and then parted, making way for her.

As she faced the three old men, Sarah felt as wobbly kneed as a bride meeting her new in-laws for the first time. Beside her, Dan gave her hand an encouraging squeeze, but she sensed the same kind of nervousness in him and knew that whoever these people were, they were important to him.

With dry mouth and pounding heart, Sarah respectfully bowed her head and murmured, "*Selamat malam*"—good evening.

There was a suspense-filled moment, and then the elders again broke into broad smiles and nodded at one another. A little chuckle of approval rippled through the crowd.

One of the elders stepped forward and said in accented English, "Welcome to our *huta*, Dr. Sarah. Daniel's friend is our friend. You will honor us if you will sleep in our house tonight. Come, we will prepare the rice table for you!"

Chapter 9

Sleep in his house?" Sarah said in a hoarse whisper as they were being escorted through rice paddies to the *huta*, the clan village.

Dan shrugged, a certain gleam in his eyes belying the innocent look on his face. "He'll have hurt feelings if we don't."

A fog of unreality was creeping over her. She shook her head, trying to dispel it. "But we can't stay here—I have to get back. Marina will be—"

"Don't worry about Marina," Dan said placidly. "I told Joka to tell her not to expect you back for a day or two."

Sarah caught her breath. Something ephemeral and wondrous blew through her, like a soft, sweet springtime wind. With laughter trembling inside her, she whispered, "You planned this? I don't believe it—you really are kidnapping me!"

"I guess I am." His smile was serene, his eyes as clear and blue as a summer sky. Both were irresistible and so different from the impenetrable mask she was accustomed to that Sarah let the laughter inside her come tumbling forth in a breathless gust of sheer astonishment.

As they came near the village the crowd around them grew, in both size and enthusiasm. Women came from the rice fields with huge baskets on their heads, children frisked and darted underfoot, old people waved at them from the steps of towering, saddle-roofed houses. One toothless old lady sitting on a high porch, braiding sisal into rope, picked up a shiny aluminum crutch and waved it as they passed, like a palm branch, Sarah thought.

"Who are these people?" she whispered in awe. "Why do you know them?" Why did they welcome him here like a hero, or a god?

Dan muttered something about a couple of his men being from this village. "I told you they were Bataks, remember?" But he seemed uncomfortable, even embarrassed, and immediately dismissed the subject by turning himself into a tour guide. And Sarah was so fascinated by the wonders he was showing her, she forgot the question.

The village was situated on a little headland, surrounded by coconut palms and banana trees. The great wooden houses with their high pilings and swaybacked roofs looked like a fleet of ships drawn up in drydock beside the waters of the lake. On one side, rice paddies and vegetable gardens ran right down to the water's edge, on the other, mountains rose into purple mist. The breeze from the lake and the mountains was cool and fresh and smelled of moist earth and growing things.

It seemed to Sarah as if nothing much had changed here in thousands of years. It was incredible to realize that these friendly, exuberant people were the direct descendants of cannibals! Here and there, however, were signs of the twentieth century: the old woman and her crutch; a young man with a boar's tusk bracelet on his arm snapping pictures with an Instamatic camera; indignant cackles and squawks coming from chickens roosting inside the rusting body of a Ford truck; stainless-steel pots on stone tables as old as time.

It was a clan village, Dan told Sarah, one of several in that general area belonging to the same clan. He explained that whenever the population of the village became too numerous, a group would splinter off and form a new *huta*. Everyone around would pitch in to help build it, first blessing the location and all the building materials, of course, to pay respects to the spirits that live in all things.

"Because," he told her, "the Bataks still remember the Old Ways."

"Not all of them, I hope," Sarah whispered, and he laughed in his new, carefree way and pulled her close to his side.

"The elder is upset with me," he confided with his lips touching her hair.

"Oh, God."

His amused chuckle teased the shell of her ear. "He's annoyed that I didn't tell him we were coming so he could notify the other clan *hutas*. Bataks love a party. He wants to throw a real blowout for us."

"But why? Do they treat all visitors like this? Why are you—"

But he silenced her with a warning squeeze on her arm. The elders were escorting them with great ceremony to the community meeting place near the entrance of the village. Carved wooden chairs were brought for them and placed at the elders' right. Tables were set up. The same women who had just come from the rice fields now disappeared inside the longhouses to prepare the evening meal.

The men gathered around. Pipes were brought out, cups of home brew and rice wine were offered. Torches were lit as lavender twilight turned into purple night.

"Well, what do you think?"

The question came as Sarah was taking a sip of the rice wine, and she wasn't sure whether Dan wanted her opinion of the vintage or things in general. She decided it didn't matter; she'd lost the ability to think.

She sipped, coughed and presently managed to say in a broken whisper, "I've a feeling this isn't Kansas."

Dan's laughter rang in the cool evening air, and all the other men laughed with him.

He's so different here, Sarah thought, suddenly filling with a vague, inexplicable longing. So happy. And then, with a kind of despair she thought, What a strange man he is! How will I ever understand him?

While small children darted in and out of the torchlight like fireflies, the women came and went in gracious silence, serving platters of rice, steamed vegetables and spicy peppered fish, green-chili relish and pots of savory curried stew. The stew was delicious and so hot it made Sarah's eyes water, but when she asked Dan what kind of stew it was, he replied with ominous brevity, "Don't ask."

After the feast, for Sarah's benefit the elders told the story of the great hero Si Raja Batak and how he became the ancestor of all the Batak tribes. They told it in the stylized manner of an epic poem, with intricate hand gestures and drum flourishes, while one of them translated into crude English. And after the story was done, the dancing began.

A reed instrument with a lilting, woodwind sound joined the drums. The music was haunting and sweet, joyful and sad. There was something about it that got under Sarah's skin and seeped into her flesh and bones. She wanted to move with it as the dancers moved. But though she could sense the rhythm in Dan's body, too, he didn't join the dancers, and she somehow understood that it would not have been proper to do so.

Men and women danced, sometimes together, sometimes separately. The dances always began with delicate finger movements, then added the feet and finally the whole body, sometimes with stately grace, sometimes with wild abandon, always with joy. There was something childlike about them, Sarah thought; something free and unrestrained. Their sarongs and headdresses were bright and colorful as tropical flowers, and they reminded Sarah of something, though she couldn't think what.

She looked at Dan across the space that separated their chairs, suddenly needing to make contact with him, the longing in her as strong and sweet as the homemade wine. As if he felt her need and longing, he tore his eyes from the dancers and found hers, and as it had once before, the naked emotion she saw in his face stopped her heart and breath. She wanted to look away, but he wouldn't let her go. Eyes ablaze with reflected torchlight held her captive, demanding answers to questions she didn't understand.

The reed's song stirred her senses like a lover's caress; the drums pounded in her blood. Her own emotions rose inside her like floodtide, threatening to swamp her. I'm not prepared for this, she protested in silent panic. I'm used to his masks and veils. I don't know what to do with his vulnerability.

She had no masks and veils to hide her own feelings, and as they rushed, stinging, to the backs of her eyes, a frown of concern appeared on Dan's forehead. In a soft, guttural voice he asked her if something was wrong.

"No!" she gasped, shaking her head. "Nothing."

I want to love you, her heart cried, but I don't know how.

"Are you tired? Do you want to go to bed?"

"No. No, I'm fine. Really. It's just so..." She left it unfinished and turned blindly back to the dancers.

Dan didn't say anything, but Sarah knew that now he watched her and not the dancers and that his eyes were shuttered and thoughtful again.

After a while he spoke quietly to the elders and then touched her elbow. "Come on, let's turn in. You're tired, and so am I. This is liable to go on for a while yet." His voice was still soft, but it had acquired a certain harshness, and Sarah thought with helpless anguish, I've spoiled it for him somehow.

One of the elders rose and picked up a torch. As he led them through the compound, the human mask and buffalo-horn carvings that adorned the dark, silent houses sprang to eerie life in the undulating light of the torch, seeming almost to dance to the throbbing drums and the haunting melodies of the reed.

Sarah stumbled, and Dan caught her around the waist and pulled her against his side. She laughed nervously and said, "Oops, too much wine." But he'd been watching her, and he knew she'd hardly drunk anything, or eaten much, either.

She's confused, he thought, feeling inexpressibly bleak. He didn't blame her. He'd been wrong to bring her here, crazy to expect her to understand him. Hell, he wasn't sure he even understood himself, sometimes.

He went ahead of her up the stairs and gave her a hand to help her through the trapdoor entrance to the longhouse, then turned to pay his respects to the elder's wife and to his ancient and toothless mother, the clan matriarch. When he drew Sarah forward to introduce her, it struck him that she looked like a child, lost among strangers.

The elder, having seen them safely inside his house, said good-night and went back to the party. Dan knew from past experience that he'd stay as long as the music and the supply of home brew held out. After he'd gone, small dark heads and curious eyes came popping out of the shadows, from behind curtains and screens. When Sarah smiled and gave the little ones a wave, she got a ripple of delighted whispers and giggles in return.

The elder's wife gently shushed the children and sent them scurrying on back to bed, then picked up a flickering oil lamp and motioned for Sarah and Dan to follow her. She led them through the curtained maze to a sleeping compartment that had been prepared for guests, placed the lamp on the floor, bowed graciously and went out, leaving them alone.

There was a moment of silence, and then a small, strangled sound from Sarah. Dan looked at her and saw that she had her hands clasped together just under her chin; in the lamplight her eyes seemed as liquid and transparent as warm sherry. "Is this where we're sleeping?" she whispered in halting disbelief.

Dan looked at the sleeping mat unrolled at his feet and nodded.

"Both of us." It was flatly stated, not a question.

"That's right, Doc." He smiled, but it felt crooked to him. "You're not still afraid of me, are you?" It amazed him how much it hurt, pushing those words through the tightness in his chest, and how much he feared her answer.

"No," she said, shaking her head emphatically.

"Nervous, then?"

Another head shake, this one less certain.

"Well you don't have to be," he said harshly. "Because that's all we're going to be doing—sleeping."

Sarah nodded and said, "Of course," in tones of bald disbelief.

Dan had serious doubts about it, himself. He'd had his share of rice wine, and there'd been a good reason for that. Now, looking at her, he knew he hadn't drunk nearly enough.

"They don't have a lot of room to spare," he said, making an effort to explain. "The elder's whole family sleeps here—sons and their wives and kids—everybody." He didn't tell her that normally only married couples got the luxury of privacy, such as it was. He bent down to pick up a length of cloth that had been left neatly folded on the sleeping mat. "Here," he said roughly, shaking it out and handing it to her, "you might be more comfortable wearing this."

"What is it?"

"It's a sarong. For—" he coughed and waved his hand "—you know—sleeping in."

"Oh."

"You don't have to if you don't want to—it just beats sleeping in your clothes."

"Yes." She cleared her throat and added a polite "Thank you."

He looked at her for a moment, then bent down to snuff out the lamp.

"Don't . . ." she said, so softly he barely heard her. He paused, looking a question at her, and saw her throat move and her lips part and then the slight shake of her head. She held out the sarong and whispered, "Hold this, please."

He took it from her, but his hands didn't feel it. He was conscious only of Sarah's luminous, golden eyes, her long slender fingers and the throbbing beat of the drums. His heart timed itself to their rhythm; his breathing quickened. In a kind of trance he watched her hands move down the front of her shirt and pull it slowly from the waistband of her jeans.

Her undressing was unstudied, without artifice, not consciously provocative, and Dan thought he'd never in his life seen anything so beautiful or so enticing. The lines of her body were taut and elegant, and she had a dancer's style and grace, but it was her awareness of him that made her movements sensuous. And an element of shyness that made them erotic. Watching her, he felt his body grow hot and tight; the muscles in his jaws ached with tension.

When she was naked except for modest white panties, she turned her back to him and bowed her head. Without a word, Dan shook out the sarong and held it while she turned herself into it. When she finished, she was facing him. His hands were pressed flat against her back, his fingers splayed wide over her soft skin. He could hear the drums and the harsh sounds of their breathing.

"Doc..." he said on a long, uneven exhalation, "I didn't bring you here for this." As he said it he thought how far he'd come from the first moments of knowing her, when all he'd wanted was this—her body in his arms, her mouth...

"What did you bring me here for?"

...Her mouth, hot and open under his. He couldn't remember why in the hell he'd brought her here! Tension was a high-pitched keening inside his head, a white-hot knife in his belly, a fire in his loins. Relief was to immerse himself in her—in her mouth, her body.

"There's another sarong," she whispered, her lips almost touching his. "Is it for you?"

"Yes." He felt her hands on his belt buckle and with a kind of desperation, caught her by the shoulders, digging his fingers into her flesh so hard she gasped. He cleared his throat and managed to croak, "Listen, Doc, I meant what I said. We're sleeping here tonight, just sleeping." And then, with a gently rueful laugh he added, "It's not as though we haven't done it before."

She stood back a little, keeping her hands on his waist, and said with certainty, "It's not what you want."

Dan's laugh was painful. "That's pretty obvious." He closed his eyes, then, and released his breath in a mighty sigh. "God, no, it's not what I want—" He caught her roughly to him and kissed her hard and deep. When he pulled away from her, she made a small, bereft sound and stared at him with shocked, hungry eyes. He felt as if he'd just gone twelve tough rounds with the middleweight champion of the world. "What I want to do," he growled, "is make love to you. I've wanted to make love to you since the first time I laid eyes on you. And I'm going to make love to you, you can bet on it. But as I said, when I do, it's not going to be on some damn folding cot, and it's for sure not going to be in a curtained-off cubicle with a dozen other people within earshot!" He gave her a little shake, charged with suppressed passion. "You understand?"

She nodded as if mesmerized and whispered, "Yes."

"All right then. Quit drivin' me crazy." He turned from her and drove his fingers through his hair. His arms and legs felt wobbly as a newborn lamb's. "Go to bed," he rasped, and as an afterthought added with a deep scowl and a jerky wave of the hand, "and turn out that goddamned lamp!"

Sarah lay down on the sleeping mat, but she didn't turn out the lamp. Instead she propped her head on her arm and watched Dan undress, feasting on the play of light and shadow across his body while desire ran hot and undirected through hers. The look he gave her as he leaned over her to snuff the lamp was dark with fury and frustration. If it hadn't been for what she'd just heard him say, she'd have thought he was angry with her. Maybe he *was* angry; there was so much about him she didn't understand!

They lay like stone effigies in the darkness, listening to each other's breathing and to the throbbing drums. After a while Dan made a soft, rueful sound. "Come here," he said gruffly, and snagging her with one arm, pulled her to him. "Gets chilly at night, here in the mountains. No reason we can't give each other a little warmth. Is there?"

"No reason," Sarah murmured, moving stiffly into the curve of his body. She wasn't cold, but for no accountable reason she had begun to shiver. "You?"

"Nope," Dan said firmly, "I'm fine."

She felt his lips press the top of her head as she settled against him. Her hand began an idle wander, across smooth pectorals and flat, hard-pebbled nipples, downward over hard ribs and tensed belly muscles, until it reached the sarong, and there it halted. After a moment she murmured curiously, "Can you go to sleep like that? Doesn't it . . . bother you?"

There was a thoughtful silence. Then Dan said solemnly, "Only when I laugh."

Sarah giggled. Dan chuckled. And suddenly they were both laughing like children, shaking and snorting and holding on to each other, trying to stifle gales of helpless mirth in each other, which, of course, tickled and only compounded the problem. Telling each other urgently to "Ssh!" and then sailing off again on waves of laughter.

Until gradually the chortles subsided to fitful snickers and gentling sighs. Sarah lay with her cheek on Dan's chest, right over his rapidly beating heart, her hand curled and relaxed in the hollow below his ribs, feeling his belly move up and down with his breathing, feeling it tighten momentarily with a last, residual chuckle. His face was in her hair; his hand trailed idly up and down her side, following the curve of her waist and hip.

It felt so good, so good, Sarah thought, to laugh with someone and to lie together like this, relaxed and spent. How long had it been? Probably childhood, with her sisters in their old house in San Jose, California. What a long, long way it was from her cluttered bedroom with white priscillas in the windows and what her artist-sister Terry had always called "that dorky pink fairy paper" on the walls, to a Batak long house in Sumatra and the arms of a strange dark man who might or might not be a poacher.

But Sarah knew that not since those happy childhood days had she felt such a warm and wonderful sense of belonging.

* * *

Sarah was certain she wouldn't sleep, but voices woke her deep in the night. Whispering voices and stealthy footsteps, ambiguous bumps and scuffles. The drums were silent; the party was over and the revelers were coming home to bed.

She was stiff and uncomfortable, unaccustomed to sleeping on her side with her head on a man's shoulder. She worried about Dan, too—she must be cutting off the circulation in his arm. But, oh, how she hated to leave the sweet security of his body! She tried to turn without breaking the contact or waking him, but he murmured something and tightened his arms around her.

"Don't go."

"But your arm—"

"It's fine—don't worry about it."

"My hip's numb."

"All right—try this...." He turned, and so did she, and they settled together again in cosy intimacy, like spoons.

The silence settled around them once more. Sarah lay awake, listening to the comforting whisper of Dan's breath, her own pulsebeat and then, a new and vaguely disquieting sound. It was a while before she recognized it, and when she did, a pulse began to throb in the pit of her stomach. Her skin grew hot. She closed her eyes and whispered, "Oh...dear."

Dan stirred and tightened his arms around her; his chuckle warmed her neck and sent waves of shivers down her spine. "Hey, don't worry about it. It's just loving. That's life."

Life and loving. It all happens right here, Sarah thought. Here in this house, people are conceived and born, love and die, and it's all just a part of living.

As she lay there in Dan's arms with his body hard and hot against her, trying to lie quietly while her own body swelled and throbbed in all its secret places, she listened to the sounds of loving in the night and felt part of it, in ways she couldn't understand or explain. More than that—knowing he was listening, too, she felt a part of him, a spiritual coupling far beyond the physical joining of bodies. That moment would come for them, soon—he'd told her so, and she knew it, too—and when it did, it would be easy, joyous and right.

What would it take for you to be easy with me, huh, Doc?

She thought ruefully that after this incredible night, it would be hard for Dan ever to be a stranger to her again.

Sarah woke slowly, floating to consciousness on clouds of music. Lovely music, far off in the distance—voices singing, sweet and true as angels—lilting melodies, hauntingly familiar. She lay with her eyes closed, recalling Sunday morning sunshine streaming through her bedroom window, she and her sisters buckling on black patent leather shoes and brushing each other's hair, while Dad whistled "Ode to Joy" in the shower and Mom called from downstairs, "Hurry up or we'll be late to church!"

"Is it Sunday?" she murmured, still half dreaming.

Dan's chuckle brought her awake. "Sure is, and morning, too."

He was sitting up beside her, arms resting on drawn-up knees, smiling in the cool, dim quietness. With her heart turning over at the sight of him, Sarah yawned, stretched and muttered, "No kidding? I lose track of what day it is." And then, doing a delayed double take. "Are they singing *hymns*?"

"I guess so." Dan paused for a yawn of his own. "That's what people usually sing in church."

"Church! Here? Who—"

"The whole village, I reckon. Pretty much everybody goes—what are you grinning at?"

"You, ah reckon," Sarah teased in a husky drawl, filling up with sunlight warmth and inexpressible joy. "But don't mind me—how did former cannibals in the middle of a Moslem nation get to be Christians?"

"It was Lutheran missionaries that converted the Bataks from the Old Ways." He frowned suddenly. "Hey, listen, did you want to go to church? There's time, if you'd stop lolling around in bed...."

His voice died away. The silence of the empty house echoed around them. Sarah stirred, stretching languorously, her body responding automatically to the velvety caress of Dan's eyes. "I don't know," she murmured. "What about you? Do you want to go?"

Dan looked away, and she knew that he'd missed her hint. She was glad she couldn't see the shutters come down over his eyes, but she heard them anyway, in his voice. "I'm not much for churches," he said distantly, "but if you want to go, I'll take you."

A new hymn rose into the morning like a chorus of angels, taking Sarah's spirits with it. She hesitated, but only because she was torn between her own desires—to go, or to stay in that quiet, private place with Dan—and not because of his retreat back into that private place where she couldn't follow. This was Dan, she reminded herself, the man she loved. And no shutters or masks were going to keep her from loving him.

"I would like to go," she said, "but isn't it too late? I'm—we're not dressed." She thought of the wrinkled, work-stained things she'd taken off the night before. "And I don't have anything—"

"You don't have a thing to wear!" Dan said, laughing at her. "Yeah, yeah, I know, just like a woman."

"What?" Sarah came bolt upright with a gasp of outrage. Dan easily fended off her mock-attack and dropped a length of red fabric into her lap.

"There," he said smugly, "no more excuses."

"Oh..." Sarah breathed, running her hands over the sarong. "It's gorgeous. Where on earth did you get this?"

"I can't take the credit—I wish I could. I think one of the elder's daughter's-in-law has lent us her Sunday best. I have one, too, see?"

Both sarongs were the same rich red, with intricate patterns woven in metallic gold. Dan's was waist-length, meant to be worn with a shirt and stole, while Sarah's was the women's full-length style. Dan showed her how to wrap and fasten it over the softer, shorter sleep sarong, which would serve now as an undergarment.

"How do I look?" she asked him breathlessly as he drew the matching stole over her shoulder.

For a moment his hands rested there, one on her upper arm, the other on the opposite shoulder, and then the knuckles of that hand brushed across her collarbone, the thumb touched her chin. She saw a gleam in her eyes, the quick flash of a grin. "You'll do," he said.

She felt her heartbeat in her throat. Suddenly shy, she fluttered a hand to her cheek, the back of her neck. "My hair...I wish I had a brush—"

His hands enclosed her head, palms over her ears, fingers burrowing under her hair to lie warm against her scalp while the thumbs pressed damp wisps back from her temples. She felt the tension in his hands, the heat of his body, heard the slow, steady sound of his breathing. In the dim and shadowed longhouse it was impossible to see his eyes, but he seemed to be examining her hair, studying her face as if she were an exquisite treasure. She felt the frustration in him, the passion—all that he wanted to say and could not.

But Sarah wanted to tell him that he didn't need words. She'd never felt so complimented or more beautiful.

"You look fine," he whispered, then gave her head a little shake and released her. "Let's go—don't want to be late."

The church was set apart from the village, among the rice paddies and banana groves. It was quiet as they approached. Through the open windows Sarah could see dark heads bowed in prayer.

"What's the matter?" Dan asked her when she caught his arm, stopping him. "Don't you want to go in?"

She could feel the tension in his muscles. "I don't know," she whispered, "I feel funny, going in late. I don't want to interrupt the service. Do you know—I mean, do you usually..."

For a moment or two he went on gazing over her head, his face closed to her. Then he tossed her a crooked smile. "No, I told you, I'm not much for churches." He looked away again. After a pause, he said slowly, "There's a place I like to go sometimes, whenever I'm here. It's kind of a special place—you know, pretty...." He laughed and threw her another look, a quick one, just long enough for her to see the wariness and vulnerability in his eyes. "I guess it's kind of like my church." There was another pause before he asked cautiously, "Would you like to see it?"

Sarah realized then that she'd been holding her breath, as if she were watching a wild animal come closer...closer. "Yes," she whispered, hardly daring to stir the air with her words, "I'd like that."

His smile was spontaneous and brief. "This way then—it's a little walk."

They took the road that lead past the church and up into the mountains, walking hand in hand, barefoot in the morning mist. As they climbed, winding through the forest of ferns and pine, they kept drifting in and out of low-hanging clouds so that one minute the mist was cool and wet in their faces and the next minute the sun burned hot on their shoulders. It reminded Sarah of the Northern California coast in the summertime, and she told Dan so, and about childhood picnics to the redwoods and the fog that would blow in from the Pacific and turn the groves into places of magic and mystery.

They paused for breath on a wooded promontory high above the turquoise waters of the lake. Below them on the left was the village and, almost at their feet, the little church. The service was over, apparently, because people were spilling out into the yard and onto the road like flower petals in a whirlwind, their voices rising like wind chimes on the clear, pure air.

"Yeah," Dan said, "it reminds me of when I was a kid, too."

"Really?" Instead of slowing down, Sarah's heart accelerated. Because they were looking at the church, and she was remembering pictures she'd seen of quaint villages and white steepled churches, she said before she thought, "What, you mean New England?" But even before he answered she was thinking, Idiot! He hated New England. He wouldn't even come here if it reminded him of that part of his past.

"No," Dan said quietly, with another of those skewed smiles, "Mexico."

And she thought, Yes! That was it—the thing that she hadn't been able to put her finger on last night, watching the dancers in their colorful costumes! It reminded her of Mexico.

Suddenly she understood.

Chapter 10

What was it Marina had said?

"Children and bright colors, sunshine, laughter... playing barefoot in the sand...."

"Mexico," Sarah said softly. "You were born there."

"Yeah," Dan murmured, not looking at her. "How did you know?"

"Marina told me."

His laugh was brief and wry. "That's right—I guess maybe I did mention it to her. So she told you, huh?"

"I asked her."

"Yeah?" Sarah saw an elusive gleam of pleasure in his eyes as they both turned back to the climb. "What else did she tell you?"

She held her breath, counting footsteps while jitters danced like butterflies along her nerves. "That you were happy there, and that when you were still very small, your mother took you away." She waited, still not breathing, and when he didn't say anything, ventured bravely, "Dan?" His profile was like stone. Only the vastness of her need to know and the memory of lying in his arms in intimacy and laughter made it possible for her to go on. "I'd love to know what you were like," she said haltingly, "as a little boy."

She watched him struggle with it, aching for him when at last he cleared his throat and drawled gruffly, "Well, I'm not much good at talkin', not about myself. Never have been."

"You told Marina," Sarah reminded him gently.

He considered that and then said, "Yeah, I did. She's a nice lady, easy to talk to."

"And I'm not?"

She'd kept her voice light, half-teasing, but he glanced at her and then quickly away, as if the sight of her pained him. "No," he said dismissively. "You're different."

They walked a little way farther in silence, not touching, just listening to their footsteps and the sounds of their breathing. Sarah heard a bird's song she didn't recognize, the soughing of wind in the pines, rushing water from somewhere up ahead.

After a while Dan paused, frowned thoughtfully at a ladder of sunlight streaming through the trees and said, "Annie—that's my ex-wife—used to tell me I didn't show my feelings enough. She said I keep too much inside."

Sarah bit down on her lower lip and kept her eyes on the path ahead. Dan cleared his throat and went on, both words and steps carefully measured. "I always knew she was right. We just didn't know how to fix it. Eventually she got fed up with being shut out all the time. She said—" He coughed and stopped walking. Sarah stopped, too, looking at him questioningly, but his gaze was focused on something beyond her. "She said I never told her I loved her."

Sarah's throat felt too tight to form words. She said in a whisper, "Did you love her?"

As he brought his eyes back to her, she saw something in them flare and then soften. "Yeah, I think I did. I just couldn't say it."

"Sometimes," Sarah said, "you don't have to say it. If you show it...."

Dan snorted softly, a sound replete with self-blame. "Yeah, well, I don't think I did that, either."

"Why not?"

"How the hell should I know?" He turned away, angry all of a sudden. "Maybe I didn't love her enough! Maybe—"

"Maybe it's just a habit," Sarah said, and paused for air. Her chest ached; she felt winded, and not from the climb. "Or fear."

His smile was dark and dangerous. This time clinging to the memory of his laughter wasn't enough. In panic she slipped into old habits of her own. "Habits can be broken," she chirped earnestly. "Fear can be gotten over, if you want to badly enough. It takes a lot of courage—"

Dan shook his head with controlled violence and held up one finger, silencing her. "Uh-uh—that's not what it takes." His words were rapid and tense; his eyes glittered with cold fire. "I'll tell you what it takes. You ever watch a little kid tryin' to learn to swim? He's standing on the edge of the water, and his daddy's holding out his arms, telling him, 'Jump—I'm gonna catch you.' And the little kid just crouches there, wantin' to jump so bad, and so damn scared... You want to know what finally makes him jump? It's not courage, Doc." He stabbed the air with his finger. "It's *trust*." He pulled in a deep breath and repeated it, softly this time but with no less intensity. "Trust—that's all, baby. He just has to know in his heart that somebody's going to be there to catch him."

He turned to walk on, and Sarah followed with hammering heart and wobbly legs, feeling shaken and more confused than ever. Because she knew that what had just passed between them had nothing whatever to do with swimming and very little to do with past loves, either. And for the life of her—the irony of it took her breath away—she couldn't figure out why *he* didn't trust *her*.

She was so deep in the puzzle of it that the next time Dan stopped, she ran into him.

He said, "Wait here a minute," and then moved on, muttering something about wanting to "check it out first." Looking past his shoulder, Sarah saw a wooden footbridge spanning a narrow chasm choked with brush and ferns. From far below came the sound she'd been hearing for the last few minutes—the muted roar of water cascading over rocks.

Her stomach gave a lurch. She'd never been good with heights, and the bridge looked as if a stiff breeze would blow it down. She'd have called Dan back, but he was already moving out onto the rickety structure. At one point it gave an ominous creak, which, of course, prompted Dan to bounce up and down on that particular spot a few times to test it, while Sarah clamped a hand across her mouth to keep from screaming, "Get off of there, you idiot!"

Safely across, Dan called to her from the other side of the chasm. "I think it'll be okay. If it held me, it should hold you. Come on over, but be careful."

As if she needed telling! Gripping the hand rails for dear life, she stepped onto the bridge, her heart drowning out the thunder of the water that leaped and tumbled over rocks and boulders on its way to a turquoise inlet far below. Her legs were cold and boneless—how she made them move was a mystery to her. Her hands were numb, and so was her brain. All she saw was Dan's face guiding her like a light at the end of a long tunnel.

She was almost across when she heard a sound like rifle fire and then an agonized groaning. She stopped dead, her hands cemented to the rails, afraid to move, afraid to take a step, afraid to breathe. In what seemed like slow motion she saw Dan's face change and then freeze into a mask of stark horror. In her mind she was screaming his name, but no sound came out.

She heard him shouting at her. Her name: "Sarah! Sarah, for God's sake, jump! Let—go—and—*jump*!"

His hands reached toward her across the chasm, an impossible distance away. The bridge swayed. She heard a terrified whimper, like a child's.

"Come on, Doc—*now*!"

She jumped, and hard hands caught her.

The earth crumbled beneath her feet; she felt herself slipping. But even as a small, terrified cry burst from her, the bands of steel that held her tightened and lifted, warmth and safety enveloped her. Behind her was chaos, but all she heard was Dan's voice crooning, "It's all right, I've got you now.... Shh...it's okay...."

Inside, he was screaming, "Sarah, oh, my God, Sarah," and holding on to her as if the earth were heaving beneath his feet and she the only solid thing in the universe. God, what if he'd lost her?

She was shaking like a reed in a windstorm, but then, so was he. He held her more tightly and whispered, "Doc..." Never wanting to let her go. Afraid to let her go.

She stirred, finally, nudged his chest with her face and gave a funny little laugh. He caught her by the arms and held her away from him, staring at her as if he'd never seen her face before or might never see it again, etching it on his memory—classic features, pale as marble, trembling mouth and blazing golden eyes. Then he let go a breath and took her mouth with a fierce and violent passion, plunging deep in what was so much more than a kiss, both a giving and a taking, claiming and surrender, a declaration and a plea.

She was his, and he'd almost lost her! And so he tried with that kiss to bind her indelibly to him, to brand her mouth with his and to leave his essence with her, to take the taste of her into himself and sear her into his being. To defy even the gods to try to take her from him again.

He kissed her heedlessly at first, aware of nothing but his own need, his own fear. But as the cutting edge of that fear dulled, he began to notice other things—like the soft, desperate sounds she was making in her throat; her hands, clutching so frantically at his shirt front that the fastening had torn off; her shoulders, satin-smooth and trembling beneath his hands.

"You lost your stole," he said thickly as he lifted his mouth from hers.

She said, "Hmm? Oh..." And then, sounding dazed, "I'm sorry."

Fear became fury. He shook her and yelled, "Forget the damned stole! Don't do that to me again, do you understand me? Not ever again!"

"Do what?" she whispered, her eyes round and bewildered.

"Scare me to death, dammit! Why did you freeze out there? Why didn't you jump when I told you to jump? You know what almost happened? If you'd waited another second, you'd be down there with the goddamn stole right now! Look." He hauled her over to the edge of the chasm and pointed to where the red cloth lay like a bloodstain on the rocks far below. The bridge, still attached to its moorings on the far side, swayed drunkenly, creaking in erratic rhythm.

He was being unfair, he knew, but even so he was surprised when she began pounding on his chest with her fists full of his shirt—to its further destruction—and yelling, "Don't do that! Don't—do—that!"

"Don't do what?" It was his turn to be bewildered.

"I—hate—heights!" Pushing away from him with a shove that knocked him backward, she went stalking off up the trail, limping slightly.

Every inch the Golden Girl, even in a sarong and bare feet, Dan thought, staring after her in amazement. Except that he'd seen the tears on her cheeks and felt the quaking in her body, and now he knew beyond any doubt that the cool elegance she wore with such self-assurance was as much a mask as the one he'd been wearing for most of his life.

"Why didn't you tell me?" he asked softly when he caught up with her. "Why'd you get on that thing if you were afraid?"

Sarah dashed tears from her cheeks with a quick, angry gesture, but her retort was blurred and liquid. "I guess...I trusted you." She gave a short, high laugh and tipped her head to one side, as if hearing her own words for the first time, then looked up at him with wet face and swimming eyes and whispered, "I *trust* you. I guess I must—I jumped, didn't I?"

She went on looking at him with her mouth half-open as if there were something more she wanted to say. Dan had a feeling he knew what that something was—it was all there in her rapt face and shining eyes. Because the thought of her saying it made his chest tighten and his throat clamp shut, he touched her lips with his thumb and said huskily, "Don't do that."

"Don't do what?"

He smiled and brushed the backs of his fingers across her cheeks. "This." Then he leaned down and, as gently as he knew how, took the moisture of her tears from her lips with his own. "I caught you, didn't I?" *I'll always catch you, Doc....*

"Yeah." He heard the little catch in her voice and felt her lips form a smile.

Her mouth blossomed under his. He felt her hand on his ribs inside his torn shirt, and beneath it, deep inside him, a hot, insistent throbbing. It was a familiar feeling, and it was proceeding in a familiar pattern, spreading heat through his belly and into his loins. It was a feeling he'd been having a lot, lately—especially last night, trying to sleep with her bottom tucked against his aching parts—but it surprised him a little to be having it now. After the emotional bombardment he'd just been through, he was glad to know that he still had enough energy left for desire.

"Hey," he murmured, stroking the tops of her shoulders, the back of her neck. "We're almost there."

"Almost where?"

"The place I told you about. Are you going to be okay, or shall I carry you?"

Her sleepy eyes widened. "Why on earth should you carry me?"

"You're limping. I thought maybe you'd hurt yourself when you jumped."

She gave a little gurgle of laughter and said cryptically, "No, not this time. I'm fine. Don't worry about me."

For a minute he just looked at her, feeling her soft skin in his hands, the throbbing in his body. He had an urge to pick her up and carry her anyway, in the time-honored tradition of masculine possession, but he knew the moment still wasn't right. He'd waited this long, and he could wait a little longer. There was something he wanted to show her first. So he chuckled and said, "Okay, then, get along," and turned her around and headed her down the trail. He let her go ahead of him because he wanted her to see it the way he'd seen if the first time.

The first thing Sarah thought of when she saw the lake was Dan's eyes and how so often they'd reminded her of just this—sunlight shining on crystal-blue water.

"Oh . . ." she whispered, enchanted, and then for a few minutes she just stood still and looked. It was like a jewel, she thought; a sapphire in a nest of green velvet. The water danced and shimmered, breezes blew soft and sweet, birds sang, and ferns and flowers grew lush to the water's edge. "It's the way the earth was meant to be," she said in a hushed voice when Dan came to stand behind her. "Like Eden."

Her response was all he'd hoped for—Sarah looking at him with glowing eyes and her heart in her face. But again he felt a swelling pressure in his chest, that aching tightness in his throat. Again a desperate need to forestall her before she could say the words.

So he chuckled low in his throat, ran his fingers lightly and suggestively across the tops of her shoulders and murmured, "Eden?"

Either she was very quick or her mind had been running along the same track. Her breath caught, then emerged on a ripple of laughter as she stepped back from him, her hands going to the fastening of her sarong. Dan folded his arms and waited, holding in his own laughter, daring her with a look.

White teeth clamped down on a quivering lip—a look of elfin mischief. He wanted to laugh out loud with pure joy at the sight of her, but instead he kept his face skeptical, calling her bluff. She took another step backward, and another, then slowly unwound the sarong and let it drop.

Dan said, "Hmph," letting her know he wasn't impressed. Not much, he wasn't; in the short, soft sleep sarong she looked like a Greek goddess, a myth come to life. He half expected to hear the music of reed pipes come wafting on the breeze.

Then Sarah lifted her head, holding it at a quizzical tilt, smiling a smile of secret enchantment; her eyes looked far away, as if she heard the pipes, too. For a long moment she held the pose, and her body became poetry, settling into lines of such elegance and beauty it made Dan's throat ache just to look at her. She became the music of the pipes, the shimmering sunlight, fern fronds swaying in the wind. The sarong fluttered to the mossy ground as she whirled and ran with a dancer's grace to the water.

It wasn't quite what she'd expected. "Oh—God—" she shrieked as the air rushed out of her lungs, "it's cold! Why didn't you tell me?"

"Well now, I don't recall you askin'," Dan drawled, standing there on the bank with his arms folded on his chest, laughing at her. He'd taken off his shirt; without it, she couldn't decide which he reminded her of more—an Aztec prince or the King of Siam. Either one was much too arrogant and assured, she decided, too high and mighty. He wanted bringing down a bit, preferably down to where she was, ignominiously freezing her fanny off!

"Don't just stand there—come on in!" she called with what she hoped was a beguiling smile, trying not to let her chattering teeth spoil the effect.

"Do I look crazy? I know what that water's like."

"Oh, come on, it feels good. I just didn't expect it to be cold, that's all." It was true. Now she was getting used to it, it felt wonderful—fresh and, in a strange way, exciting. She began to enjoy the caress of the water on her naked body, like cool fingers...sliding between her thighs and over her belly and breasts, teasing her nipples to pebble hardness....

"I never thought you'd be chicken," she said, her voice throaty and without any inclination at all, now, to shiver.

Dan's grin looked dangerous. He thumbed back an imaginary Stetson and, in an exaggerated accent, drawled, "Ma'am, Ah don't think you know who yer talkin' to—nobody calls a Texan a chicken and gits away with it."

"Chick-en," Sarah sang, flapping her hands like wings. She gave a gurgle of laughter when his hands went to the fastening of his sarong, but in the next minute swallowed it with a gasp as, for one split second he stood there, poised, naked, his body gleaming golden in the sun. Then he cut the water with a shallow dive. Her next sound was a squawk of dismay as he caught her around the waist and ducked her.

She surfaced sputtering and splashing with all her might, so Dan picked her up in his arms and threw her right back into the water. She came up laughing and fighting, asking and giving no quarter. This time, when he'd managed to subdue her enough to pick her up again, she wrapped her arms around his neck and hung on, so that they both went under together.

"Okay," Dan sputtered when he was able to speak again, "if that's the way you want it—" He hefted her once, tightened his grip and began striding with purpose toward the bank.

Now, in the perverse way of women, she pummeled his shoulders and demanded to be put down!

He halted and looked deep into her eyes, feeling her body smooth and slippery against his, her thighs firm and solid in his grasp, her hands cool and light on his neck. "Are you sure that's what you want?"

She nodded. He caught the reflexive movement of her swallow and transferred his gaze to her throat, letting it rest for a moment on the little puddle of water in the hollow there before beginning a slow journey, past drops of water quivering on the pink crests of her breasts and running in silvery rivers down her ribs, to the flooded depression in her abdomen and the dark wet triangle beyond. He heard a barely whispered, "Yes, please."

He let go of her thighs, allowing her to slide with excruciatingly slowness down his body to stand facing him in waist-deep water, wet and sleek, regal as a goddess, graceful as a sprite, so beautiful she didn't seem real.

But she was real, that was the miracle of it—real and warm, playful and funny, loving and passionate. Water drops spangled her lashes, her cheeks, her parted lips, like flower petals in the rain; each breath pushed belly muscles against the lapping water and lifted breasts shivered round and hard with cold.

Her nipples were drawn so tight, he thought. Painfully tight. He lifted his hands and carefully placed one over each breast, nesting their tender tips in his palms.

Her breath sighed sharply through her lips. He felt a tremor run through her body, and then her eyes closed and she swayed forward into his touch.

"Dan...."

"What?"

He felt her cool fingers touch the backs of his hands. "Are you going to make love to me?"

Something—unnamed emotions—shivered through him, crowding his chest. "I mean to, yes." The contrast of his hands on her skin mesmerized him as he moved them in gentle rotations and felt her breasts warm and soften.

"Dan?" Her voice grew faint and breathy as he set about pebbling her nipples again, in his own way.

"Hmm?" He was smiling slightly, his eyes slumberous as he watched her nipples harden under the stroking of his thumbs.

Sarah's breath caught; she swayed and clutched at Dan's arm, shocked at the intensity of the feeling. It was so little—such a light touch, and only there—but she felt the stroking everywhere—from the deepest parts of her body to the tips of her fingers. And already, inside she was beginning to tremble.

She gasped, "Now?"

His chuckle was rich and unrestrained, full of masculine delight in her response to him. "Oh, yeah."

"Umm, right here?" He was tracing the undercurve of her breasts with his thumbs, fanning his fingers over her ribs, spanning her waist with his hands. It made it very difficult to talk while he was doing that—his hands felt so good on her skin.

"Well," he said, laughing softly, "I think we'll probably move to dry land."

He was teasing her, toying with her! So strong and in control, while she was trembling in earnest, now, wondering how much longer her legs were going to hold her. She gripped his forearms and gazed at him in helpless frustration, unable to tell him how shaken she felt inside, how much she wanted him.

Wide, warm-honey eyes stared at him, shimmering with reproach. Dan smiled at her, tenderness brewing inside him and rippling across his lips like a storm wind riffling the surface of the lake. Almost imperceptibly his hands tightened on her slender waist, and she came into his arms, her hands sliding up to clutch at his shoulders, his hands slipping beneath the water to cup and lift the cold, firm swell of her bottom, bringing her hard and tight against him. As a dancer she was used to being carried; it didn't dismay her. Almost instantly her legs parted and came around him, wrapping him in that silken embrace he'd imagined so long ago, it seemed to him now. It was nothing like he'd imagined.

Nothing in his imagination could have prepared him for the reality of her. He'd known her body would be beautiful—he'd pictured it in his mind a thousand times, seen her silhouetted in darkness, caught glimpses of her in the shower—but he found that the way he felt now had very little to do with her body. He'd fantasized making love to her, the images in his mind carnal and graphic, sensual ban-

quets of tangled limbs and heated bodies, hot, moist join-
ings, hungry mouths and cries of mindless passion. He
hadn't known how fresh and sweet and clean her skin would
smell or how her face and eyes would light at the sight of
him. He hadn't known.

He groaned when their mouths met. Sarah wondered
about it—wondered and reveled in it, desire welling up inside her to emerge in a soft, deep-throated sound of her
own. She welcomed his tongue's sweet invasion, joyfully
making a place for him, inviting him in and then joining
with him in a dance of feverish abandon that left them both
gasping. His mouth seared her throat, the long, arched col-
umn of her neck, not bruising, but hot and open, warming
her wherever it touched.

Her fingers tangled in his hair. She said things, meaning-
less things, she didn't know what. His name. The part of her
that was pressed most tightly against him was throbbing
so—he must surely feel it. She was a pulsing, mindless vessel, wanting only to be filled.

She laughed when he carried her out of the water and laid
her down on the soft, grassy shore, on the clothing he'd
discarded there—soft chuckles of pleasure and relief that
sounded almost like sobs. As he hovered above her, lacing
his fingers through hers, stroking damp hair back from her
face, she mumbled, "Did you bring me here for this?"

It wasn't until later that he remembered what he'd said to
her in the night. He said softly, "To this place? Yeah, I
did."

"It's okay, isn't it? To...do this? Nobody will—"

"It's okay." He smiled tenderly down at her. "Nobody
will come." He paused, touching soft kisses to her lips, her
throat. "Does it bother you? I suppose I could have taken
you to a motel...."

"No," she whispered, her eyelids drifting down, her
mouth blossoming into a smile, "This is...right."

Chapter 11

Yes, Sarah thought, this was right. As she'd known it would be. Crushed ferns for a bed, a warm breeze for the softest of covers, the sky stretching clear and blue to infinity and birds singing.

And then Dan's arms were under her, lifting her, and his body heat became her cover. The sky was in his eyes, and the singing was inside of her.

He raised her higher and, when her head fell back, covered her bared throat with his open mouth, arching above her like a stallion. He timed her leaping pulses with his tongue, and when he moved on, he left a wandering trail of kisses—her ears and neck, the base of her throat, the first gentle rise of her breasts—while she gasped softly and tangled her fingers through his hair.

Still holding her with one arm, he covered her breast with his hand. And then once again he tugged and chafed the nipple to excruciating hardness, treating it more roughly than before so that she whimpered with the pleasure-pain of

it and writhed in his grasp, desperately wanting the soothing warmth of his mouth there.

When she finally felt his liquid heat envelop her tender
nipple, she gave a whimpering laugh and pushed against it.
But that brought her no relief; his hand simply moved to her
other breast and began the same sweet torture there, while
the laving strokes of his tongue and the rhythmic, drawing
pressure of his mouth tugged sharply at the secret places
deep inside her.

Her breath screamed through her chest and emerged in
agonized whimpers. She caught at his shoulders and gasped,
"Dan—please—I can't . . ."

With a chuckle of satisfaction he released her breast and
slid quickly up her chest, trapping her protest in her mouth.
His tongue slipped into her mouth and probed deeply, demanding, mastering, until she felt as if her body's own
rhythms were timed and controlled by its thrusts. At the
same time, his hand was stroking and soothing her aching
breasts and moving downward to spread wide and warm
over her belly and beyond. His hand was so strong, so sure.

"Darlin'" he whispered against her mouth, "am I still
makin' you nervous?" Her thighs were locked tight—a re-
flex; he doubted she was even aware of it.

"Hmm?" He smiled at her valiant effort to focus her
eyes. Amusement rippled through him. "No," she whispered, puzzled. "Of course not. Why—"

He drew his hand lightly down the top of one leg and back
up the other, stroking against the nap of her fine, golden
hair. "In that case," he said, with tenderness and laughter
rising like bubbles in his throat, "do you think you could
relax, just a little bit?"

"Oh—" She gave an embarrassed laugh and put her hand
over her eyes. "I'm sorry." She swallowed and whispered,
"it's difficult."

He said "I know," in tenderness and sympathy as he took her hand and moved it away from her face. Then, holding her head cradled in his hand, he slowly raised her up to him and watched her as he took possession of her mouth, noticing the way her eyelids quivered and the little stress frown that formed between them.

After a moment he lifted his head and murmured, "Doc, look at me."

She tried, but her eyes were glazed and unfocused. When he brushed the soft insides of her thighs with his fingertips, her lashes fluttered and threatened to drop. "Uh-uh, look at me," he insisted, and felt her escaping breath flow like warm wine over his lips.

The palm of his hand cradled the warm, moist mound at the apex of her thighs. "No...no, don't close your eyes." His fingers began a slow and gentle exploration, searching for and finding her most sensitive and secret places. "I'll never hurt you, you know that, don't you?"

A quick, shallow nod. "Yes—it's just...it's been a while, that's all." Her breath caught and then continued in erratic gasps as she tilted her chin and touched his lips with random kisses. A fine sheen of sweat glinted like gold dust on her skin.

He felt the trembling in her, the tension, the pressure rising in her like magma. "It's all right—we've got all the time in the world...."

He knew how badly she wanted to close her eyes, but still he compelled her with words and will to look only at him, holding her gaze as he held her body, in intimacy and absolute control. When her breathing had become high and sharp and her eyes dark with panic, he lifted her and turned her face into his neck, absorbing her shuddering with his body while his fingers coaxed wave after wave of ecstasy from her depths.

Afterward, while he still housed the throbbing, pulsing part of her in the warmth of his hand, she clung to him shivering, laughing a little—with release, perhaps, or joy or even embarrassment. He held her with confidence, soothed and gentled her and murmured the words of reassurance he knew she needed to hear, not letting her know that in his heart he felt as fragile and shaken as she.

Presently he cleared his throat and said softly, "See? I told you I wouldn't hurt you—you just have to learn to trust me."

Sarah's laughter had a liquid sound. "Well, I jumped, didn't I?"

He began to laugh, then. But while they held each other tightly, smothering husky chuckles against each other the way they had in the night, Dan was remembering something she'd said earlier. *It's been a long time.*

When she was quiet, he kissed the top of her head and said with great care and gentleness, "Darlin', you're not protected, are you." He didn't make it a question; he knew it with such certainty. He told himself he should have known, but it simply hadn't occurred to him that she wouldn't be—a woman her age and a scientist, to boot. But then, he'd thought a lot of things about her that he was discovering weren't true.

She drew back a little and looked at him, a frown of consternation marring her forehead. "I used to be, but I stopped when...out here, I didn't think— You don't...?"

He shook his head, laughing painfully, kicking himself. "Sorry, sarongs don't have pockets." Why hadn't he known? He'd been so blinded by the image he'd built of her. Sophisticated, worldly. Golden Girl.

His hand still held her neck in a light embrace, so he felt the constricted movements of her throat as she swallowed—once and then again. Because he understood that her distress was for him, he damped down his own frustrations and smiled. "Hey, I'm not a kid. It's okay."

She licked her lips. Her frown deepened. Dan knew the struggle that was going on inside her, knew what she was going to say even before she did, carefully clearing her throat first. "It would probably be all right—"

He silenced her rationalizations with a finger touched to her lips and firmly shook his head. "No, darlin', no way." No way he was going to make the same mistake his father had made, thirty-some-odd years ago. At least, he told himself bitterly, he'd learned that much. "No sense taking chances," he said gently. "There'll be another time—I guarantee it."

But something was flaring in her eyes, something fierce and purposeful. Tiger eyes. Her lips curved in a smile he'd never seen before, and for some reason, a little pulse began to throb deep down in his belly.

"No way?" she said dangerously, and throwing her weight against his chest, knocked him over backward into the ferns.

She'd caught him off guard. Before he knew what was going on, she was lying on top of him—every silky golden inch of her. He laughed indulgently. "What do you think you're doing?"

Her chuckle was husky and more. "Improvising."

"Cut it out, Doc." He tried to be stern, but it wasn't possible, not when she had her knees between his thighs and was wriggling her taut, slender hips into the cradle of his body, kissing his neck, chest, tracing his hard, flat nipples with her tongue.

Well, it was a difficult situation, he told himself. She was very fragile; he had to be patient, but firm. "Hey listen, Doc..." He wrapped his arms around her, but she slipped downward, right out of his grasp. Funny, he didn't seem to have any strength in his arms. "Sarah, come back here," he said less firmly and with much less patience.

"Be still." He felt the words like a kitten's kisses on his stomach. Her soft laughter blew moist puffs across the quivering muscles of his abdomen.

"Sarah—" He tried once more, but his voice was ragged and lacked conviction. And shortly thereafter, all he could do was groan.

A strong man's groan, torn from the depths of his being, born of a need Sarah was only beginning to fathom. She heard the sound, felt the need and instinctively opened herself to him with all her heart and soul, making herself a vessel for those needs and vulnerabilities he was too strong to allow himself to show.

She held his powerful, surging body with hands and mouth and heart and all her being and felt a fierce and primitive exultation. His vulnerability became her strength, his need became her power. She felt warmth and light and joy welling up in her to burst finally in a blinding supernova of love—fierce and invincible, tender and cherishing, full of awe and wonder.

Lying with her cheek on Dan's heaving belly, for the first time in a long time Sarah felt confident and in control. Now, for the first time since she'd seen him standing in the road with his conflicts in his eyes, she knew where she stood. This strange man of masks and enigmas was her man. She loved him. She wasn't certain where the path was going to lead her, but at least her feet were on the ground.

Dan was very quiet. Sarah could hear the birds again and feel the sun and the breeze on her back. As his skin cooled and his heartbeat slowed, she slid up over his body and lightly kissed him.

He opened one eye and said thickly, "Improvising?"

"Where's there's a will, there's a way," she said primly.

Dan wrapped his arms around her and held her tightly, their bodies bumping together in delicious, silent laughter. The breeze came and stirred her hair across his lips, like feathers of silk.

"Mmf," he said, rubbing his mouth, "that tickles. "

"Sorry." Her hand went to smooth her hair and got in the way of his doing the same. He caught her hand and kissed it, and then the top of her head.

"It's all right," Dan murmured, sounding sleepy. "Soft." His hand moved in her hair, stroking it back from her face. "Short."

Sarah teased him lazily. "Hah, and you, I suppose, like all men, like it long?"

"Hmm, not necessarily." She felt his fingers exploring her hairline, stroking around her ear and down. "I like your neck."

"Well, I've always had that," she mumbled, stirring sinuously under the warmth of his hand. "Even when my hair was long."

"No kidding?" Sarah heard the ripple of amusement in his voice, but was too sleepy to realize she'd said anything to cause it. "You used to wear it long?"

"Yeah, when I was dancing. But I always wore it up." She smothered a yawn. "Dancers wear their hair up, you know, so their necks look long and graceful."

"Hmm." His fingers were moving slowly up and down the cords of her neck, weaving a starry web of goose bumps over her skin. "When did you cut it?"

She stirred again, restlessly this time, and drew one leg up over his. It wasn't something she liked to remember. "When I was in the hospital. It was too hard to take care of it."

"When you broke your leg, you mean? Were you in the hospital a long time?"

She nodded. "Almost six months."

Dan didn't say anything for a minute or two. His hand had begun a seemingly random journey across her shoulder, down her back, over the curve of her hip. "Must have been a bad break," he murmured as he gently massaged her bottom.

Sarah's reply was indistinct—she didn't want to talk about her leg, not right now. Not when Dan's hand was gliding along the back of her thigh, clasping her knee, drawing it up over the hard ridges of his legs, caressing the soft, sensitive place behind her knee, then moving down....

His hand stopped. She felt his body tense, and with a sharp hiss of indrawn breath, she tried to jerk her leg out of his grasp. But it was too late.

He hadn't noticed it before. Her legs had always been covered—by the jeans she normally wore, by darkness, a sarong and cold, crystal water. Or he'd been preoccupied, noticing other things. Now he traced the hard ridges of scar tissue with his fingertips and felt his heart contract and a coldness wash through him. She tried to pull away from him, tried to sit up, but he held her tightly until his exploration was done. Then he exhaled slowly and carefully through his nose and said very softly, "How did this happen?"

"I told you—I fell."

"Off what, a building?" His voice lacerated his throat.

"No! I tried something I wasn't ready for, and I landed wrong, that's all. It happens—in sports, gymnastics, dancing—"

"How, goddamn it?" Rage boiled up in him—he couldn't keep it inside! He felt the injury as if it were an insult to his own body. "Who let this happen? Why were you doing something you weren't ready for? Tell me, dammit!"

"Dan..." She lay quietly in his arms, her hand making soothing circles on his stomach. "It doesn't matter anymore, really. It was a long time ago. I'm perfectly fine—I don't even limp, except when I jump off collapsing bridges.''

But his anger was implacable, and when he didn't respond to her efforts to make light of her injury, she sighed and said resignedly, ''It wasn't anybody's fault but my own. I was alone, practicing, dancing beyond myself, trying to prove something. And I used poor judgment—no judgment at all, really. I was upset, angry...crying.''

''Why?'' He was quiet now, too, but there was something dangerous—even deadly—in his voice, and for the first time in a long time, Sarah thought of the panther.

She held on to him tightly while she told him about Michael and Irina and the death of a dream. She told it simply, with few words, although it hadn't been simple at all and there had been a time when she'd thought there weren't enough words in the world to express the pain of her loss and betrayal.

She'd been so young when she'd joined the company— just out of high school. Her parents had wanted her to go to college, but she hadn't been able to see anything but dancing. Oh, she'd been so starry-eyed and sure. She was going to be a principal dancer, a prima ballerina, the toast of San Francisco, New York, Paris, London—the greatest since Fontaine! And then...

''I fell in love,'' she said wryly. ''With the company's artistic director. Michael was a brilliant dancer—I was thrilled that he singled me out for attention. And he was so very charismatic, I suppose I couldn't help falling in love with him.''

She supposed she should have known she was making a fool of herself. But Michael had had a talent for making her feel special—sometimes. And at other times, as if she were nothing at all. He would praise and compliment her and then ignore her completely. Make love to her in secret and stare through her in public. For months she'd ridden an emotional roller coaster, one minute in the clouds and the next minute in the depths of despair. And still, because she loved him so much, she'd believed Michael's promises. Michael's lies.

Until she'd come face-to-face with a truth she couldn't ignore. Proof.

"He'd been acting cool toward me. I didn't understand what was wrong, so I went to his office to talk to him about it. I found him there—with Irina Panova." Her voice became detached. "You may have heard of her—it was big news when she defected—it was in all the papers, television...no? Anyway, she was a tremendous dancer and a big star. She'd joined the company a few months after I did. I admired her so much...." She had to pause, even after so much time, to let the pain relax its grip on her throat. Dan began to stroke her back, moving his hands slowly and mechanically up and down.

"I remember the look on Irina's face—it was so smug and pitying. I don't remember what I said, but I remember Michael saying something rather contemptuous about my having a lot to learn. It was such a shock. I tore off to the practice room, determined to show them both, I suppose, though I don't remember that clearly what I was thinking. I suppose I wasn't thinking. I was dancing blindly, in anger and passion." She paused again, and after a moment said slowly, "I don't remember any pain. Not when it happened. It was the sound that was so awful, like shots—"

He caught her to him and smothered the rest against his chest. He made of his arms a fortress around her, his soothing words an incantation to banish the ghosts of memory.

After a while Sarah stirred and said matter-of-factly, "The breaks were so bad, they thought for a while they might have to take my leg. But I decided I wasn't going to let Michael cost me my leg. He just wasn't worth it."

"Bravo," said Dan softly. He cleared his throat but still tasted his rage, like brass on his tongue. There was a lot he'd like to have said, but he was afraid of betraying too much. So he waited until he knew he could control his voice and then asked quietly, "What about dancing? Can you still do that?"

She shrugged. "I don't know. I haven't wanted to try."

"Are you afraid?"

There was a long silence, and then she drew in a quick, restless breath. "In a way, I guess I have been. Not so much of dancing...."

"What, then?"

She released the breath. "Of taking risks, trusting, loving." She lifted her head suddenly and gazed down at him as if she were seeing him for the first time, her eyes liquid and luminous as melted honey. Her lips parted in a smile that almost stopped his heart. "I think I must be cured, though, because I trusted you, didn't I? Twice. And I lo—"

Dan's head came up, and his mouth covered hers with controlled violence, once again intercepting the forbidden words she offered so innocently. The way Eve offered the apple, he thought bitterly as he rolled her over in the fragrant foliage, thinking of her remark about Eden. Oh, it was a tempting gift, but he knew the rest of the story. She thought that what she was offering him was beautiful and nourishing. She didn't know, as he did, that that same sweet apple had the power to destroy them.

So he distracted her with gentle roughhousing, kissing her until their laughter became sporadic chuckles and then wordless sounds of pleasure and surprise.

"Improvising?" she asked him teasingly, with a catch deep in her throat.

He made a complacent sound, like a tiger purring. "Well, Ah reckon there's more'n one way of doin' it, don't you?"

"Oh, yeah. I wonder—" She gasped and dug her fingers into his shoulders. "I wonder how many—"

"I don't know, darlin'," Dan drawled softly, "but we've got all afternoon to figure it out."

But it had been a long time since the rice cakes and cold fish they'd grabbed before leaving the longhouse that morning, and they'd used up a considerable amount of energy since. So before the afternoon was fully spent, hunger of another kind drove them down from the mountain.

It was just as well, Dan pointed out; he needed to get Sarah home by nightfall anyway. Marina would worry.

No! Sarah wanted to protest. It's too soon! One day in Eden is not enough!

Beyond this tiny island of paradise there was ugliness and violence, fear and uncertainty. There were things she didn't want to have to think about or deal with.

"I wish we could stay here forever," she said fervently to Dan as they approached the Batak village.

He didn't answer her, but the arm across her shoulders tightened in silent sympathy. As if that small gesture had somehow triggered something, like a pebble an avalanche, Sarah suddenly turned into him in a blind rush; her arms went around him, and she held him with a desperate urgency, pressing her hands into his back, wishing with a child's single-mindedness that she didn't have to go, almost believing that if she wished hard enough and held on tightly enough, that her wish would come true.

He lifted her chin and took her mouth with the same urgency, kissing her hard and deep, but at the same time with a measure of restraint. When they turned to walk on again, Sarah saw that his eyes were remote and sad.

She thought, how quickly the sun can disappear and the world turn gray and cold! She could feel him slipping away from her. She wanted desperately to hold on to him, to cry out to him, Wait! What just happened between us? Am I crazy to think it was something important and wonderful? You took me to Eden—don't leave me out in the cold now!

The roller coaster again. For a moment panic fluttered through her stomach. And then she set her mouth and lifted her chin and said, No. No, never again. Her feet were on the ground, and even though the path ahead was full of shadows and she might have to grope her way one step at a time, she was moving under her own power. Never again would she allow herself to be swept helplessly along by the tide!

Dan's hand reached for hers, enclosed it in a warm grasp and lifted it. She felt his exhaled breath flow over her palm and then the firm but gentle pressure of his lips.

No, she thought, as love and certainty rinsed through her and settled into a reservoir of calm resolve, Dan wasn't Michael. He wasn't lying to her, and he'd made no promises, and if he retreated from her sometimes into that lonely, secret world where she couldn't follow, there must be a reason. She would simply have to find out what it was.

They ate supper with the elder's family in the longhouse—rice, steamed vegetables, spicy boiled fish and a mixture of nuts and chopped lime. Then they changed back into their own clothes. Sarah was sorry to give up the soft, comfortable sarongs. It seemed symbolic, somehow, to be leaving behind the graceful simplicity of the sarong to encumber herself once more with the complexities of buttons and zippers, shoes and socks.

She tried to explain to the elder's daughter-in-law about the loss of the stole—with profuse apologies—but the woman just nodded and smiled and pressed the folded sarong back into Sarah's hands.

"She wants you to keep it," Dan said when she looked to him for an explanation.

"Oh, no, I couldn't possibly! It's much too beautiful—"

"It's a gift," Dan said with a shrug and a half smile. "It would be an insult to refuse."

Sarah hugged the shimmering red-and-gold material to her chest and looked from his shuttered eyes to the Batak woman's smiling face. And then, because she felt overwhelmed by the kindness and generosity and because she didn't know the words for "thank you" in Batak, she put her arms around the daughter-in-law and hugged her, too. The children put their hands over their mouths and giggled, the men shuffled their feet and coughed, and the daughter-in-law looked embarrassed, reminding Sarah belatedly that Indonesians aren't normally demonstrative.

But the awkward moment passed, and with much smiling and bowing and handshaking, they took their leave of the elder's longhouse. Most of the village escorted them to the helicopter, trailing out behind the elders like a colorful, undulating Chinese dragon. There was laughter and singing, and when they reached the helicopter, more smiles and bows and shaking of hands.

The three elders took turns shaking Sarah's hand and wishing her happiness and good fortune in broken English. They turned to Dan and did the same, and then the head elder took both of their hands and said something to Dan in Batak that made the whole crowd respond with cries of delight and approval. Dan glanced at Sarah, and with a shrug and a little half smile, replied in the same language. Then, before she could ask for a translation, he hustled her aboard the chopper. If it hadn't seemed so unlikely, she'd have said he was blushing.

"What was that all about?" she shouted when they were in the air and flashing across the shimmering turquoise waters of the lake.

Dan leaned toward her, pretending innocence. "Hmm?"

"What did the elder say to you?"

"Oh, that. He was just inviting us to come back." His eyes were focused intently through the windshield; his hands were firm on the controls. "I told him we'd have to see about that."

Sarah didn't say anything, though she was sure there must be something more he wasn't telling her. She turned to look back at the island and the mountain where just a few hours ago she'd lain naked in Dan's arms, warmed by the sun and sated with love. It was shrouded in clouds now and lit by the red-gold glow of the setting sun, like Bali Hai. Eden.

"Dan," she began softly, and then, realizing he couldn't hear her above the chopper noise, raised it to a shout. "Dan? Why did they welcome you like that, like some long-lost brother? It's almost like they consider you one of them."

He nodded and threw her a smile. "They do. They've adopted me."

"No kidding! Why?" Is there no end to this man's facets? she thought as she watched him struggle with his reticence, wondering with held breath whether he would finally confess his secret.

But after lifting a shoulder and coughing and squirming a little, he said, "Couple years ago during the monsoon, there was quite a bit of flooding on the island—which isn't that unusual—and the village was isolated. The elder's son—that's the husband of the woman that gave you the sarong, by the way—picked the wrong time to have an attack of acute appendicitis. I just happened to be there with a chopper—I'd just made a supply run—and I got him to the hospital, that's all. No big deal. I was just in the right place at the right time, but...they were real grateful. But these people are like that—once you're their friend, you're a friend forever—like family."

When Sarah didn't say anything, Dan looked over at her and found her gazing back at him with eyes that reminded him of little bits of sunset. His chest contracted, and his stomach turned over, and he turned back to the darkening horizon, feeling as if that darkness were creeping over his heart.

Be careful what you wish for—you might get in. So he'd gotten what he'd wanted. He'd made her fall in love with him, carried her off to a romantic island paradise—what had she called it? Eden. Of course, she'd succumbed to the magic, just as another young woman with stars in her eyes had fallen under the spell of the tropics so long ago in Mexico.

Behind them, the island, the lake and then the sun itself dropped below the horizon. Sarah turned in her seat to give them one last look and then faced front again, and Dan knew she was still seeing that rosy glow reflected in the chopper's dark window. Still seeing paradise, thinking it would last forever.

But Dan knew it wasn't real and that it couldn't last, and all he saw in the same reflection was the tragic specter of history repeating itself.

"You don't have to come with me," Sarah said as the chopper's rotors slowed and died. "It's so far, and I know you need to get home, too. I'll be fine." She didn't want to say goodbye to him at the camp in front of Marina, and maybe the rangers, too. She didn't want to say goodbye to him at all.

"Aren't you forgetting something?" Dan's eyes glinted at her in the near darkness. She saw the pale flash of his smile. "The crate," he said softly when she looked him without comprehension. "You'd have a hard time carrying it all by yourself."

He jumped down from the chopper's doorway and held up his hands, and this time there was no hesitation in her. She put her hands in his and felt his muscles bunch and brace, and then she was in his arms, reaching for him, finding his mouth in the darkness, opening her mouth and taking him in like a diver starved for oxygen.

"I don't want—" she began in a panicky little gasp, the way a person might say, "I can't breathe."

Dan's hand came to nudge her chin and then cup it. "Shh," he said as he kissed her, gentling, soothing, bathing her lips with his tongue and his breath, "It's okay…it's all right."

That was all, but it was what she needed. It was going to be all right. She was going to see him again. And in the meantime there were things that had to be done. She nodded and swallowed the lump in her throat and separated herself from him. She bent down and picked up the crate's carry-pole and—at Dan's quiet "Ready?"—shouldered it. Dan clicked on the flashlight, and they set out down the trail to the river.

Marina was waiting for them on the reserve side of the crossing. When she saw the flashlight, she began swinging her lantern in a wide arc and shouting excitedly, something Sarah couldn't quite make out above the water noise. No, she thought. Not again. Her heart began a terrible pounding.

She whispered, "Oh, God, what now?"

Dan gave her a quick, hard look and didn't say anything, just steadied the boat with one foot while they carefully balanced the crate across its gunwales.

The crossing took forever. Not even waiting for them to step ashore, Marina splashed out to meet them, chattering breathlessly as she helped them beach the boat and unload the crate.

"Oh, Sarah—I'm so glad you are finally here—I heard the helicopter fly over. I have been waiting for you—I have such news! I was afraid you were not going to arrive in time—you will have to hurry, but I think you can still make it. Dan can take you in the helicopter—"

Sarah dropped her end of the crate on the riverbank and waved away the swarm of river gnats and mosquitos that were singing around her head. "What are you talking about? Where is Dan supposed to take me? Has something happened? Is it the poachers?"

"No, no, nothing like that! It has been very quiet, everything is fine. No—we've received a letter—it should have arrived last week—just today Joka found it on the floor of the Land Rover! Anyway," she went on excitedly, forestalling Sarah's frustrated exclamation, "it is from the Foundation. They want one of us to speak to the Earthcare Conference in Singapore. Sarah, you have to go. It could mean thousands of dollars in funding for the rehab project and to help stop the poaching—"

"Wait, wait—hold on!" Sarah managed to catch hold of Marina's wildly waving arms and interrupt the cascade of words. "I agree with you, it's great opportunity, but why me? Are you forgetting? I just went on a trip. It's your turn to go."

"Oh, will you forget about whose turn it is?" Marina cried, slapping Sarah's hands away. "You are a much better speaker than I am, especially in English, and you are good in front of people, you know you are! This is too important to be silly about whose turn it is!"

"All right, I'll go!" Sarah clapped a hand to her reeling head. The world, her work, her life were crashing in on her before she was ready. She'd just spent twenty-four hours in Eden—she needed time to adjust! "All right, let's see...when is it?" She needed time to write a speech, get some slides together, figure out something to wear.

Marina caught her breath in a small hiccup and said, "It's tomorrow."

"Tomorrow! But that's impossible! I can't even get to Singapore by tomorrow, and even if I could—"

"It's tomorrow night. You can get there by tomorrow night, if Dan takes you to Medan and you catch a flight to Singapore—"

"But even if we did that, I'd need time to get things together, to pack—"

Dan put his hand on the back of her neck and gave it a gentle squeeze, and she realized only then that he'd been there all along. "We'll work it out," he said quietly.

Marina gave him a grateful look, but Sarah turned to him and whispered, "I can't ask you to do that."

"You're not askin', I'm offerin'," he replied in that drawl of his, the soft, dangerous one, not the exaggerated, fooling-around one that always made her laugh. And then, in his normal voice he said, "Listen, how about this? I need to refuel the chopper anyway. Why don't you take tonight to get ready, and I'll come back for you in the morning."

"But . . . I don't know if I can get a flight so late."

"Don't worry about it—I'll take you to Singapore. Hey—" He tightened his hand on her neck, silencing her protest. "AMINCO has a plane at Medan. It's the fastest way. There's some business I've been meaning to attend to in Singapore, anyway."

She heard an odd note creep into his voice and turned toward him in unspoken question, but it was too dark to see his face. His hands settled on her shoulders. "Go on," he said softly, "get yourself ready. Get a good night's sleep. I'll see you in the morning." There was nothing in his voice now but warmth and encouragement, and Sarah wondered if she'd imagined that curious hollowness.

"Yes, go!" Marina chimed in briskly. "We have so much to do. Come on, I'll help you."

Dan was already climbing back into the boat. Marina grabbed Sarah's arm and pulled her toward the path, and it felt to her as if she were being stretched on a rack.

All the way home, Marina chattered excitedly about the trip—what slides to take, points Sarah must be sure to get across in her speech, what to wear, what sights she must see in Singapore. Sarah was glad to leave her at the quarantine cages and enjoy a few minutes of silent aloneness as she made her way in the dark to the cabin. Her head was swimming. It had been so full already with Dan and his enigmas, with her new and overwhelming feelings, with all that had happened in the last twenty-four hours—and now there was Singapore and an opportunity to speak to an international environmental conference on the plight of the orangutans! It was too much! What she needed now was peace and quiet and a chance to think!

She pushed open the door to the cabin and walked in. Momentum carried her halfway across the lighted room, but her legs had already turned to water. For a moment or two her mind remained empty, every thought driven from it by the small rectangular object that was lying on the table.

Chapter 12

It was her pack of cigarettes, there wasn't any doubt about that. The same brand, a little bit crumpled, a few cigarettes missing....

Sarah found herself standing beside the table looking down at it with no recollection of having walked across the room. A hand that had no connection with her reached down and picked it up. There was a tiny crackling sound. The faintest odor of tobacco.

"I washed your sheets," Marina said from the cabin doorway. "I thought it would be a good time, while you were gone." She waited, her dark gaze steady, neither asking nor accusing.

Sarah cleared her throat and said stiffly, "I'm sorry. I should have told you."

"Why didn't you?"

Blunt, straightforward, honest—that was Marina. No masks, no secrets, no enigmas. "I found them," Sarah said tonelessly. "Last week."

"Last week! But why—"

"I found them in the Land Rover, under the seat."

Marina threw up her hands in exasperation and crossed the room. "In the—but that's crazy, how would they get there? No one uses the Land Rover except you and me and the rangers, and none of us smokes."

"They're Dan's," Sarah said in a hard, flat voice she'd never used before. "He left them there the day he took me to see old Beau. He put them on the dash, and they must have slid off when we hit a pothole in the road. I didn't really notice then, but I remembered when...I found them." She took a deep breath and dropped the cigarettes onto the table. They lay there with the lantern light glinting off the cellophane wrapping, like a single, malevolent eye.

Marina caught Sarah's arm and peered searchingly into her face. "And you were afraid?" she said slowly, her voice soft and incredulous. "Did you think Dan was our poacher?"

"Well, I—" Feeling a sudden overwhelming need to sit down, Sarah groped for a chair and sank into it. "I don't know. I guess I did. I thought it was possible." She felt nauseated, even saying the words.

"Dan? Oh, Sarah!" In a passionate little flurry, Marina kicked back a chair and sat down, too, leaning toward her across the table. "How could you think such a thing! Just because of a pack of cigarettes?"

"It's not just the cigarettes—although, you know something weird? He hasn't smoked this brand since that day. If he's innocent, why did he suddenly switch brands, huh? It's other things, too—little things. It's like they say in cop shows, you know? Motive and opportunity. Motive is obvious—" Marina interrupted with a snort. Sarah faltered and then rushed on. It was difficult to imagine Dan motivated by greed, but she was playing her own devil's advocate and wasn't about to be sidetracked by common sense.

"And he certainly has the opportunity. He's already close by, and he has the helicopter whenever he needs it."

"There are others who have the same opportunity," Marina said darkly. A tiny spasm tightened her mouth as she added, "And much more motive."

"Yes, but Dan is the boss, he can come and go as he pleases. And he knows quite a bit about orangutans, Marina. I was surprised by how much he knows. And other things I can't really explain." Some things had no words; they were just feelings, images, impressions. A look in the eyes, a tone of voice that made her think of a panther lying in ambush. Catlike reflexes and a whip-hard body, and the way he'd come through an open window in total darkness in the face of a hunting rifle and, in a matter of seconds, disarmed and subdued her. One thing she knew for certain—Dan Cisco was no stranger to violence.

Marina had been listening to all this with a thoughtful frown on her face. When Sarah paused, she suddenly interjected, with characteristic bluntness, "You have just been with Dan, is that true?"

Sarah's stomach did a slow flip-flop. She swallowed and whispered, "Yes."

"And after this, do you still think he could be a poacher?"

Suddenly Sarah's throat hurt too much to talk. She was afraid that if she said one more word she would start to cry. But Marina was waiting, and that terrible question was dangling there! She swallowed several times and finally managed to whisper, "I don't know what to think." Then in spite of all her efforts, she was crying anyway, shading her eyes from Marina with her hand. "Oh, God, Mari, when I'm with him I don't even think of it, it's just not possible. I think I know what kind of man he is and that he could never do something so horrible. I see that he's kind and gentle and compassionate. And then I see this—" she batted the cigarettes angrily with her hand "—and the ugly thoughts come back. I just can't help it. It makes me feel so awful to think that *I* think that someone I love could do such things. When I'm with him, I know that I would trust him with my life, but then—"

"Do you love Dan?" Marina's question was matter-of-fact, almost conversational.

Sarah drew her hand across her eyes and sniffed. Then she wiped her cheeks with both hands, took a deep breath and said dully, "Yes. I do."

"Well, then—"

"But that's the reason I can't trust him, don't you see?" Sarah cried in a sudden breathless rush of excitement, because the realization had just that moment come to her. "What if I'm being blinded by the fact that I love him? I keep thinking about all these criminals you read about and the poor women who love them. Did they know, deep down in their hearts, or were they completely fooled? I just don't know."

Marina was emphatically shaking her head. "But you are not a fool. You are an intelligent, healthy woman—" she tapped her head to show what kind of health she meant "—and I think you would know. You should trust yourself."

"But that's just it—I can't trust myself! I have terrible judgment where men are concerned. It's happened to me before, when I fell in love with a man I thought was one thing and he turned out to be something entirely different."

"You are talking about Michael."

"Yes! I thought he was so wonderful, and he turned out to be a total jerk. How do I know Dan—"

"Dan is not Michael," Marina stated flatly. "Michael was a liar. Dan may not say very much, but what he does say is the truth. I am sure of it."

"You don't think he is guilty, do you?" Sarah said wistfully, envying Marina her conviction.

Marina had picked up the cigarette pack and was turning it this way and that, staring at it. "No," she said slowly, "I don't. But it doesn't matter what I think, does it? It's what you know in your heart. You have to be certain."

Sarah gave a high, hopeless laugh. "I wish I could be. I don't know what to do."

"Well," said Marina, "I know what I would do."

"What's that?"

"I would show the cigarettes to Dan and tell him everything. Then I would ask him to explain." She shrugged, and Sarah had to laugh. Yes, she thought, that was exactly what Marina would do. "I know there is an explanation," Marina said confidently, and dropped the pack onto the table, its faint *smack* putting an emphatic period to the sentence.

When Sarah didn't say anything, Marina pushed the cigarettes slowly across the table toward her. "Sarah," she said softly and with a curious intensity, "trust me. You will be with him in Singapore tomorrow. Please—ask him."

The grand ballroom of the brand-new, steel-and-glass Hotel International in Singapore was all aglitter, a veritable sea of crystal and white linen. A classy affair, Dan acknowledged, though he preferred the old Raffles Hotel, himself. He liked something a little smaller and quieter, something with lazily whirling fans on the ceiling, instead of crystal chandeliers that looked like upside-down wedding cakes, and maybe with a few potted palms and a seedy-looking fat guy in a crumpled white suit drinking beer at the next table.

He ditched his cigarette in the receptacle beside the huge double doors and moved back into the shadows behind a bank of flowers, trying to see across that vast and crowded room, searching the assembly for one shining golden head.

Somewhere up there in the front of the room, under the huge stylized hand and globe that was the international symbol for Earthcare—that was where Doc would be.

She'd wanted him to join her there, and he'd actually rented a tux from the hotel's men's shop for the occasion, but he'd known he didn't really belong there, among the dignitaries and scientists, the celebrities and the merely rich. In the end he'd made his excuses and, after escorting her to her place at the speakers' table, had slipped into the back of the ballroom with some members of the press corps.

While dessert was being served and the dignitaries introduced, he'd gone out in search of some fresh air and a cigarette. For a while he'd wandered around the lobby, watching people come and go, quite a few of them in evening clothes. Then he'd caught a glimpse of himself in a wall of plate-glass mirrors, and it had given him a considerable jolt to realize that he did look just as though he belonged there.

But, as he was finding out, looks could be deceiving.

He thought about the way Doc had looked when he'd escorted her across this same lobby about an hour ago. She'd worn the Batak sarong, but she sure hadn't looked anything like the girl on the island. She'd seemed about a foot taller, for one thing, in a pair of gold high-heeled sandals she'd bought that afternoon in the hotel boutique. She'd also bought a jacket made of some kind of shimmery material that set off the gold threads woven into the sarong. She was wearing earrings, long, gold ones, and for the first time since he'd known her, she'd put on makeup.

But in her case the change was more than just the clothes and the makeup. It was the way she stood, the way she walked, the way she held her head—so cool, elegant, self-assured. Like a damned duchess, Dan thought, remembering the laughing, barefooted girl with the sun in her hair and mischief in her eyes, and remembering the way she'd looked slipping out of the sarong, running to the water.

The memory jolted him in a predictable way, and it was at that point he'd decided it was time to go back to the ballroom.

Applause stirred the gathering like a breeze through dry leaves. There were anticipatory noises—coughs and chair scrapes and the minute clink of ice cubes. The ballroom darkened, leaving only the illuminated globe to shed its cone of light on the speaker's lectern below.

Dan's mouth quirked wryly at the theatricality of it all, but the smile faded as he watched Sarah move into the light. He thought she seemed very small and far away. He suddenly needed a drink. He hadn't been this nervous since he'd had to lead the Pledge of Allegiance at his eighth-grade graduation.

As she stepped to the lectern, he saw her sweep the room with a searching glance and knew she was looking for him. Not finding him, she settled her shoulders and set her head at that graceful tilt he was beginning to find so familiar— and, for some reason, so poignant—and began to speak. Her amplified voice filled the room, mellow as church bells on a soft spring morning.

As he listened, her voice seemed to fade into background hum, and instead he heard words and phrases from the past, fragmented like children's voices overheard from a distance. Visual images in warm-gold colors swirled like leaves through his memory.

Sarah's hair, gleaming in the light of flickering torches; her laughter, the very first time he heard it; his hand and hers lying side by side on an orangutan's rusty coat; a smug and throaty "Improvising"; water drops trembling on a cold-firmed nipple; honey-gold eyes, swimming with tears; "I wanted to be a dancer...."

And finally, the thing that rose to a crescendo with the applause and stayed to echo in the silence that followed it: "I was going to be the toast of San Francisco, New York, Paris, London...."

It was where she belonged, Dan thought bleakly, poised and elegant, all dressed in gold, dining on fine china and basking in the limelight and applause. He knew it, and in her heart, so did Sarah. He didn't know what she was trying to prove by living in a jungle, playing nanny to a bunch of apes. Maybe she was still hiding from the hurt and rejection she'd suffered at the hands of that bastard—what was his name?—Michael. Maybe she was just trying to put her life back together. Either way, sooner or later she was going to get it out of her system and go back where she belonged. They always did.

Suddenly he felt his chest contract and his stomach twist into a painful, throbbing knot. His throat closed, and something stung inside his head like a burgeoning sneeze. He wanted to tear out of that place, out of the city, to run until he found a place where the sand was hot under his feet and the sky wide and empty over his head, where there was no one to hear him release his frustration and loneliness.

It was a feeling he hadn't had in years, not since he was a small boy. And since he had nowhere to run, now as then, he dealt with it the only way he knew how, the way he'd taught himself to do, so long ago. In his mind he made himself armor of stone; inside it he was strong and untouchable, and no one could see his pain.

When he was sure his armor was firmly in place, he slipped through the double doors and into the lobby, where he calmly lit a cigarette and leaned back against the wall to wait for Sarah.

She knew the moment she laid eyes on him.

She'd come off the dais on a cloud of euphoria, shaky with adrenaline, dizzy with success, glowing from the accolades of people she admired and respected—and with a great, empty void inside her. As soon as she could, she'd gone looking for the one person who could fill it, moving through the crowd of well-wishers with the single-minded purpose of a thirsty animal heading for a water hole.

When she saw him in the lobby, she cried, "Dan!" and started forward in a joyful surge. He looked up, dropped his cigarette into a receptacle and straightened slowly. And she halted while her insides did a double flip-flop, once with love, once with fear.

For a few moments she just stood there trembling, so desperately needing his arms around her, pouring strength into her, needing to share her triumph with him, knowing it all meant nothing unless he added his praise to it. And then she thought, Dammit, no! She wasn't going to be intimidated by that mask of his, not anymore. She didn't care how impenetrable it appeared, she'd seen him without it. Dan, the man she loved, was in there somewhere, and right now she needed him!

So she marched up to him and bravely and breathlessly announced, "Hi, I need a hug."

He gave a little chuckle of surprise and drawled, "Well, I reckon I can oblige."

His arms came around her, hard and unfamiliar in the rented jacket. He smelled unfamiliar, too, of tobacco and wine and the hotel barber shop's after-shave. But the smooth, hard line of jaw against her temple was Dan's, and so were the fingers burrowing into her hair, tracing her hairline behind her ear and around to the back of her neck. Sarah closed her eyes and felt the trembling ease and warmth and calm pour into her, and she wondered when this strange, unapproachable man had become her refuge and strength.

After awhile she stepped back, laughing, and said, "Well, I think that's done it for the time being. So, what did you think? How did I do?"

A spark of amusement glittered through the veil of lashes. "Doc, you know good and well how you did. You were dynamite. And you looked like a million dollars up there, to boot."

Sarah took a breath and said, "Ah, now I feel better." Laughter bubbled up in her, part exhilaration, part relief.

"So," Dan said, "are you all done here?"

"All done." She lifted her arms and let them fall. "Boy, am I glad that's over with! I'd forgotten how nervous I get when I have to speak in front of people."

"You'd never know it," Dan muttered under his breath. He looked at his watch. "So, what would you like to do? This *is* Singapore, world-reknowned for its nightlife. Want to go paint the town?"

Sarah caught her breath and pinned her lower lip between her teeth. "You know what I'd really like?"

"No, what?"

She searched his face, trying to find a way to penetrate the mask, and settled finally on his eyes. "I want to take a bath," she said, and saw something flicker in them. "A real, honest-to-goodness bath, with bubbles and everything. Do you know how long it's been? Ages. You know, I think that's one of the things I miss most."

Dan's chuckle was indulgent. "You're pretty easy to please. Okay, so you just want to go up to the room, is that it?"

"That's it." *The* room—not *our* room.

"Don't you have anything—purse, whatever?"

"Oops, yes, and my slides, too. I left everything in the ballroom. I'll go get them and meet you at the elevators."

"Yeah," Dan murmured, "you do that."

Sarah hesitated, wondering at the preoccupied tone in his voice, then said with determined brightness, "Okay, see you soon."

Dan waited just until the ballroom doors had settled behind her, then crossed the lobby to the bank of pay telephones. He took a business card out of his shirt pocket, stared at it for a moment or two while he worked a muscle in his jaw, then dialed one of the numbers on the card. While he listened to the ring, he took in air and huffed it out, like an athlete psyching himself up for the performance of his life.

"Hello," he said when the receiver crackled to life, "this is Dan Cisco. I'm sorry to call so late— Oh, just fine, thanks. Listen, I'm in town, and if you've got time tomorrow, I'd like to talk to you about that job in the States, if it's still open.... Good, good.... Yeah, tomorrow morning will be fine.... Okay, sure.... Don't worry, I'll find it.... What's that?" He laughed softly. "Yeah, well, let's just say I've changed my mind. But you're still going to have to make it worth my while.... Yeah, well, I'll see you tomorrow, then. 'Night." He cradled the receiver and stood still for a long time, staring at it.

He waited for Sarah by the elevators. When he saw her coming, he looked at the cigarette in his hand with distaste and put it out; for some reason he'd been smoking a lot this evening.

She opened her purse and took out the key to the room the conference coordinators had reserved for her and handed it to him. Her head was high, and her chin had that self-confident tilt he'd resented so much the first time he'd seen her. But her eyes—they licked at him like candle flames.

Mentally checking his armor for chinks, he took the key from her and punched the elevator call button.

Sarah hated the elevator. It was one of those glass things that go up and down on the outside of the building, giving passengers a breathtaking view of the city and the harbor. This afternoon it had made her so dizzy, watching the ground drop away from her, that she'd had to close her eyes and take deep breaths to battle the nausea.

Tonight, probably because of the darkness, it didn't seem so bad. As the elevator rose higher and the spangled carpet of lights spread out below them, she turned to the window, risking a look. "It's beautiful," she said, mostly just to break the silence.

"Yeah, it is, from here." She could hear him fiddling with the key in his pocket. "You sure you don't want to go out?"

His voice was remote; he seemed as far out of reach as those pinpoints of light beyond the elevator's glass walls, and he was slipping farther away from her by the minute. Panic rose in her like a hiccup. She didn't know how to stop it!

"Positive," she said evenly as the elevator bumped gently at their floor.

Dan unlocked the door, then went ahead of her into the room and turned on the lights. It was a nice room, a big room, with a single king-size bed. Neither of them had said anything earlier about the accommodations or the sleeping arrangements, and they didn't do so now. They both knew it would have been pure hypocrisy.

And yet—suddenly Sarah wasn't at all sure. Dan had dropped the room key on the dresser and was standing in the middle of the room surveying it as if he were the bellman, giving it one last check before departing. She hesitated, then quickly shut the door and slipped past him to dump her things in a pile on the table—and found that her heart was hammering as frantically as if she'd just walked in and discovered a stranger in her room. As she looked at Dan's closed, dark face and rigid profile, she thought that was just what she had done. He was a stranger. She didn't know him.

She couldn't reach him! She drew a quick, panicky breath and turned blindly toward the window, noticing irrelevantly that it had much the same view as the one from the elevator. As she stood in front of it fighting desperately for control, she felt Dan move to stand behind her, but keeping a little distance away.

"Thought you didn't care for heights." The words were flippant, but the sound was like tearing cloth.

"I don't." She shivered and turned her head slightly as he moved up beside her. They stood there, not touching, not talking. Tension filled all the space inside Sarah's head, like a scream amplified to torture pitch. She wanted to put her hands over her ears to block it out.

"Didn't you want to take a bath?"

Sarah cleared her throat and said, "Yes. I'm going to."

The tension-scream, which had subsided a little, began to rise again. Just when she was sure she couldn't stand another second of it, Dan took out his cigarette, lit one and waved the match to extinguish it. Something about the familiar action seemed strange to her, but it wasn't until he stepped away from her to reach for the ashtray on the nightstand that she realized what it was. His movements were jerky and disconnected; what was missing was his natural, fluid grace.

She thought, He's having as much trouble with this as I am. For some reason that awareness made her feel stronger. She thought about the incriminating pack of cigarettes in the top drawer of the nightstand, just inches from his hand. Maybe this was the best time to ask about them. Things were already so strained between them, it seemed as though she might have nothing to lose.

She caught a quick breath and opened her mouth, but the words that came out weren't quite what she'd expected.

With a host of butterflies carousing inside her, she smiled and said shakily, "Dan, am I makin' you nervous?"

His head came up. He gave a short little laugh of surprise and shook his head, exhaling smoke.

"What would it take for you to be easy with me?" Sarah quoted softly, not waiting for him to reply.

Dan stubbed out his barely smoked cigarette and came toward her. "I'm sorry, Doc," he said in a rusted voice, stopping an arm's length away, his crooked smile tugging at her heart. "You just look so damn different."

"Not as different as you do," she pointed out, her own voice as uneven as his. "At least I'm still wearing a sarong."

"And a few other things." He touched the sleeve of her jacket.

She shrugged out of it and let it drop to the floor. "There, is that better?"

"It's a start."

She stepped out of her shoes. Her eyes were warm and liquid. Dan began to feel slightly disoriented, as if he were floating in them. Slowly he lifted his hand and pulled off one of the golden earrings and then the other. She gave a soft little sigh and brushed back of his hand with her cheek. There was quivering deep inside of him, like the trembling of muscles under unbearable strain. Did she feel it? He held his breath, feeling his armor weaken.

Something moved—her lips, his hand . . . who knew for certain? It might not have been movement at all, but just the impact of his thoughts, his emotions, his desires, colliding with hers. Then suddenly his mouth was meeting hers in a collision of another kind—bruising and passion violent, a shocking penetration and gasping reception, her hands tangling feverishly in his hair, his hands spread wide on her hips, pressing her hard against him in bold and blatant possession.

Yes! he exulted in silent triumph as desire raged through him. It was all right! He felt powerful, invincible, in control. He could take her like this, on a purely physical level, and still keep his armor intact. He could have her quivering and whimpering in his arms and never give away the magnitude of his own need.

Yes, Sarah thought, rejoicing in the bruising strength of his hands, the raw hunger in his mouth, the masculine power in his body. It was all right. She was in control again, confident of her own strength and power. Hers was a quiet strength, an inner strength, as old as humankind, the power of a nurturing body, a soft voice and a gentle hand. The knowledge that, though he was strong, he needed her. He was hungry, and she had food to give him.

The desire to give felt like an earthquake, an explosion in her soul. She'd never known anything so devastating—much greater than purely physical desire. She felt as if she might burst with it—she couldn't hold him close enough, kiss him deeply enough! She wanted to take him inside her and, at the same time, fill *him*. Most of all, she wanted to say it, shout it, trumpet it for all the world to hear: *Dan, I love you. I love you!*

This time it was he who stripped her sarong from her— she didn't know exactly how or when, but she whimpered a little in protest at the rasp of coarse fabric and buttons against her sensitized skin. Dan gave a low-throated sound of masculine satisfaction and picked her up in his arms.

"Dan—" she gasped when he laid her down on the bed, holding on to his neck and gazing at him with dark, stricken eyes.

"What?"

"I'm still—I'm not—"

He laughed and leaned over to silence her with a deep, slow, stroking, pulsating kiss. When he pulled away from her at last, her lips looked wet and swollen and her eyes intoxicated.

"It's okay," he said huskily, kissing her one more time. "The only good thing about a tux is that it does have pockets."

He watched her eyes, waiting for it—the tiger's glow. He laughed when he saw it, in exultation and delight, and kissed her again and again, teasing and tormenting her, arousing her to whimpering, gasping frustration while her fingers trembled on his zipper and buttons. Her hands reached for him, discarding clothing without any care at all, rubbing and stroking his skin as if she couldn't get enough of touching him. Her fingers pressed deeply, urgently into the small of his back, but he held himself away from her, kissing her breasts, her stomach and the downy mound below, drawing small, helpless cries from her when he tugged each turgid nipple deeply into his mouth and when he probed the shallow depression of her navel with his tongue.

He eased her legs apart and kissed the silky soft places on her inner thighs and felt her breathing grow sharp, the muscles under his cheek tense and tighten. Ruthlessly, he caught her legs and held them open, and the hummingbird quivering he felt deep in the muscles beneath his hands awoke a similar trembling in him.

She gasped, "Dan—I need—please..." and tangled her fingers in his hair, but still he held her and, raising her to him, kissed her deeply and intimately, stroking her, coaxing her closer and closer to the brink. He held her without gentleness while her body writhed in mindless struggle and wave after wave of shudders rocked her, needing to control, fighting for mastery not of her but of himself.

Maybe... if he held her tightly enough, he could hold on to the last crumbling remnants of his armor.

She sobbed his name once more. Her fingers flexed, spread wide and pushed at him with a new desperation.

Then at last he straightened and, still holding her open to him, came to kneel between her thighs.

Her body had a dusky, sultry look, her skin a moist, golden sheen. He could feel the heat in her, passion to match his own. She waited for him now, her chest and belly heaving with every breath, her mouth beestung, her eyes slumberous.

He whispered, "Now, Doc..." on a long exhalation, and leaned forward, holding her still with just the pressure of his body as he caught her hands and began, with excruciating slowness, to enter her. She drew in a long, shuddering breath and held it, clamping down on her swollen lower lip with her teeth as he gradually increased the pressure, drawing out the suspense, carrying her with him, forcing her to stay with him, controlling her, controlling himself. And then she opened her eyes. Tiger eyes. They clung to his face while he brought himself at last into her body, and he felt as if their light and warmth were coming inside him.

Awe and wonder washed through him like a tidal wave, taking the last shards of his armor with it. He knew what it must have cost her—he hadn't asked it of her, she'd done it of her own accord, done it for him, like an offering or a gift. Never in his life had he received such a gift. Reverently, he framed her face with his hands, hardly daring to believe the gift was his. Looking into her eyes, he felt as if he were falling, tumbling from a great height into the sun.

When he was sheathed in her as deeply as he could be, he felt her smile, and with her eyes still warming him with their own sunshine, he heard her say the words at last.

"I love you, Dan."

I love you.

Oh, yes, Sarah thought, it was all there in his smoky, pain-filled eyes and ravaged face. She wanted to tell him it was all right, that he didn't have to say the words out loud. She felt it as surely as she felt his body, deep inside her. She knew it as surely as she knew she loved him and that he could never, ever harm her.

She touched his face, smoothing the lines of strain in his cheeks and forehead, brushing his lips with the gentlest of caresses. And finally, with profound relief and overwhelming joy, she let her weighted eyelids fall and gave herself up to him completely—hard, surging body in her arms, sweat-slippery back beneath her hands, passion-whispers in her ears—half words, half thought—and in her mind only one word: Dan.

Then her body and her mind came together, a wrenching, grinding collision of physical and emotional passion that she feared would tear her apart. She cried out and dug her fingers into Dan's back while her body clenched and tightened and she fought to hang on, to hold herself together just a little longer, until she heard his cry torn from him by the forces of his own collision, and knew that there was no longer any need to hold on.

The explosion left her shattered and incoherent, like the shocked survivor of a calamity. Half laughing, half crying, she felt Dan's body settle gently onto hers, felt his breath blow softly by ear as he joined his shaken laughter with hers. He half lifted her into his arms and rolled sideways with her, keeping her warmly and securely enfolded. It was a long time before she settled down, and when she did, sleep came like the twilight's subtle eclipse by night, almost without her noticing.

So this is what it's like, she thought, waking in the night with her legs and Dan's still intimately entwined, his heart-beat in her ears, the scent of him in her nostrils and his body heat her only blanket. His breathing was regular and deep, wholly masculine, but at the same time oddly childlike. Vulnerable. A small aftershock of awe and love shook her to her core, and she thought, This is what he's like without his mask.

She remembered the cigarettes in the nightstand drawer and smiled. Tomorrow, she thought, just before she snuggled back down in the warm embrace of sleep. Tomorrow she would throw the awful things away. She knew now beyond any shadow of doubt; she didn't need to ask him about them anymore.

Dan woke up to a delightful and unfamiliar sound. Singing—well, humming, actually. It was coming from the bathroom. Doc's voice. He realized that he'd never heard her sing before. He thought the tune she was humming sounded familiar, but it took him a while to place it, and when he did, the smile on his face spread through his whole body. It was a Batak hymn, one of the ones they'd heard that Sunday morning on the island.

He stretched, then added Sarah's pillows to his and hoisted himself to a semisitting position. Her scent still clung to the sheets and pillowcases, flooding him with sensory memories of the night just past, making him smile all over again.

The digital clock on the television set across the room said 8:25. Plenty of time to get to his ten-thirty appointment. A tiny spasm twisted his belly when he thought about that, but he knew he was doing the right thing—more than ever, after last night. If he had to choose between fieldwork and Doc, it was no contest. He didn't know why it had been such a hard decision in the first place—it seemed so simple to him now. Sarah didn't belong in the jungle, and eventually she was going to go back to where she did belong. So he'd go with her. This, he vowed, was where history stopped repeating itself.

Wonder where I'll end up? he thought as he reached for his cigarettes. Houston or Dallas wouldn't be too bad—at least it was Texas. On the other hand, there was New York. But Doc might like New York.

Damn. He was out of matches. Well, he thought, there ought to be some here someplace. Hotel rooms always had matches. He pulled open the top drawer of the nightstand.

Chapter 13

Dan stared at the open drawer for several full seconds before he reached in and took out the cigarettes. His first thought—that the maid had fallen down on her job—didn't stay with him long. After that, thoughts fell on him like an avalanche, and it took him a while to dig himself out of the pile and figure out what in the hell was going on.

He recognized the pack, at least he thought he did. What he couldn't figure out was what Sarah was doing with the damn things and why they were in her nightstand drawer in a Singapore hotel room. However, he didn't spend much time worrying about that point because there were too many other things to sort out, and the more things fell into place, the less he liked the picture.

Sarah had stopped singing. All Dan could hear coming from the bathroom now were water noises—splashes and sloshes and occasionally a running faucet. Keeping one eye on the bathroom door, he picked up the telephone and got the long-distance operator. While he was waiting for the connection, he kept turning the pack over and over, frowning at it. He had a bad feeling about this.

"Good morning, AMINCO. *Selamat pagi.* How may I—"

"Yeah, this is Dan Cisco. Hey listen, is Tank Guthrie around?"

"Oh, hello, Mr. Cisco. I wasn't expecting to hear from you today. How is Singapore?"

Dan silently ground his teeth and said patiently, "Fine, real good. I need to speak to Tank—is he there?"

"I'm sorry, Mr. Cisco, he isn't. He is in Medan, on business. He didn't leave a number where he could be reached. May I have him get in touch with you when he returns?"

"Any idea when that'll be?"

"Sometime tomorrow, that's all I know. I'm sorry."

"So am I," Dan said dryly.

Just as he was hanging up the phone, Sarah came out of the bathroom wearing a towel that reminded him of the sleep sarong she'd worn on the island. He managed to palm the cigarettes and slip them under a pillow, but not even her smile and the kiss she gave him, fresh and sweet and warm as summer rain, could hide the fact that his bad feelings had just gotten a whole lot worse.

"Oh, who was that?" she asked, innocently curious. And then, pulling away from him to look at his face she said, "Uh-oh, bad news?"

"Yeah, I'm afraid so." He drew in a breath of her fragrance and held it, letting it rinse through him like cooling balm. So clean, he thought, drinking her in, his face buried in the moist curve of her neck, his mouth exploring the silky drape of her collarbone. So soft. The towel was down around her waist. Her breasts were pillowed against his chest, and his hands were making long, gliding strokes up and down her back. Soft and sweet, clean and fresh—and damned precious to him!

He let his breath out and reluctantly put her away from him. "Trouble at home," he said with a grimace. "Gotta get back."

"Now?" He could see in her eyes that she didn't really understand. Damn, he thought, why did everything have to show in her eyes?

But he couldn't let her get caught in what was coming; he had to keep her out of the way until he'd gotten to the bottom of this thing, no matter what it took. He just couldn't risk it. He didn't know what he'd do if anything happened to her now.

"Yeah," he said, throwing back the sheet, "right now, in fact—soon as I can get my pants on."

"Sounds serious," she said, her gaze following him across the room. "Is it? Serious, I mean? Can you tell me what's wrong?" When he didn't answer she got up and came to him and put her arms around him from behind. "I'm sorry," she whispered. "If you don't want to tell me, I understand. I don't mean to pry, it's just that I don't want anything to happen to you. I don't even want you to cross a street—"

"Hey, Doc," he growled, turning in her arms, "you can pry all you want to. Remember now, I want you to be—"

"Easy with me, I know," she finished with him, laughing. "Okay then, is it?"

"Serious? No, not really," Dan said with an inner grimace of distaste. There wasn't anything in the world he hated as much as lying. He did his best not to. "Just some trouble with one of the men. But I'm probably the only one who can fix things—you know how that is."

"Yeah." But she said it with a sigh, laying her forehead on his chest, and he couldn't resist pulling her close, wasting precious seconds just to feel her soft, silky body all down the length of his.

He could see them in the dresser mirror, standing naked with their arms around each other, dusky and golden, dark and fair. He liked what he saw, and he liked what he felt, and he knew that the decisions he'd made in the last twenty-four hours were the right ones. They were going to be good together, for a long, long time.

But there was something he had to take care of first.

"Gotta go, darlin'," he said hoarsely, putting her away from him.

"I'll get dressed."

She headed for the bathroom, but he pulled her back. "No." It came out so harshly she turned to look at him. He cleared his throat. "Look, there really isn't time. Soon as I get my pants and shoes on, I'm outa here. You've still got hair and all that other stuff—" He waved his hand vaguely, and then rushed on, heading off her argument. "And there's the tux—I'm going to need you to take that back for me. Listen, Doc." He put his hands on her shoulders and looked into her eyes. "I hate to cut this short for you. Singapore's a great city. I think you should stay, do some shopping, see some sights. The conference is paying for your travel expenses, right?"

She nodded. "I guess so."

"There, you see? You can stay as long as you want to. Take a commercial flight. When you get to Medan, call AMINCO, and I'll come get you in the chopper. How's that?"

She nodded again and said gamely, "All right, sure. I guess I can do that." But he could see she wasn't happy about it.

Neither was he, but it couldn't be helped. He kissed her— not very satisfyingly—then took her firmly by the shoulders and headed her back into the bathroom.

He dressed quickly, slipping the cigarettes into his shirt pocket while Sarah's back was turned. He wasn't sure what he meant to do with them, but they represented a lot of questions he wanted answered. And he figured the best person to give him the answers was the person those cigarettes belonged to.

After Dan had gone, Sarah sat in her hotel room feeling gray and lonely. She hadn't really wanted to stay. The conference was over, sight-seeing wasn't much fun without someone to share it with, and she didn't feel like shopping. She'd had fun yesterday, picking out the shoes and jacket to go with the sarong, but then, Dan had been with her. Except maybe for some new underwear, there just wasn't anything she needed, and besides, she was worried.

She'd known from the way he'd tried to shield his eyes from her that something was bothering him. Whatever the problem was at home, he was worried about it. But he'd seemed so genuinely sorry about disappointing her that she'd agreed to stay just to make him feel better. Now she wished she hadn't. What in the world was she going to do with herself all day?

Well, she thought dispiritedly, there was the tux to take back. She could do that. And there were those stupid cigarettes, too. She'd promised herself she was going to get rid of them. She might as well take care of that right now.

She opened the nightstand drawer.

Dan was sitting in the back of a taxi that was stopped at a red light when he remembered the appointment he'd made for ten-thirty that morning. He swore under his breath and tapped the driver on the shoulder. It was going to cost him some time, but his whole future with Doc was riding on that interview, and he wasn't about to blow it.

The light turned green. Dan shoved some bills at the driver, grunted, "Keep the change," and dove out into traffic as horns blared and brakes squealed. Tough, Dan thought. He'd been sworn at in more than one language in his lifetime.

The sights and sounds and smells of Singapore ebbed and flowed all around him, but as far as Dan was concerned, looking for a phone booth was pretty much the same no matter where you were. He may just as well have been in New York, or Fresno, for that matter.

He finally found one outside a Chinese restaurant, slipped in just ahead of a huffy American lady with a camera and a pair of sunglasses hanging around her neck and dialed the number he wanted. Shutting the phone booth's door kept out the American lady and most of the noise, but not the odors from the Chinese restaurant. His stomach began to growl, reminding him that he hadn't had breakfast.

"I'm sorry, Mr. Rockwell is on another line," said a pleasantly accented voice in his ear. "Would you like to hold?"

Dan looked at his watch and swore under his breath. "Yeah, all right, but, hey, don't forget me, okay? ... Dammit." The line was already dead.

Resigned and hungry, he settled down to wait under the baleful glare of the lady with the camera.

I don't understand, Sarah thought as she sat on the edge of the bed with her hands clasped between her knees. She'd put them there originally to keep them from shaking and to warm them up, but they still felt like chunks of ice.

It had to have been Dan. She had put the cigarettes there last night, before she and Dan had gone down to the banquet. No one else had been in the room, not even the maid. But why? Why hadn't he said anything about them to her? She supposed he could have just been looking for cigarettes and assumed—no. She didn't smoke, so why would she have a partly used pack of cigarettes, that just happened to be his own brand, in her nightstand drawer? He wouldn't have taken them without asking her about them, unless he hadn't wanted her to know he'd found them.

What was going on? She trusted Dan. She did. But something was up. After finding those cigarettes, Dan had made a phone call and then had gone tearing back to Sumatra. And he'd insisted on leaving her behind. Something was going on back home, and if he thought she was going to sit here in a Singapore hotel room and worry herself sick about it, he was crazy!

Setting her mouth in determined lines, Sarah picked up the phone and dialed hotel information. She was almost certainly too late to catch Dan, but she could still get a flight to Medan, and from there to the reserve—well, she'd work something out. She didn't need Dan's helicopter. She was a big girl; she could find her own way home.

By the time Dan taxied his plane off the runway and into the hangar in Medan, his frustration levels were reaching safety-valve blow-out stage. He needed something to kick, like a trash can or, better yet, somebody's butt. His current favorite candidates were the receptionist who'd kept him on hold for ten minutes and the mechanic at the airport in Singapore who hadn't refueled and serviced his plane as he'd been told to.

He was looking for somebody to yell at, and he got his opportunity.

"What do you mean, the chopper's not here?" he demanded of the hapless Indonesian in airport coveralls he found working in the AMINCO hangar. "Where in the hell is it?"

Looking affronted at the unseemly display of emotion, the Indonesian loftily informed Dan that he did not know where the AMINCO helicopter was. "Someone come and take it away," he told him, holding one hand over his head and imitating a chopper's rotors with one oil-stained finger.

Dan swore and scrubbed a hand across his face. "What did he look like, can you tell me that? The man who took the chopper."

"Big man," the Indonesian said, using his hands again. "American." He grinned suddenly, showing crooked teeth. "Hair like orangutan."

Dan uttered a short, sibilant Anglo-Saxon word he was almost certain the Indonesian would understand and headed for the parking lot, loping across pavement still wet and steaming from the daily cloudburst. The smell of wet asphalt reminded him of home—AMINCO's jungle compound. His sense of urgency grew stronger.

Tank's company pickup was in the parking lot, mud-caked and locked. Dan didn't let that stop him. He rummaged around in the back until he found a good sturdy length of pipe, cast a quick look around then broke out the window with it. Once inside it was no sweat. As the truck's engine roared to life, Dan wondered wryly what Doc would say if she knew his talents included breaking and entering and hot-wiring cars.

He thought about Sarah as he jounced out of the lot and began threading his way through traffic, imagining her golden, sunshine eyes lighting up at the sight of the gardens and shopping streets of Singapore. Her first time in the island city. He wished he could have shared it with her. God, how he'd hated to leave her behind! But the way this thing was shaping up, he was more than ever glad that she was safe and sound and five hundred miles away.

The rain caught Sarah as she was nearing the AMINCO compound. She had to pull over and wait for it to pass because she couldn't figure out how to turn on the windshield wipers in the ancient Jeep she'd borrowed from the ranger headquarters in Medan.

While she sat in the saunalike cab, listening to the drumming of rain on the canvas roof, she thought about the last time she'd driven this road—the first time she'd seen Dan, standing in the road like a pagan prince, sweat gleaming on his smooth, coppery body. Then she thought about the last time she'd seen that same body, and suddenly he was there with her, sharing the steamy cab and the sultry thunder of the rain. She could smell him, taste him, feel him. Desire rocked her to her core, shocking her a little; she hadn't known she could feel like that!

She told herself that it wouldn't be long now until she would be seeing him again in the flesh.

The girl at the reception desk at AMINCO headquarters was the same one Sarah remembered from her first visit. She obviously remembered Sarah, too, as she greeted her with a smile and a friendly, "Oh, hi, Dr. Fairchild. How is the baby orangutan?"

Sarah told her Sweetie was fine and asked for Dan. The receptionist looked dismayed. "Oh, I'm sorry. Mr. Cisco is still in Singapore. He isn't expected back for several days." When Sarah just looked at her without saying anything, she went on hopefully, "Umm, can someone else help you?"

"No," Sarah said, and cleared her throat carefully. "Are you sure? I thought—are you sure he didn't change his plans?"

The receptionist shook her head. "No, he didn't say anything about changing his plans."

"Then you've heard from him?"

"Oh, yes, he called early this morning, to talk to Mr. Guthrie, but he didn't—"

Tank. He'd called Tank! Maybe *he*'d know what was going on. "I see," Sarah said carefully. "Umm, is Mr. Guthrie here, by any chance?"

"Oh, I'm sorry, no, he's not. That's what I told Mr. Cisco. Mr. Guthrie is away on business, also. In Medan."

"I see," Sarah whispered, and turned and walked away. At the door she paused. "Is there someplace here I can get something to eat? Maybe a vending machine?"

"Oh, yes, certainly!" The receptionist seemed overjoyed to be able to comply with a request at last. "There is the cafeteria—follow the road to the left. Just past the infirmary."

Sarah found the cafeteria without any trouble and went in and ordered a roast-beef sandwich and a cup of coffee. She ate the sandwich sitting at a Formica-topped table that might have come straight from her high-school cafeteria back in San Jose, except it didn't have obscenities scribbled all over it. She was sipping cooled coffee and becoming more depressed by the minute when someone walked by her table, paused, then turned around and came back.

"Excuse me," a cultured, slightly accented voice said softly. "You must be Marina's friend from the reserve. I believe it's Dr. Fairchild, isn't it?"

"Yes," Sarah said uncertainly, frowning at the slightly built man with graying hair and dark-rimmed glasses. "I'm sorry, I don't..."

"I'm Dr. Soekardja. I treated a small friend of yours." Behind the thick glasses, compassionate brown eyes were crinkling with amusement.

"Oh!" Sarah took the slender brown hand he offered her and felt the warmth of instant liking. "Of course! You treated J.J., Dr. Soekardja, I don't know how—"

"Call me Joe. Or Doc Sako, if you prefer—it's what most people here call me."

Sarah laughed. "Joe's fine. And I'm Sarah. Please, sit down."

"Only for a minute, I'm afraid. I just came for coffee. But tell me, how is my patient?"

"J.J.? Oh, he's much stronger. I think he's going to be fine. Of course, it will be a while before he's able to climb again. I don't know how I can ever thank you for what you did, Doc—Joe. I just can't tell you how grateful we are.''

''I'm glad I was able to help.'' The doctor's eyes and voice altered subtly. ''And . . . Marina? How is she?''

''She's fine, too. I haven't seen very much of her lately though.'' She went on to tell him about her trips to Singapore and Samosir Island, but although he listened politely, Sarah had the distinct impression that her travels weren't what the doctor was interested in.

''So you see, I've been gone quite a bit,'' she concluded, coming to both a realization and a decision. She had been gone a lot, and it wasn't fair to Marina. Dan wasn't here, and she didn't know when he was going to come back. She couldn't stay here, and if she didn't start home right away, she wasn't going to make it to the reserve before dark.

She began to gather up her sandwich plate and napkin. ''I'm just on my way home right now,'' she said. ''I just stopped to get a bite to eat, but I'm afraid I need to be getting on my way. It was very nice meeting you.''

The doctor stood up when she did and held out his hand. ''Please, say hello to Marina for me. Tell her I hope to be seeing her again very soon.'' The soft expression in his eyes and the warmth in his smile were unmistakable.

Sarah went out to her car thinking, Marina and Dr. Soekardja? Then she shook her head, smiling. No, it was too impossible—the doctor was a wonderful man, but those two were poles apart! Imagine someone as quiet and reserved as Dr. Soekardja putting up with Marina's ebullience, her bluntness! Besides, he was years older than she was. And inches shorter!

No, she told herself, it was ridiculous, on Marina's part, anyway. Anyway, Marina was interested in Tank.

Dan had gotten his wish. He'd finally found something to kick. The only thing wrong with that was, the ''something'' happened to be the pickup's left front tire. It was flat.

So was the spare. The way Dan saw it, that left with him three choices. He could try to hitch a ride with somebody going his way; he could hitch a ride back to Medan and start all over again in a more reliable vehicle; or he could ride the damn truck on its rim all the way to the reserve. The odds on the first weren't good—it was quitting time, and in this country that meant the traffic would be all going the other way, back to the city from the plantations and lumber mills and oil refineries in the countryside. The second was going to cost him more time than he had to spend. So, after a futile attempt to trade an old man the truck for his three-wheeled peddle cart, Dan touched the ignition wires together one more time and lurched back out onto the road, swearing bitterly.

If he hadn't known it was probably impossible, he'd have been convinced Tank had planned this.

Once he got going, it wasn't too bad. Even on three wheels the truck wasn't much bumpier than most Sumatran roads during the rainy season. It was slow going, though, so while he was gallumping along, he had a lot of time to think about Tank and a few other things. The pieces were all beginning to fit together.

One of the biggest pieces, of course, was that pack of cigarettes. He remembered when he'd bought them, the night before he'd met Doc for the first time. He'd bought them from the machine in the cafeteria. The damn thing had been out of his own brand. He remembered straightening up with the pack in his hand, and Tank coming up behind him and clapping him on the shoulder.

"Dan, my man!" Dan could almost hear him saying it. "Hey, old buddy, do me a favor, will you? Lend me a buck in quarters?"

"Forget it," Dan had told him. He knew better.

"Come on, man, all I got's a twenty, and the cafeteria's closed. Hey, a couple cigarettes, then. Just to last me until I can get change. Swear to God, I'll pay you back. I'll get some tonight, in fact. I'm takin' the chopper to Medan. Got a date," he'd said, smiling, pleased with himself.

Dan had given him the cigarettes, of course, even though he knew better. He could see Tank's hand, tucking them in his shirt pocket as he went out the door, saying, "Thanks, buddy, I owe you one."

That was the biggest piece, but there were others. Like the fact that good ol' Tank knew just how long it took to get to the reserve, even before he'd ever actually been there.

Sarah was almost to the reserve when she heard the chopper. It seemed to rise up out of nowhere all of a sudden, skimming the treetops right over her head, the thumping of its rotors flat and heavy above the racket the Jeep was making. There was no doubt that it was Dan's helicopter—red and white, with the AMINCO logo on the door—and she knew it must have taken off from the landing at road's end. She waved and honked the Jeep's horn frantically until it disappeared beyond the trees, and then she slumped back, swallowing repeatedly and blinking back tears of frustration and disappointment.

She'd missed him. While she'd been wasting time at AMINCO looking for him, he'd been here. It was almost funny.

She had an irrational impulse to turn around and chase the helicopter back to AMINCO, but reason prevailed. It was late, and she was so close to home now. She absolutely had to check in with Marina and see how J.J. was getting along, and Sweetie. She'd been away too long as it was.

The sun was just setting behind the treetops when she reached the end of the road. The rangers' truck was gone again. She wondered which ranger had taken it this time and for what reason, but it didn't really concern her. She had other things on her mind as she shrugged into her backpack and started down the path to the river—such as the insects, which were always at their worst this time of evening. She really should have put on more repellent.

The path was muddy and well-trampled, but that didn't concern her, either. She figured it was probably just another van load of tourists come to watch the afternoon feeding.

Other than that, everything seemed as usual. The sun went down, clouds of river gnats and mosquitos rose like ground fog, and the bats darted here and there in the lavender twilight, gorging themselves on the bug banquet. The river chuckled peacefully along, and the frogs started tuning up for their evening concert. It was a serene time of day.

Sarah thought about stopping at the ranger station to ask if Dan had been there, but it looked deserted, so she passed it by. Marina would tell her soon enough. Anticipation quickened her heartbeat and her footsteps. Now that she was this close, she could hardly wait to get home, to hear all about what had been happening in her absence. She wanted to know what Sweetie was eating and whether Luki was leaving J.J.'s bandage alone and whether Bad John had ever tangled with his new rival. This was her work and her home, and she'd missed them.

Just as she was coming into the clearing near the quarantine cages, Sarah tripped over a bucket in the path. She banged her shin on it, then swore and kicked it. Stupid place to leave a bucket!

And then she stopped. Marina would never leave a bucket lying around like that; she was so neat and tidy it was positively irritating, sometimes—a regular Dutch cliché! Sarah bent over and picked up the bucket. She turned it upside down and frowned at the few drops of milk that fell from it onto the top of her tennis shoe. A milk bucket—the one they used at the feeding platform. What was it doing way down here?

She went on, slowly now, her heart hammering against the walls of her chest. A few steps more. She stopped and called, "Marina?" But there was no answer.

She dropped the bucket and began to run. She ran as if in a nightmare, not feeling her feet, seeming to make no progress at all, and yet in an instant she was there. The quarantine cages were looming before her.

Empty.

They were gone, all of them. The cages had been smashed, the doors ripped from their hinges. Sweetie, old Beau, Luki and J.J.—all gone.

Sarah stood in the midst of the wreckage, shuddering, unable to comprehend what had happened. She screamed Marina's name once more, felt as if it were being ripped from her throat. As the echoes of her screams died away, she realized that she was sobbing.

Chapter 14

Sarah found Marina lying half under old Beau's cage. She was certain at first that she must be dead. Icy cold and whimpering with shock, she dropped to her knees in the wet grass.

"Oh, God, Marina—"

Marina's face was swollen and discolored, but she wasn't dead. At the sound of Sarah's voice, she lifted her head and tried to sit up. She said something—Sarah's name, perhaps—but it was barely a whisper, more like a sigh.

"Oh, God, you're alive, Marina—" Laughing and sobbing, Sarah tried to hug her, but Marina's hand fended her off. She leaned closer and heard a faint whisper.

"...Hurt."

Hurt. Sarah put her hand over her mouth to hold back a sob. She didn't know what to do! After a moment she said brokenly, "Mari, can you move? Can you talk?"

Marina's head moved slightly, back and forth. "Can't," she whispered. "Think...something's broken."

Sarah realized then that she was trying to talk without moving her jaws. She touched Marina's face and felt her flinch.

"Mari, can you tell me where you're hurt? What happened? Did they shoot you?"

Again she felt Marina's head move. No. "Hit me," she whispered. "I was...up...on the platform. I tried...they took—"

"I know." Sarah gulped down a sob. "Who was it, Mari? Who did this?"

"Poachers."

"I know, but do you know who they were? Did you see their faces?" Her voice was patient, gentle, but in her mind she screamed it. Because she already knew who it had to be. She'd seen his helicopter, missed it by only a few minutes. If she hadn't stopped to talk to Doc Sako, would she have walked in on this? Would she have met him face-to-face?

"No," Marina whispered. "Wore...masks."

Masks. Hysterical laughter rose in the back of Sarah's throat. Of course.

"I've got to get help," she gasped, fighting for calm, fighting for control, trying to think. Trying not to think.

She started to stand up, but Marina clutched at her arm. "Wait...I know—"

"Shh, don't try to talk anymore. I'm going to go get help, okay?" She put out her hand, blinded by tears, afraid to touch. "Wait, I'll be back as soon as I can. Please—hold on."

She went first to the cabin for water and a blanket. She bathed Marina's lips with the water and covered her with the blanket, but when she started to rise, Marina again caught at her hand.

"Wait...I know—"

"Marina, I have to go," she said desperately, pleading. "I can't get you to a doctor by myself. I'm going to the ranger station to radio for help, okay? Just...hang on. I'll be right back."

Marina sighed and closed her eyes.

Sarah ran all the way to the ranger station, forcing herself beyond her own limits so she wouldn't have any energy left for thought. Only one thing mattered now, anyway, and that was getting help for Marina.

She almost stepped on Joka. He was lying on the floor of the ranger station, just inside the door, and in the twilight she didn't see him until her foot bumped his side. She heard a low groan.

Whispering over and over again, "No...oh, no," Sarah knelt beside the unconscious ranger. A bump on the head, she thought, exploring gingerly with her fingers. She didn't know what else. That was bad enough, but it was what she saw when she looked beyond him that made her turn cold. Even in the near-darkness, she could see that the radio had been smashed to pieces.

Later, when she remembered that terrible night, it seemed to Sarah that all she did was run. Like one of those chase dreams, where you keep running on and on, sides splitting, lungs bursting, legs like lead, just one step ahead of something dreadful. And maybe that's what she had done—run as hard and as fast as she could, trying to keep that one vital step ahead of her own thoughts.

Pausing only to cover Joka with a blanket as she had Marina and to find a flashlight, she pounded back down the stairs and ran to the river crossing. There was only one place she knew of where she was sure to find help, and that was AMINCO.

She didn't remember the crossing; she only remembered running. Running down the long dark path from the river to the Jeep, watching her flashlight beam bob up and down, counting to the thump-swish of her footsteps. And then she was driving, driving like a crazy person, jouncing through potholes, careening around corners, narrowly missing a head-on collision with a mud-caked pickup truck limping along on a flat tire. But even that narrow escape didn't slow her. She was deliberately pushing the Jeep to the brink of disaster, hoping that by using all her concentration just to avoid it, maybe she'd make it without falling apart.

But if she allowed herself to start to think about Dan and a red-and-white helicopter rising from the trees, passing right over her head so she could see emblem on the door—the same helicopter that had borne her to Eden and back....

The AMINCO compound looked oddly beautiful at night, like an amusement park, Sarah thought, with lights illuminating all the drilling sites and the pumps going up and down.

She drove straight to the infirmary. She didn't know where Dr. Soekardja lived, and if he wasn't still there she didn't know what she was going to do. Start banging on doors, she supposed. But for once she was lucky. The doctor was in his office. He half rose when she burst in on him, then threw his glasses down on the papers he'd been studying and came around his desk to take her by the arms.

"Dr. Fairchild! Sarah—what is the matter? Here, sit down. Tell me—"

"No, I can't." She clutched at his hands—doctor's hands, soft-skinned, long-fingered, cool and strong. "It's Marina—she's hurt. Joka, too—I think they hit him on the head. The poachers came, and she tried to stop them. They beat her—" Her voice broke. "I didn't want to leave her there, but I couldn't get her to the Jeep. I had to leave her there. Please—"

"Shh, it's all right," Dr. Soekardja said in his quiet, soothing voice, but he was already reaching for the telephone on his desk. "I will take care of it, don't worry. You have done the right thing, coming for help." He spoke briefly and tersely into the telephone, then cradled the receiver and turned, reaching for his bag. "No, no," he said when she rose to follow him out the door, "you have done what you can. Now you must leave it to others. You stay here and try to rest."

"But I want to go with you," Sarah protested.

The doctor shook his head. "I know how you must feel. But to be honest, there is not enough room in the helicopter for you to come along. With two injured people—unfortunately, I am not a pilot, so that makes four. I'm sorry."

Sarah was staring stupidly at him. "The helicopter? But I thought Dan—I mean, I thought the helicopter wasn't here."

Dr. Soekardja glanced at his watch. "I heard it return an hour or two ago. And I have just rounded up a pilot who knows how to get to the reserve, so I must be going." He squeezed Sarah's hands and said kindly, "In no time at all we will be back with Marina. In the meantime, lie down on one of the beds in the infirmary and rest." He smiled suddenly, briefly. "Doctor's orders." And then he was gone.

Sarah stared after him with eyes that felt like dry sockets. She was exhausted, but there was no way on earth she was going to be able to follow the doctor's orders.

The helicopter was back. That meant that Dan was here, too. Right here in the compound. She had to find him—confront him. In spite of her terrible fears, she didn't really believe it—she wouldn't believe it. Not until she'd seen him, talked to him, face-to-face.

"Come on, man—talk to me, dammit! Who did this? Where's Marina?" With a noise of pure frustration, Dan let go of Joka's shoulders and scrubbed a hand over his face. Damn! He'd known something was wrong. He'd known it in his guts.

Well, one thing was certain. The ranger wasn't going to be any help, staggering around with a bump on his head the size of his fist, muttering incoherently in Indonesian. He obviously didn't even remember what had hit him. And the radio was useless.

Wasting no more time on either one, Dan grabbed up his flashlight, vaulted down the steps and took off for the re-hab station as fast as he could run. For once in his life he wasn't worrying about snakes.

In the darkness he went straight by the quarantine cages. He headed straight for the main cabin, yelling for Marina. When he didn't find her there, he went looking for her.

It didn't take Sarah long to realize that she didn't have any idea how to go about finding Dan. She had no way of knowing which of the pleasant suburban cottages was his, and there didn't seem to be anyone around she could ask, now that Dr. Soekardja had gone.

Okay, she thought. What now?

Now that she knew help was on its way to Marina and Joka, she felt absolutely calm. She was thinking clearly.

There wasn't anything she could do about finding Dan until Joe came back. So instead she thought about the he-licopter. She remembered that Dr. Soekardja had said the chopper had returned a couple of hours ago. The way she saw it, unless it had landed somewhere else first—which seemed unlikely given the time frame and the fact that there was nothing but jungle for miles in every direction—that chopper should have been carrying passengers when it landed. At least four very small, very hairy passengers. Where were they now?

It wasn't likely that four small orangutans could be car-ried across a brightly lit oil drilling compound without risk of being seen, so it seemed reasonable to assume that if they were being kept on the compound temporarily, it would be somewhere near the landing pad.

Much later, when it was all over, that was the way Sarah explained how she'd come to be snooping around an aluminum storage shed at the edge of the forest not far from the helicopter landing area in the middle of the night. At the time, her thoughts weren't quite that orderly and reasonable. She'd acted on impulse as much as anything, putting together thoughts and feelings and impressions and arriving at a conclusion, then acting on it before examining all the consequences. But then, hadn't she always?

Standing in shadows, staring at the storage shed, Sarah had to admit that perhaps she hadn't been thinking that clearly. These were dangerous, violent men she was dealing with. Vicious criminals. She was one medium-sized woman, all alone, with only a flashlight for a weapon. She should have gone to someone first, gotten help. This was an oil company compound—there would be security people around somewhere. She should report her suspicions to security and let them handle it.

When she heard the scuff of footsteps on the gravel landing pad, her heart stopped; adrenaline blasted her with a stinging shower of nerve impulses. She whirled, every muscle in her body tensing reflexively. Then she began to laugh with sheer relief.

"Tank," she said, "thank God it's you!"

"It was Tank," Marina whispered when Dan lifted her into his arms. "I tried to tell her...."

Tears were trickling down the side of her head. He could feel them soaking into his shirt as he carried her along the dark path to the river. "I know," he said hoarsely. He was surprised he could talk at all; icy rage had turned him to stone. "You saw him?"

He felt her head move. "No...mask."

"Yeah. It's okay, we'll get him." He'd already told her not to talk; it was obvious her jaw was either broken or dislocated. But she'd had something on her mind, something important enough to her that she was going to tell him, even if every single word hurt her like hell.

"I *know*," she said with a violent shudder. "I knew when he touched me. He tried...that night I stayed with J.J. And again, the next day...when he brought me home. He is very strong." Her voice broke.

"Shh," Dan whispered. "It's gonna be okay."

Her body was jerking in his arms. He assumed that she was crying until she spoke again. "I got away," she whispered, shaking with painful laughter. "J.J. bit him...in a very bad place. I pushed him out of the truck and locked the doors. It was raining, and he got very wet. He was angry...."

"I'll bet he was," Dan said grimly. He knew Tank's way. He'd seen him in action before.

"I...didn't trust him. I should have told somebody. When he...touched me tonight, I knew his hands. I tried to tell her—"

She'd said that before. "Who'd you try to tell?" he asked softly.

"Sarah. I tried—"

Dan stopped walking. His whole body had gone numb. "You say you tried to tell Sarah? When?"

"A while ago. She was here...and then she went for help." Marina's whisper became a squeaky little sob. "I don't know what's taking her so long...."

Dan didn't answer. He'd started walking again, putting one foot in front of the other, while all around him the dark jungle grew silent, waiting for him to pass. But the darkness he felt closing in on him wasn't night and the flashlight he carried in his hand couldn't penetrate it. It was the darkness of his worst nightmare; the blackness of the void; the specter of a future without Doc.

Sarah woke in a panic. She was being buried alive—it was dark, she couldn't move. There was something thick and heavy over her face. She couldn't breathe!

She began to struggle, which pumped new oxygen to her brain and helped fine-tune her perceptions a little. She discovered that the thing on her face only covered the bottom part—her mouth, in fact. She could breathe, although it wasn't pleasant to do so. The air was hot and smelled of crude oil and sweat. If she opened her eyes, she could see the shapes of objects around her in the darkness. And she could move, after a fashion, although her hands and feet were tied.

None of this made any sense to her until she moved her head and felt a stab of pain. Then she knew that she was lying on the concrete floor of a shed, that several of the objects nearby were wooden crates and that she had a very tender bump on the back of her head. She remembered a shed. She'd been looking at it, thinking about calling security, when she'd heard something. She'd turned around, and....

Joy swept her like a spring wind. All she could see was sunshine, and the air smelled fresh and sweet. Tank. Not Dan, but Tank.

Clearly now, she saw Tank's face—his smile, so breezy and open—and the gun in his hand. But it hadn't been Tank who'd hit her—that had come from behind. She thought about that, but only for a second. So there was at least one other person involved besides Tank. It didn't matter, as long as she knew it wasn't Dan. It couldn't be Dan, because she knew he would never, ever hurt her. He loved her.

Sarah's joy turned to despair. He loved her. Would she ever see him again? What would happen to him when she was gone? Would he simply put on his stone mask again and go on with his life, never letting anyone close, never letting his grief show, never loving or letting himself be loved?

Hopeless sobs shuddered through her, and tears trickled coldly through her hair. She was going to die. She was the only person who knew the identity of the poacher. He would have to kill her; the only questions were when and how?

For a few moments she allowed herself to fantasize about being rescued. She thought wistfully about Dan coming to find her, sweeping her up in his arms. She could almost hear his voice, his broken whisper, "Doc, I love you."

But Dan wasn't going to rescue her. How could he, when he thought she was safe and sound in Singapore?

"I don't know where she is," Doc Sako said. "I left her here and told her to rest." He took off his glasses and rubbed his eyes. "Maybe she has gone somewhere else to rest. Dan, I am going to tell you to do the same. Go. Go away, now, and let me take care of my patients!"

It was the closest thing to an emotional outburst Dan had ever heard from Dr. Soekardja, and as he watched him bending over Marina, he thought he understood the reason for it. From the look on Doc Sako's face and the way Marina had clung to him in the chopper, it seemed a good bet that there was one particular patient the doctor was going to be taking care of for a long, long time.

Watching them together, Dan felt envy and a new wave of despair. He wondered if he and Sarah were going to have that chance. Damn her, why hadn't she stayed in Singapore!

He stormed out of the infirmary with eyes burning and chest heaving. *Doc, where are you?* In the wide, empty parking lot he halted and threw back his head and spread his arms wide, looking up at the starry sky as if searching for the answer there.

Where are you, Doc? You're a part of me now. Why can't I see you, hear you, feel you? Tell me where you are, Doc, I'm listening!

And suddenly he was listening. He was hearing everything she'd ever said to him and all the things she hadn't said. He was inside of her. He knew everything about her, everything she felt, the way her mind worked!

Sarah wouldn't rest. She'd go looking for those orangutans of hers, that's what she'd have done once she'd known help was on its way to Marina.

Somewhere out there, Dan thought grimly, staring off across the compound, looking beyond the festive lights and giddily bobbing pumps. Wherever her orangutans were, that's where Doc would be.

In the quiet time before dawn, Sarah lay awake staring into gray darkness, thinking about things—people and places she wasn't ever going to see again, things she wished she'd done and said. Crying silently. She'd tried to be brave, but she was scared. It wouldn't be long now before they came for the crates—and her.

As she lay there in absolute hopelessness, it seemed to her that the silence around her intensified. It seemed almost to take on substance and life of its own, shivering her skin with goose bumps, lifting the fine hairs on her arms and the back of her neck. She found that she was holding her breath, listening. Waiting.

Then she heard the sound. The sound she and all the other animals in the forest had been listening for, waiting for. The sound the tiger makes when he prowls the jungle, just before dawn. A distinctive coughing sound—she'd heard it only once before in her life, but it was unmistakable, and she'd never forgotten it. She'd even told Dan about it that first night they'd spent together in the cabin.

A tiger! Unbelievably, it seemed to be right outside the shed. But it was impossible—there couldn't be a tiger here, so close to all the logging and drilling. There hadn't been any tigers seen in this area in years!

And suddenly she knew. Not a tiger—Dan. Somehow, incredibly, he'd found her. He was there, somewhere in the jungle, close by. He was talking to her, telling her it was going to be all right.

Dan was here. He couldn't come for her because the poachers were guarding the shed, but he was here. She wasn't alone. She wasn't helpless. Her mind began functioning again, trying to figure out some way to increase her chances and Dan's.

A scuffling sound from one of crates reminded her that there were other hostages in the shed, too. If she could just get the crates open, she thought, it might give the orangutans a chance to escape. They were too tame and too placid to run, but if they were loose in the shed when the poachers came for them, maybe in the confusion of trying to recapture them, Dan would find his chance.

It was a long shot, but it was all she could think of. Sarah closed her eyes, took as big a breath as she could manage with the gag in her mouth and began working her way over to the nearest crate.

It was fully light by the time she'd finished the last one. Like some weird alien species, a long hairy arm emerged from the opening and grasped a handful of her hair. Hello, old Beau, Sarah greeted him silently, tears springing to her eyes. Now go—find yourself a place to hide!

Slowly, painstakingly, the orangutan crawled from the box. And not a moment too soon! Footsteps were crunching on the gravel outside! Sarah heard voices—Tank, certainly; the other she didn't recognize. The door to the shed opened, letting in a blinding flash of light. Shrieking with fear, the orangutans—tiny Sweetie clinging like a burr to

Luki's back—scuttled toward the rear of the shed, away from the intruders.

"What the hell—" Tank was looming above her, a huge angry silhouette against the light. Swearing, he lunged at old Beau. The orangutan screamed and tumbled across the crates. Tank hissed, "Ouch, goddamn it," and jerked his hand back. "Damn thing bit me! Come on," he snarled at someone behind him, "hurry up—get 'em back in the crates. Let's get out of here." He knelt down and began to untie the ropes around Sarah's ankle. The second man moved forward into the light.

It was Salim.

Of course, Sarah thought. It almost had to be. The way the poachers had always seemed to know when the coast was clear.

Outside the world suddenly erupted. Sarah heard cars arriving, doors slamming, running footsteps on gravel. A bullhorn crackled, and an unfamiliar voice with a heavy Indonesian accent bellowed, "All right, you in the shed— throw out your weapons and come out with your hands up!"

Sarah felt an absurd impulse to laugh. Someone had obviously been watching too much American television! But Tank wasn't amused. He swore violently and grabbed her arm, yanking her to her feet. Her feet were numb and wouldn't support her, but he pulled her along anyway, half dragging her by her bound wrists.

"Leave 'em!" he shouted to Salim. "Let's get the hell out of here!"

When Dan saw Tank come out of the shed with Sarah, he knew he'd blown it. He was ready to kill the idiot with the bullhorn—he'd been trying for a surprise ambush when they all came out of the shed. Now it was too late. If he made a move, Sarah was a dead duck. And they had a clear run to the helicopter.

Apparently they'd decided to leave the orangutans behind, except for the one the ranger had in his arms—darned if it didn't look like old Beau.

Now they were getting into the helicopter—Tank and Sarah, Salim and the orangutan. Just for a moment, Sarah looked back at him—and the blackest rage Dan had ever known in his life exploded inside him. He'd never forget the look in her eyes, not if he lived forever. Huge, dark as amber above that damnable gag, they were saying goodbye to him! Goodbye.

Goodbye, hell—he'd only just found her! He wasn't going to let it happen!

The helicopter's engines fired. The rotors began their slow revolution, picking up speed. Dan lifted his revolver and took careful aim. The chopper started to rise, a few inches and then a couple of feet. He fired. There seemed to be some kind of scuffle going on inside the chopper. He saw Tank grab his shoulder. The chopper wobbled, but kept on rising. Dan fired once more. And then he was running toward the chopper, yelling with everything he had in him, "Jump, Doc—jump!"

Inside the helicopter it was pandemonium. Old Beau was throwing a real tantrum; it looked as if both Salim and Tank had their hands full. It looked like they might be about to crash the damned chopper!

Dan could see Sarah's face in the doorway, her eyes huge and scared, looking down at him. Damn, he'd forgotten her fear of heights! She wasn't going to do it—in another second or two it was going to be too late. Then, if she did jump, she'd kill them both.

"Doc," he pleaded, holding out his hands, "for God's sake, jump!"

And then she did. She let go of that chopper door and came floating down just like an angel, right on top of him.

She knocked the wind out of him, so it was a while before he could say anything. He just lay there with her great big golden eyes staring down at him, and felt as if he were the one who was falling, right into the sun.

"Doc," he finally croaked, "what the hell took you so long? What are you tryin' to do, kill me?"

She was shaking her head frantically. He remembered the gag and pulled it off. It took her several tries before she could whisper, "I jumped, didn't I?"

He started to laugh, then. Laughing, and maybe some other stuff, too. Finally he just wrapped his arms around her slender body and with pandemonium in his ears and the smell of burning in his nostrils, growled, "Ah, Doc, I love you."

"You know what I wish?" Sarah said. "I wish we could get married in that little church in the Batak village. Do you think—"

"Hmm," Dan said, nuzzling the soft warm place behind her ear, "the elder's way ahead of you."

"What do you mean?"

"Remember when we were leaving, the elder said something to me, and you wanted to know what it was? Well, what he said was, we should be sure to come back for the wedding so he could throw us a real party."

"You didn't tell me that!" Sarah pulled back to look at him. "Why, were you embarrassed?"

"No," Dan said, remembering the wave of hopeless longing that had swept him then, "not embarrassed. I guess... I just didn't think you were for real."

"Why? You must have known I loved you."

"Yeah, I did. But I was afraid—" Dan shifted uncomfortably, looked away and finally said, "I was sure you'd leave me, eventually."

There was a long silence while all that he'd told her about his mother and father and his own loneliness sang in the air around them. Then Sarah said huskily, "I'm not going to leave you. You have to learn to trust me, you know." She kissed him and then pulled back suddenly. "There is one thing you have to promise me, though."

"Yeah, what's that?"

"Promise me you won't even consider taking a job in the States, at least not for a long, long time."

"Hmm. What about when we have kids? How can you raise a child on an orangutan reserve?"

"What better opportunity to observe the developmental stages of a human infant as compared to an orangutan infant," Sarah informed him in her very best scientist's tones, the effects of which were spoiled somewhat by the fact that she was lying naked in his arms in a nest of crushed ferns.

They were married in the Batak village, in the little church in the rice fields. The elder finally got his wish—he threw them a party to end all parties. All the clan members from all the neighboring *hutas* were invited, and the feasting and dancing went on for three days.

* * * * *

Silhouette Intimate Moments

COMING NEXT MONTH!

LIEUTENANT
GABRIEL RODRIGUEZ
in
Something of Heaven

From his first appearance in Marilyn Pappano's popular *Guilt by Association*, Lieutenant Gabriel Rodriguez captured readers' hearts. Your letters poured in, asking to see this dynamic man reappear—this time as the hero of his own book. Next month, all your wishes come true in *Something of Heaven* (IM #294), Marilyn Pappano's latest romantic tour de force.

Gabriel longs to win back the love of Rachel Martinez, who once filled his arms and brought beauty to his lonely nights. Then he drove her away, unable to face the power of his feelings and the cruelty of fate. That same fate has given him a second chance with Rachel, but to take advantage of it, he will have to trust her with his darkest secret: somewhere in the world, Gabriel may have a son. Long before he knew Rachel, there was another woman, a woman who repaid his love with lies—and ran away to bear their child alone. Rachel is the only one who can find that child for him, but if he asks her, will he lose her love forever or, together, will they find *Something of Heaven*?

Next month only, read *Something of Heaven* and follow Gabriel on the road to happiness.

Silhouette Intimate Moments
Where the Romance Never Ends   IM294-1

"GIVE YOUR HEART TO SILHOUETTE" SWEEPSTAKES
OFFICIAL RULES
NO PURCHASE NECESSARY TO ENTER OR RECEIVE A PRIZE

1. To enter and join the Silhouette Reader Service, rub off the concealment device on all game tickets. This will reveal the potential value for each Sweepstakes entry number and the number of free book(s) you will receive. Accepting the free book(s) will automatically entitle you to also receive a free bonus gift. If you do not wish to take advantage of our introduction to the Silhouette Reader Service but wish to enter the Sweepstakes only, rub off the concealment device on tickets #1-3 only. To enter, return your entire sheet of tickets. Incomplete and/or inaccurate entries are not eligible for that section or section (s) of prizes. Not responsible for mutilated or unreadable entries or inadvertent printing errors. Mechanically reproduced entries are null and void.

2. Either way, your Sweepstakes numbers will be compared against the list of winning numbers generated at random by computer. In the event that all prizes are not claimed, random drawings will be made from all entries received from all presentations to award all unclaimed prizes. All cash prizes are payable in U.S. funds. This is in addition to any free, surprise or mystery gifts that might be offered. The following prizes are awarded in this sweepstakes:

(1)	*Grand Prize	$1,000,000	Annuity
(1)	First Prize	$35,000	
(1)	Second Prize	$10,000	
(3)	Third Prize	$5,000	
(10)	Fourth Prize	$1,000	
(25)	Fifth Prize	$500	
(5000)	Sixth Prize	$5	

   *The Grand Prize is payable through a $1,000,000 annuity. Winner may elect to receive $25,000 a year for 40 years, totaling up to $1,000,000 without interest, or $350,000 in one cash payment. Winners selected will receive the prizes offered in the Sweepstakes promotion they receive.
   Entrants may cancel the Reader Service privileges at any time without cost or obligation to buy (see details in center insert card).

3. Versions of this Sweepstakes with different graphics may be offered in other mailings or at retail outlets by Torstar Corp. and its affiliates. This promotion is being conducted under the supervision of Marden-Kane, Inc., an independent judging organization. By entering this Sweepstakes, each entrant accepts and agrees to be bound by these rules and the decisions of the judges, which shall be final and binding. Odds of winning are dependent upon the total number of entries received. Taxes, if any, are the sole responsibility of the winners. Prizes are nontransferable. All entries must be received by March 31, 1990. The drawing will take place on April 30, 1990, at the offices of Marden-Kane, Inc., Lake Success, N.Y.

4. This offer is open to residents of the U.S., Great Britain and Canada, 18 years or older, except employees of Torstar Corp., its affiliates, and subsidiaries, Marden-Kane, Inc. and all other agencies and persons connected with conducting this Sweepstakes. All federal, state and local laws apply. Void wherever prohibited or restricted by law.

5. Winners will be notified by mail and may be required to execute an affidavit of eligibility and release that must be returned within 14 days after notification. Canadian winners will be required to answer a skill-testing question. Winners consent to the use of their name, photograph and/or likeness for advertising and publicity in conjunction with this and similar promotions without additional compensation. One prize per family or household.

6. For a list of our most current major prizewinners, send a stamped, self-addressed envelope to: WINNERS LIST, c/o MARDEN-KANE, INC., P.O. BOX 701, SAYREVILLE, N.J. 08871

If Sweepstakes entry form is missing, please print your name and address on a 3" ×5" piece of plain paper and send to:

In the U.S.	In Canada
Sweepstakes Entry	Sweepstakes Entry
901 Fuhrmann Blvd.	P.O. Box 609
P.O. Box 1867	Fort Erie, Ontario
Buffalo, NY 14269-1867	L2A 5X3

LTY-S69R

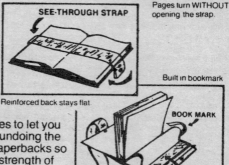